A Plague of Traitors
Copyright © 2021 by D.V. Berkom
Published by Duct Tape Press

ISBN: 978-1-7348599-3-5

DV BERKOM

A LEINE BASSO THRILLER

A PLAGUE OF TRAITORS

1

Mirovia Lab, Libya

The airlock closed with a hiss. Yanus waited until the interior door buzzed, signifying it was safe to enter, before he pushed through. Another scientist, Milos, was already seated at the console. A quick glance through the massive glass windows showed two subjects lying on gurneys in separate sealed-off cubicles. The two men's wrists, heads, and ankles had been secured with cushioned metal bands.

"Did he sign the waiver?"

Milos answered Yanus's question with a curt nod. All of the subjects the government supplied were told to sign—Yanus supposed anything was better than a bleak Siberian winter with little heat. The warmth of the Libyan desert must have been a welcome respite from the freezing temperatures of the Russian steppe.

The subject in the second cubicle had no qualms about signing the form. The subject in the first cubicle had been reticent, but then finally did.

They all did, eventually.

Milos leaned forward and activated the mic on the console in front of him. "We're ready to begin."

A third scientist, Sasha, entered the area dressed in protective clothing, a face shield, mask, and nitrile gloves. She walked into the first of two cubicles where a man lay on a gurney positioned next to a metal tray on a stand. A fresh hypodermic needle, a vial, and several alcohol swabs could be seen on the tray, next to a covered glass filled with four ounces of clear liquid.

The man on the gurney, a thirty-year-old dissident sentenced to "reeducation" at a camp in Russia's far north, eyed her with suspicion.

"Prepare the subject," Milos said into the mic as he checked the notes displayed on the console in front of him.

Sasha proceeded to fill the syringe with the contents of the vial. Setting down the now-empty container, she flicked at the hypodermic to remove any air bubbles. Lifting the short sleeve of the dissident's shirt, she cleaned the exposed skin with an alcohol wipe and threw it into a trash receptacle. She said something in a low voice to the dissident and he visibly relaxed. Yanus smiled to himself. Sasha had been the right choice. No need to alarm the subject.

Administering the shot took less than two seconds. Sasha placed a small bandage on the injection site and pulled his sleeve back into place. Again, she said something, and he cracked a smile. She disposed of the syringe, then uncovered the glass filled with liquid and held it to his lips. His gaze riveted to hers, he swallowed the contents. Once he'd finished, she then disposed of the glass.

"Good work, Sasha," Yanus said over the mic. "Prepare Subject Two."

Sasha repeated the process with the subject in the second cubicle. A career criminal who had been sentenced to death for killing his landlord, he watched her with interest—whether his interest was in her or the vial was unclear—but otherwise he appeared calm. The prison tattoos on his arm suggested the landlord's murder hadn't been his first. Finished, Sasha then rolled the tray to a far corner and walked toward the exit. Subject Two called out to her and she turned.

"When this is over, will I see you again?" he asked.

Sasha smiled. "Perhaps." She left the room.

Yanus nodded at Milos "Time stamp."

Milos logged the time on the console and leaned back. "And now we wait."

Shortly afterward, the sound of the airlock announced Sasha's arrival in the observation booth. She had removed the protective equipment and left it in the hazardous materials receptacle, gone through the sanitizing booth, and now wore only a lab coat over a pair of pressed khakis and a button-down shirt.

"How are their vitals?" she asked.

"No change yet." Yanus was again struck by the sparkle in his colleague's eyes. Sasha had a way about her—raw femininity combined with sharp intellect—that had every man at the lab try their luck, including the married ones. But she was all business. Obviously, it helped that she was one of the only attractive female scientists in an isolated lab overpopulated by introverted, horny male scientists.

Such a cliché. But they were clichés for a reason.

Several minutes later Milos pointed to the screen populated with Subject One's vitals. "His heart rate has increased, as has his temperature." They all turned their attention to the man in the first cubicle. Beads of sweat formed on his forehead. The steady rise and fall of his chest quickened.

Sasha glanced at the monitor. "Look at his liver enzymes."

Yanus's gaze lasered in on the numbers—they were high and escalating. He and Milos exchanged looks.

Sasha peered more closely at the monitor. "My God." She looked up as the patient shuddered violently. "He's going into convulsions." She checked the elapsed time. "It's been less than fifteen minutes. Something's wrong. This is too soon. I'm going to administer the vaccine—see if we can arrest the onset of symptoms."

Yanus moved to the console and hit a button. There was a *click* as the door leading into the observation room locked.

"What are you doing?"

"Do not intervene. We must record the subject's reactions without interruption." He stared, fascinated, through the glass as the man in the first cubicle struggled against his restraints. The convict strained against his as well, attempting to see what was happening to Subject One. Other than an elevated heart rate, Subject Two's vitals were normal.

Sasha shook her head, distress obvious in her beautiful eyes. "This isn't how the mice reacted to the virus. There's something wrong."

"There's been a small change."

Sasha gave him a puzzled look. "What do you mean?"

By now, the man was convulsing. Sweat poured off him, soaking the gurney's sheets. Angry red pustules had erupted on his face and arms.

"This was supposed to be the preliminary test of the vaccine." She pointed to the first patient. "That isn't how the virus behaved in any of my studies. Symptoms occurred within days, not minutes. And they weren't this severe." Sasha rattled the door forcefully. "Let me in there now, Yanus."

"I can't do that." He walked toward her, speaking softly. "We're scientists. We observe. That is our job." He nodded toward the man on the second gurney. "Your vaccine is working."

"But the first subject is worsening, quickly. If we don't do something, he'll die."

"Then he dies."

Sasha shook her head in disbelief. "You can't mean that. Human subjects aren't disposable." She turned to Milos. "Let me in there. I'll see to him. He obviously received the placebo. I have several vials of the vaccine—it might save him. You don't have to report it."

Milos watched their subject, absorbed in the swift progression of symptoms. "My God, Yanus. It's even better than we imagined." He turned to his colleague, the glow of excitement in his eyes.

Yanus checked his watch. Twenty-three minutes. "I thought our predictions for infection were high, but this." He shook his head in wonder. "This has far exceeded my expectations."

Sasha stared disbelievingly at Yanus. "You *meant* for this to happen?"

When both men avoided her accusing stare, her face blanched white. "The vaccine I helped create was for a virus found in a bush market in Zaire. This is not that virus."

"But it is, Sasha. The basis of the original virus is still there. That would explain the vaccine's efficacy." Yanus smiled, excited to share this triumph with her. "You have just witnessed the effects of a successful lab-created chimera. Our earlier tests showed one hundred percent mortality rate via drinking water. Think of the possibilities."

"The possibilities? What have you done? What if the vaccine fails?"

Yanus remained quiet, allowing her to come to her own conclusions. She'd see the brilliance of it once she figured things out for herself.

Milos responded. "She's right, of course. Any failure of the vaccine will not be tolerated. There must be a failsafe or the virus can't be deployed. We will observe Subject Two over the course of seventy-two hours to ensure the vaccine's initial efficacy. Sasha's team will be notified if anything further is required."

"What else, Yanus?" Sasha asked. "What did you add to the virus?"

Jubilant, he replied, "We introduced a lab-created component that highjacks the gene sequence to create its own chimeric proteins to expedite invasion, replication, and spread."

The alarm on Sasha's face was not what Yanus had expected. He continued, certain she would come around. "Don't you see? This super virus is an unimaginable victory, as is the apparent efficacy of the vaccine. We must test a larger group immediately. With this kind of transmissibility and potency, Russia will be safe from our enemies' attempts to destroy us. The threat of release will be more than enough to deter an attack."

"This 'super virus' is sanctioned by our government?"

He turned on her, righteous anger rising in his chest. "And why wouldn't it be?" Who was she to question what they were doing? She wasn't tier-one, like he was. She'd known the lab was working with a newly discovered virus—they all did. What wasn't widely known was that they were actually creating a more robust version.

He thought she might be his protégé. This was why he'd included her in the experiment.

He should have known better.

Startling sounds emanated from the other room and the three of them turned in unison. Blood streamed from the dissident's ears and nose as he gasped for breath, before he projectile vomited, expelling foaming, bright red blood and bile. The angry red pustules on his face and arms had broken open from his contortions, had started oozing a combination of pus and blood.

"For the love of God, help him," Subject Two shouted.

Sasha turned away and covered her ears. Yanus grabbed her by the shoulders and spun her so that she faced the large windows. "Watch," he demanded. She kept her gaze lowered. He shook her. "*Watch.* Learn."

To Yanus's immense satisfaction, Sasha raised her head and did as he instructed. Ramrod straight, her gaze forward, she stared at their subject, unshed tears glistening in her eyes.

Perhaps she would make tier-one yet.

2

———

Los Angeles, California

Leine Basso wiped the sweat from her eyes with her forearm and focused on her opponent. His menacing expression told her there would be no quarter. Hands in a defensive position, she crouched low.

She didn't have to wait long.

Her attacker feinted right, then predictably went in for the coup de grace with a side kick intended to shatter a knee. Leine blocked him and stepped laterally, planning to sweep his feet out from under him. At the last moment, he changed tack and slid onto his side, scissoring his legs and turning her move against her.

Leine pivoted, eluding his grasp. She fell on top of him in a body blow, knocking the wind from his lungs as she drove her knee into his chest. Then she quickly straddled him, trapping his arms to his sides.

Wheezing, he grappled for a handhold in an attempt to extricate himself, but she twisted and rolled them both to one side. Wrapping him in a chokehold, she hooked her ankles together and squeezed.

His face flushed scarlet as he pounded the floor, unable to breathe. Leine gave one last squeeze before she slackened her hold and glanced at the onlookers.

"See what I mean?" She untangled herself from her sparring partner, Spencer Simms, and climbed to her feet. "Questions?" Simms let out a soft groan as she gave him a hand up. That brought a few giggles.

One of the new recruits raised her hand.

"Emmy?" Leine nodded at the pretty fourteen-year-old. A rising star in the SHEN training program, she had shown a lot of potential.

"I didn't recognize all of the moves you used."

"Good observation." Leine glanced at the rest of the class of a dozen young women and men. "I improvised. When you're attacked, you use whatever you can to fight off your adversary. Your training can only get you so far. The rest is instinct, wits, muscle memory, and eventually, experience. Read your opponents' tells and craft your plan on the fly. If you're too focused on doing things the right way, you won't have a chance."

"She knows of what she speaks." Simms cracked his neck and shrugged his shoulders to loosen them. His streaked blond hair gave him the quintessential "California Surfer" look, even though he'd been born and raised overseas. "Improvisation will take you farther than rote learning. Like she said, read your opponent, but you should also read your surroundings. Look for possible weapons and escape routes."

"Exactly." Leine grabbed her water bottle and took a drink. One of the interns from the office appeared at the door to the gym and motioned to her. "Excuse me for a second." Leine walked over to the young woman. "What's up, Nikki?"

"There's someone here to see you." Nikki's gaze flickered to a door down the hall from them. "He's in the Woo-Woo room."

The Woo-Woo room was the academy's nickname for the meditation room, a space used to achieve one of the three main tenets of the anti-trafficking academy: calm, logic, and kicking ass. Being able to draw on the ability to remain calm in a crisis often meant the difference between a successful operation and chaos. Leine liked to describe the skill as "being in the eye of the hurricane." Meditation practice was one of the best routes to that end.

"Did he give you a name?"

Nikki shook her head. "No, but he's got two bodyguards stationed at the entrance."

"Huh. What's he look like?"

"Jacket and tie. Expensive shoes. Kinda uptight. Like he's a CEO or something."

Curious, Leine thanked the intern and headed for the room. Clients who required bodyguards weren't unusual fare for the group at Stop Human Enslavement Now, better known for its anti-trafficking work as SHEN, but they normally didn't pay the academy a visit. Intake was done at the downtown office by Lou Stokes, a good friend of Leine's and her old handler from her days as one of the government's elite, off-book assassins.

She opened the door and stepped into the room. Sparse accent lighting kept the space in near darkness. The smell of incense, coupled with soft instrumental music floating through the strategically placed speakers, encouraged relaxation. Leine's heart rate instantly slowed, responding to the familiar stimuli. Colorful cushions lay scattered across the floor, joined by several multi-hued yoga mats rolled and stacked against a wall like giant crayons. She scanned the room, looking for her visitor. She found him near the back, shrouded in shadow. Even in the low light she immediately recognized the familiar broad-shouldered silhouette.

"Hey, Scott."

The man at the back of the room nodded his acknowledgement. His glasses glinted in the low light. "Good to see you, Leine."

"To what do I owe this surprise visit?" It wasn't every day that the director of national intelligence stopped by.

Scott Henderson cleared his throat and stepped forward into the circle of light cast by one of the spots in the ceiling. He looked around the room, his gaze settling on a low cushion. "Is there somewhere we can talk?"

Henderson wasn't accustomed to being quite so far out of his comfort zone, which tended toward marble, mahogany, and wingback chairs, not incense, zafu pillows, and meditation music. The tall, buttoned-up powerhouse of the intelligence community didn't strike her as the kind of guy who enjoyed a good yoga session.

Although, she'd been wrong about him before. His political instincts had gotten him the position, his ability to coordinate between so many disparate organizations with ease and a no-nonsense approach to the value of each helped him keep it.

"The conference room is being used for a class. We could go to my office, except we'll be sharing it with a handful of people stuffing envelopes for a fundraiser." Backed by wealthy patrons who were often past clients, the academy helped raise funds for several organizations that supported SHEN's mission. This month, the recipient was a women's shelter that took in trafficking victims and helped them get the counseling and resources they needed to survive and thrive.

Henderson nodded. "Then let's take a drive, shall we?"

Leine checked the time on her phone. "I have an hour

before my next class. If you can get me back by then, I'd be happy to listen."

"I should be able to handle that."

If Henderson was annoyed by Leine's lack of deference, he didn't show it. One rarely told the DNI what he should or shouldn't do. At this point in her life, Leine couldn't have cared less. A few years back, she'd declined Henderson's offer of a spot on a covert team of operatives he was running. Since then they hadn't been exactly close.

Which was the way she preferred things.

With Henderson's security contingent in tow, Leine climbed into the black Suburban with the director. The sleek SUV had several aftermarket goodies–glass-clad polycarbonate windows that could withstand an attack from a crew of gunmen wielding assault rifles, military grade reinforced flooring that would survive an IED, as well as other reinforcements that could withstand a rocket propelled grenade. The only vehicle safer was the infamous Beast, used by the president of the United States, but not by much.

They rolled out of the academy parking lot and turned south, headed for the Harbor Freeway. Henderson opened the door to a small cooler at his feet and produced a bottle of sparkling water, which he offered to Leine. She shook her head. He opened the bottle and took a drink.

"What's so important that we need to do the cloak and dagger stuff?" Leine caught his gaze.

Henderson broke visual contact first and glanced out the window at downtown Los Angeles speeding by. He straightened his tie and cleared his throat a second time. "We've got a new program in its early stages and your name came up."

Leine smiled. "You're not on board with this, are you?" She chuckled. "Well, now I *have* to find out the particulars—especially since the idea of my participation makes you so uncomfortable."

Henderson gave her a look that bordered on annoyance. "One of the many reasons I never pursued you for a different position in the Agency."

Leine widened her eyes in mock surprise. "You can't mean my refusal to listen to the Agency's BS? Or was it my loathing of all things paperwork?"

"Your built-in insubordination and disinclination to follow rules."

"You'll have to do better than that, Scott. My 'disinclination' saved lives when I was at the agency."

"It was only a matter of time before it cost them," Henderson retorted. He took a deep breath and exhaled. "Be that as it may, I had to agree that you are the best fit for this particular job."

"Which is?"

Henderson picked up a manila folder from the seat beside him and handed it to Leine.

She opened the cover. Paper-clipped to a report stamped Top Secret, was a photograph of a dark-haired man of about thirty-five with deep brown eyes and a scar across his left cheek. The wound was old, judging by its coloring. A knife fight in his youth? She flipped the picture up and scanned the report.

His name was Yusuf Al Shami. The son of Mustafa Al Shami, the Syrian president's right-hand man and top spy. Considered a debauched playboy by even Middle Eastern standards, Yusuf had made a name for himself as a connoisseur of sadomasochism. The report mentioned that he preferred playing the submissive—craved humiliation, in fact. His predilection had spawned a skillset favored by the president and his inner circle: enhanced interrogation, commonly referred to by less-diplomatic types as torture.

"Lovely." Leine looked at Henderson. "Getting the band

back together?" Henderson was aware that Leine's old boss, Eric, had created a black ops group within the US government and had allowed Eric autonomy in its operation. That autonomy had led to Eric hiring out his roster of elite assassins for his own enrichment. The practice didn't exactly sit well with the operatives, or the vice president.

Henderson shook his head. "Not exactly."

"But you want Yusuf eliminated."

"If it comes to that, yes."

"You know I don't do that kind of work anymore, Scott."

"I don't want you to actually do it. I want you to train and lead the team that will."

"You need to give me a little more information here. Where would the training take place? Who am I training? What's the operation? Is this a straight elimination op or does it involve extraction and interrogation?"

"Current training facilities are in Libya, at an abandoned airfield outside Tripoli. Paul Miller suggested you after your operation rescuing Yazidi girls from Izz al-Din, as well as your familiarity with Libya." Paul Miller, now chief of station at the temporary office in Tunisia, had been a field agent Leine worked with on an operation in Tripoli a couple of years before. The terrorist organization Izz al-Din was loosely linked to ISIS, and one that Leine had dealt with on occasion.

"Current? Sounds temporary."

"Although there's a so-called cease-fire between the UN- and Turkish-backed Libyan government and the warlord backed by the Russians, UAE, and Egypt, fighting between the interim government and Izz al-Din has been sporadic near the airfield. We have to be ready to fold up shop and reopen elsewhere."

"Why not locate training away from the action?"

"Paul pulled some strings to get the facility for us. Our contact within the Libyan provisional government has proven to be tight-lipped about our presence in the country, as long as we grease the right palms. That isn't true in Eastern Libya."

"Fine. Tripoli it is. Who are the recruits? Please don't tell me mercenaries trained by the Russian Federation." She'd said it half-jokingly. Russian mercs had recruited, trained, and imported thousands of foreign fighters to supplement the warlord's attempt to overthrow the Libyan provisional government.

Henderson allowed himself a ghost of a smile. "If we sent you those kinds of recruits there'd be no one left to train."

"Then who?"

"Someone who doesn't know you well offered up US-trained Afghani fighters as a possibility. God knows there's a surplus and they could use the additional training. Paul shot it down before the guy even finished."

"Smart man." Friends of Leine's that trained with Afghani forces mentioned the vast difference between the Afghani recruits and Americans, explaining that their mindset was difficult if not impossible to overcome, posing a danger in many cases. She closed the folder and handed it back to Henderson. "You still haven't answered my questions."

"Analysts have reason to believe Yusuf is about to acquire a bioweapon that the Russians created in a lab near Tripoli, which he will then hand off to his father for the Syrian president's use against the rebels in his own country."

"With his own people as collateral damage." Syrian President Bashar al-Assad's lack of concern for his people in the quest to obliterate his enemies at any cost was widely known. Innocent men, women, and children had been murdered on his orders and that of his backers, first the Iranians, then the Russians. Concerned countries, including the US, that were interested in regime change in Syria balked at "pulling the trigger," unsure who would take the current president's place.

Apparently, a familiar devil beat an unfamiliar one.

"Do we know what this bioweapon does or how it's made?"

"Our source was unable or unwilling to provide that information. All we know is that its potential is reported to far exceed anything we've seen before."

"Great. So no way to prepare." There were many possibilities when it came to bioweapons. With the advent of CRISPr technology, synthesizing and recombining deadly viruses had become easier to achieve than ever. Scientific papers sequencing multiple viruses' genomes had become accessible to the general public, allowing bad actors to get a jump start on creating synthetic or designer viruses.

"You'd think after Covid-19, we'd have learned—as a species, I mean."

"Always the optimist." Henderson's sarcasm made Leine smile.

"Since there's no information on the threat, who am I training?"

"You've heard of the YPG?"

"The People's Protection Unit." The YPG was a group of fierce Syrian Kurds who helped to successfully beat back ISIS, loosening its stranglehold on Northern Syria in the bloody war against the terrorist group. The YPG had been rebranded as the SDF, or Syrian Democratic Forces, having changed its name to appease Turkey, who considered the Syrian Kurds terrorists.

Henderson nodded. "The men selected for the training include veterans from the battles for Kobani and Raqqa."

Leine whistled. "Impressive." She cocked her head to the side. "What's your angle?"

"What do you mean?"

"You selected all men."

Henderson nodded. "That's not unusual for this type of direct action."

"What about the women fighters?"

"You mean the YPJ?" Henderson shrugged. "None of them showed up for testing."

"Which means whoever was responsible for selecting recruits didn't give them a chance to compete."

"I suppose that's possible."

"Before I commit, I'd like you to open it up to women."

"Convince me."

"I shouldn't have to. You and I both know that the YPJ excelled as commanders and fighters. They've been responsible for massive victories in the war against ISIS."

"The recruits selected for this op had the highest scores out of the group we tested. The group just happened to consist of all men."

Leine shook her head. "You want me to work this op? Go back and offer to test women fighters for at least half the positions. I doubt you'll have a hard time convincing them to try. I guarantee the op will run just as smoothly if they make the cut."

Henderson gave her a look. "Can I take that as a yes?"

"You do that, then I'm in."

3

Sasha clocked out of the lab at six thirty, her eagerness to leave imperceptible to anyone except those who knew her well—which left out most of her co-workers. She surrendered her backpack to Boris, the security guard, stopping herself from drumming her fingers impatiently on the table while he rifled through her things. He handed it back with a wink and a lascivious smile, which she ignored. No sense alienating someone who might come in handy.

"Have a hot date tonight, Sasha?"

Sasha covered her surprise at his perceptive question with an eye roll. "You know it, Boris. The male strippers are on their way to my apartment this moment. Would you like to join me?" She wiggled her eyebrows and gave him a loopy grin.

"Ha ha. No thanks. I've got the late shift tonight," he answered, as though she hadn't been joking.

"Have a good night, Boris." Sasha threw the pack over her shoulder and walked out of the nondescript, concrete building, straight to her well-used Saab. The crushing Libyan heat radiated upward from the parking lot, heralding yet another endlessly dry afternoon and evening, making her miss her home in Moscow even more than usual. At least there were four seasons in Russia. She wanted to kick herself for her rash decision to work in the desert, seeing only the extra money her government offered if she signed a three-year contract.

She still had twelve months to go.

Ten minutes later, she pulled into her apartment complex, built specifically to house the scientists who worked at the lab. Similar to many new building projects in her homeland, the complex was only partially realized. Several of the one-bedroom apartments were left unfinished, creating a feeling of melancholy abandonment.

She bounded up the steps to her second-floor flat and unlocked the door. Normally, Sasha would heat dinner in the microwave, grab a contraband beer from her small fridge, and reread one of her Western-style romances. Tonight was different. She would sweep the apartment for listening devices, then use her burner phone for an encrypted chat with Tony.

The sweep took less than ten minutes. Satisfied her apartment was bug-free, she opened the app on her phone and logged into the chat room. Tony wasn't available yet—she was early. She sat back and sipped the illicit beer, her mind racing with what she was about to tell him.

She'd met Tony at a medical conference in Spain—one of her last trips before she left for the Libyan job. His maturity and unassuming manner immediately appealed to her, so different from the macho behavior of the other male scientists.

It hadn't occurred to her that he might not be what he seemed.

By the time she'd figured out his plan to groom her as a CIA asset, Sasha was all in on helping him. How could she have known the experiments her lab would ultimately conduct would have such far-reaching and insidious results? Once she knew for certain what Yanus and his associates had created, her anger and fear had threatened to boil over.

She'd been blindsided by the possible repercussions—no one she worked for or with had even hinted at the military aspect of her job. Everyone insisted they were working on a vaccine for a dangerous virus discovered at a bush meat market in Zaire, hoping to avoid a replay of the 2020 Covid pandemic.

But they'd lied. They'd been working on a bioweapon in another section of the lab.

The jobs recruiter had assured her she would be on the cutting edge of helping humanity, not creating something that could wipe out millions—something without a failsafe baked inside. The result of the experiment Yanus had allowed her to witness had horrified her beyond words.

It was then she decided to steal the formula for the vaccine and give it to the CIA.

Her initial excitement at her decision that morning had morphed into anxiety. What if Tony's people were unable to achieve the same result? What if his government wouldn't help her defect?

Don't think like that, Sasha. The plan has to work.

The app chimed in that Tony was now in the "room." She set the beer on the table and started to type.

Sasha: *I have news.*

Tony: ??

Sasha: *I have info on vax.*

Sasha swallowed, her mouth dry. It was done. She'd just told the CIA she was willing to betray her country.

Tony: *How do you know it works?*

Sasha: *I've seen it. Small trial.*

Tony: *That's great news. Can you leave the information at the drop site?*

Sasha frowned. *That wasn't the plan.*

Tony: *Things have changed. The timeline has moved up.*

Sasha caught her breath as a chill skittered down her spine. The lab wasn't that large—the scientists were close, insular. It would be obvious if the higher-ups had decided to move the virus to another facility.

How? she typed. *I haven't heard anything.* If she had, she'd have already stolen the formula and would probably be somewhere in Europe or the United States by now.

Tony: *Intercepted comms.*

Sasha: *Telling me you intercepted something doesn't make it true. Proof?*

There was a pause. Then Tony wrote: *Classified. Do you have access to the drop site?*

Sasha: *Of course.* The plan had been for Tony to extract her from Libya once she had actionable intelligence. This was most certainly actionable. She'd be able to share the vaccine globally before Russia or Russia's allies deployed the bioweapon. That meant her own timeline had been moved up.

When do I leave? If my employer finds out... She stopped typing. Best to leave her fears unspoken. Tony knew what would happen to her if she was found to have been working with the enemy. She hit send.

Soon, Tony answered. *I'll be in touch. We have 2 weeks at most. When can you do the drop?*

Sasha: *Not sure.* The vaccine was her only card, and she would play it well. She hesitated, then wrote, *When will I see you again?*

The wait for his reply was excruciating. He was taking too long to respond. Sasha watched the minutes tick by on her phone. Her emotions plummeted. He didn't really love her, didn't care about her safety. He was only using her for his own purposes. Despair boomeranged to anger, as the implications became clear. Tears welled in her eyes at her stupidity, at being played. She was an educated, intelligent woman. How could she have fallen so recklessly?

She'd come to trust him—had told Tony what she and her colleagues were working on, given him specifics. Once she discovered the truth she couldn't be a part of the experiment that her colleagues had labeled "Doomsday." And now, thanks to Tony, she would be a traitor. Sasha choked back her fear of abandonment—by Tony and by her country.

At least I will have helped rescue the world from this horrible plague my own country has created.

But how would she survive? Once the formula for the vaccine was released, everyone would know it came from her lab. It wouldn't take long before she was found out.

She'd have to wipe her laptop before that happened. Then it couldn't be traced to her. She would wait to transfer the formula until Tony gave her something concrete—a date, a time.

A moment later, her phone pinged.

Tony: *We'll be together soon. Hold on a bit longer. This obviously changes things. Have to rethink.*

Relief flowed through her. He did love her. He just had to work out the logistics.

Sasha: *All right. But hurry. I can't stay here.*

She waited, but Tony didn't reply.

$$4$$

____

Abandoned airfield outside of Tripoli, Libya

A stifling hot breeze hit Leine as she exited the Russian-made aircraft, and she removed her long-sleeve shirt, revealing a white tank top. She breathed a sigh of relief, thankful she'd dressed in layers. She put her hair up with a couple of bobby pins as she walked toward her Libyan liaison —a burly man with a permanent scowl. Dressed in faded black fatigues and a T-shirt, his aviator sunglasses and AK-47 gave him the same tired look of every mercenary she'd ever worked with.

"Hey, Sunshine." Leine gave him her most dazzling smile as she walked past him. Scowl-boy's frown deepened, and he cocked his head as though he'd just heard a dog speak. Leine stopped and turned back to look at him. "Coming?"

"I am to bring you to your quarters and then to the mess hall."

"Let's do that later, shall we? I'd like to see the space where I'll be training." She motioned toward a hulking metal hangar in the distance. "I assume it's in there?"

"Yes."

"Well, then." Not waiting for a reply, Leine strode toward the building. Scowl-boy soon followed.

The old hangar appeared past its prime, with much of its camouflage paint having flaked off through the years, but it would do. The cavernous space lent itself to the type of training Leine had determined would work best for the operation—she'd have Scowl-boy rustle up some obstacles once the group had advanced to the "war game" portion of the program.

At least they'd be out of the relentless Libyan sun.

A large whiteboard had been set up at one end of the hangar, with six chairs facing it. The rusty box fan clanking in the corner did nothing but stir the hot air. A six-foot-long metal table that had seen better days had pride of place next to the whiteboard. On it was a sampling of firearms and ammunition, from the ubiquitous AK-47 to a Czech-made sniper rifle. Leine dropped her rucksack and shirt on the table and turned to Scowl-boy.

"What do I call you?"

"Mahmoud."

"Great, Mahmoud. I'm Leine. Where are my students?"

Mahmoud shrugged. "They assumed you would want to rest after your journey."

"Well, that's sweet, but I find I do much better if I start work right away. Helps with the jet lag. Would you mind calling them in here?"

Mahmoud took his scowl out through the huge open doors of the hangar and disappeared.

Leine busied herself checking the weapons and making sure the ammunition matched. The 7.62x39mm rounds used in the AK-47s were easy to find in North Africa. Leine had her own preferences when she was on a job, but this was down and dirty training for seasoned warriors to take out a target, so preferences took a backseat to availability.

A short time later, three women and two men walked into the hangar. The women wore their hair pulled back, with colorful scarves wound around their necks. The men's buzz cuts matched the typical military recruit. All five appeared to be in their early thirties and were dressed in similar hiking boots, camouflage cargo pants, and T-shirts.

Leine motioned to the chairs. "Please, sit."

Once they took their seats, Leine continued. "I'm Leine, your instructor and your lead for this operation."

The woman who had arrived first raised her hand. Her healthy complexion and sun-streaked caramel-colored hair swept up in a loose bun wouldn't have been out of place in a Southern California surf shop. Her T-shirt bore the screen-printed likenesses of several women soldiers with automatic weapons and the letters YPJ displayed in the corner. Leine nodded at her to speak.

"I am Dani." She turned to the woman beside her, who was dressed in an army-green T-shirt with her dark hair in a pony-tail. "This is Raheema."

Raheema's cherubic face had an openness Leine hadn't encountered often in war zones. Like her counterpart, Dani, looks could be deceiving. Normally, a soldier's battle experience was written on their faces. Not this crew.

The third woman added, "I'm Naza." She wore a long braid and a white T-shirt advertising an alternative rock band. According to Naza's file, she had some medical training. All the recruits had a rudimentary knowledge of combat medicine —a necessity in war—but Naza's extra knowledge was welcome.

"Hassan," one of the men offered. His shirt bore a quote written in Kurmanci, the language of the Northern Kurds that Leine recognized but didn't speak. "And this one is Mohammed." He nodded toward the fifth recruit, a quiet, studious-looking man with glasses who also wore an army-green shirt.

Leine was glad to see that women outnumbered the men. All had come highly recommended and all had scored well on the tests used to determine their eligibility.

Henderson had been good to his word—he'd promised to send Leine the highest scoring recruits, no matter their gender.

"I thought there were supposed to be six of you?" Leine nodded at the empty chair next to Mohammed.

Dani spoke up. "Amira isn't feeling well."

"Then someone needs to take notes for her. Let's get to it, shall we?"

At that moment, another woman walked into the hangar, followed by Mahmoud. She wore the same boots and fatigues as everyone else, but her shirt was untucked, and her hair had escaped its confines, surrounding her head like a dark halo. She carried herself like a boxer entering a ring. Narrowing her eyes at Leine, she took the remaining seat and immediately crossed her arms.

"You must be Amira." Leine studied her new student. Belligerence radiated off the young woman. "Glad to see you're feeling better."

"Thanks," she answered, her tone just short of surly. "And you are?"

"Leine." Leine glanced at her handler. "You know what, Mahmoud? Apparently I'm hungrier than I thought. Is your offer of food still good?" He nodded. "Then could I bother you for a snack and some water?"

"Of course," he replied and left.

Leine turned to the recruits. "I had Mahmoud leave because the information I'm about to share is for you only."

Dani leaned over to speak directly with Amira. "This is the woman they told us about. The one who is here to teach us."

Amira scowled. "I know who she *is*. I just don't know why they flew her all the way from the United States when we have plenty of qualified teachers of our own in Syria."

"Anyone can teach you the fundamentals of assassination." Leine leaned her palms on the table. "It's not rocket science. You identify a target, scout the target and the area where the operation is to take place, then kill them by whatever means necessary. I'm here to teach you the necessary means."

"We have several snipers in our ranks." Amira sniffed and looked away.

"Amira is one of them," Dani volunteered. "We all are."

Leine nodded. "I hear that you're veterans of the fight to liberate Kobani and Raqqa." She caught Amira's gaze and held it. "From what I've been told, combat in both cities was brutal, that the SDF was at the frontlines, and you pushed ISIS out. It's because of your presence on the battlefield that the terrorists fell back and were ultimately defeated."

"But then America *abandoned us*." Amira's outburst echoed in the vast hangar. "Just like before."

Naza gave her a warning look. "Be still, Amira."

Leine nodded. "You're right. We did. And I can tell you this —every single American soldier who fought alongside the YPG and the YPJ disagreed with that decision."

"And yet you still withdrew." Amira's scowl deepened.

"Yes. But without America's air support, the battle for both Kobani and Raqqa would have been much worse with far more casualties." That brought a few nods from the recruits. "Unfortunately, the wishes of one US ally held more weight than the loyalty of our other allies. Our military takes its orders from Washington, and Washington decided in Turkey's interests."

"Turkey is afraid of us." Amira spat out the words. The other recruits murmured their agreement.

"I'm not going to get into a discussion about Turkey, or politics, for that matter." Leine straightened and walked to the front of the table. "Depending on the administration, America's alliances shift with the circumstances. Now that there is new blood in Washington, you can be certain there will be yet another shift. I'm not here to argue the merits or lack thereof. I'm here to teach you how to eliminate a dire threat—a threat to your people, and the world."

Naza leaned forward, her elbows on her knees. "We have been told very little about this operation, only that it involves a person of high rank in the Syrian president's circle, and that we would receive training."

"That's correct." Leine noted her refusal to use the president's surname, along with the brief look of distaste. She didn't blame Naza. President Assad made no secret of his distrust of the SDF, even though they'd been successful in helping to defeat ISIS.

"Then why are we here?" Amira asked. "Couldn't we have trained back home in Syria? The terrorists are building in strength. Our people need us there to fight."

"And to rebuild," added Hassan.

"We're in Libya because the operation will take place near Tripoli." Leine leaned against the table. "We've received information that Yusuf Al Shami is to accept delivery of a dangerous bioweapon developed at a lab controlled by the Russians."

"You mean Mustafa Al Shami's son." Dani's eyes widened and she let out a low whistle. "They weren't kidding when they told us it was a high-ranking target."

"What kind of weapon?" Leine almost didn't hear Mohammed's question. His quiet delivery stood in stark contrast to everyone else's. "I know you said it is biological in nature," he continued, "but is it something that is easily dispersed? Are there special protocols for handling it once we take possession?"

"All good questions," Leine answered. "Unfortunately, we know very little. I hope to have updates as we train, but there's always the possibility that we won't know until it's been delivered to our scientists."

The six recruits exchanged uneasy glances.

"I understand your concerns." Leine looked each of them in the eyes. "As long as we keep the weapon's transport case intact, there shouldn't be anything to worry about."

"Shouldn't is the operative word here." Amira rolled her eyes. "Typical American doublespeak."

Dani shushed Amira, and nodded at Leine. "Please, go on."

"Yusuf will attempt to deliver the shipment to his father," Leine continued, "who is planning to deploy it against the resurgent rebel army in Syria. Our mission is to prevent Al Shami from taking possession of the deadly substance. Which means," Leine moved to the whiteboard, "that we must stop the handoff here in Libya."

Hassan studied Leine. "We are meant to kill him, then?"

"If the need arises, yes. The main objective is to acquire the weapon. If that means taking Al Shami out, then so be it. The only caveat is that we must make it look like Izz al-Din is responsible for his execution. Obviously, your involvement and that of the US can't be disclosed."

Amira snorted. "Like I said, typical."

"Do we know where the handoff with the Russians will be?" Raheema asked, ignoring Amira's comment.

"Not yet. One of our agents will put a tracker on Yusuf's vehicle when he arrives. We'll also monitor his calls and any visitors once he arrives."

"But why did he choose Tripoli for the handoff?" Dani asked. "There are far friendlier forces in the east."

"I'll get to that in a minute."

Mohammed gave Leine a puzzled look. "Does the Libyan government know of your plans?"

"Very little," Leine conceded. "They're letting us use this hangar, although the story is that we're training soldiers to fight Izz al-Din."

"Then what?" Raheema asked.

"Once we know where the meet will be, we create a plan to acquire the weapon."

"Why don't we just take them by force?" Amira asked.

Hassan nodded. "It seems that would be the most direct course of action."

"Yes," Amira added, her anger forgotten for the moment. "With the right amount of firepower, we can overcome his security and retrieve the weapon."

"That's certainly an idea." Leine nodded. "If that was all that the US intended, then they'd authorize a larger strike force. The idea is to get the case from him with as little fanfare as possible."

"Right." Amira scoffed. "And just how are we going to do that? Yusuf will have tight security. He won't let this weapon leave his sight."

"That's true. Now for the reason he chose Tripoli. Yusuf is into bondage and discipline; he'll be looking for a dominant, as he's a masochist. So we're looking to provide him with a woman who knows her way around a whip and a pair of handcuffs. There's also a pop-up sex club in Tripoli well-known to the international BDSM crowd."

Amira perked up. "And you're hoping he decides to sample the nightlife?"

Leine grinned. "Exactly."

5

———

Training took five of the allotted seven days. The recruits were some of the best Leine had ever worked with, and they took to role-playing and espionage tactics with the ease of a cohesive group that could improvise on the fly. Leine observed all six with a practiced eye, watching for individual strengths and weaknesses.

Naza was fast on her feet and could work a room, bringing everyone together. That, coupled with some medical training, would come in handy. Dani's ability to switch from teasing seductress to lethal assassin reminded Leine of herself when she was Dani's age. Raheema's cherubic face hid a mathematical wizard—her uncanny ability to judge a target's distance, level of drop, and crosswind in rapid succession made her a natural spotter. Hassan did best on reconnaissance, and Mohammed, though quiet, had an almost preternatural ability to read a situation and come up with several tactical options.

The chip on Amira's shoulder was the only variable that gave Leine pause. She was good with a sniper rifle, the best of the six, but her attitude could easily put them all in danger if she let her anger get the better of her.

During the third day, the trainees were role-playing a possible scenario with Yusuf and his security entourage. Leine had Mohammed act as Yusuf's driver behind the wheel of a black SUV with tinted windows. Leine, acting as a bodyguard, rode in the back with Naza, who would play Yusuf. The other recruits followed at a distance, then would maneuver their vehicle, a white pickup, close enough to clip the SUV with what was called a PIT maneuver, sending "Yusuf" and his entourage into a tailspin.

Dani drove first, but she didn't hit the SUV in the correct place, allowing Mohammed to keep control. Her second attempt worked much more effectively. The SUV went into a 360-degree rotation and stopped. The other recruits easily overcame the occupants of the SUV.

Amira took the second turn at the wheel of the white pickup and hit the correct spot on the first try. The SUV went into a spin and then stopped. Leine and Mohammed exited the vehicle and took up defensive positions as the other recruits began to fire blanks from behind the pickup. Naza remained inside. Soon, Mohammed and Amira were locked in a firefight while Leine fended off the other three.

Focused on her targets, Leine didn't realize that Amira had come out from behind the pickup and was headed straight for Mohammed. Leine fired, but Amira kept advancing.

"Amira—stop. You've been shot," Leine shouted. Amira ignored Leine and, with a blood-curdling scream, broke into a sprint toward Mohammed, a feral look in her eyes.

She's not playacting.

Leine raced toward her, hoping to intercept the enraged recruit. Mohammed crouched in a defensive position, holding his empty rifle.

"Amira—*stop!*" Dani shouted. Amira lifted her rifle as she

reached Mohammed. Leine was a split-second from them when Amira brought the rifle down, aiming for his head. Mohammed held his hands up to ward off the blow as Leine tackled the woman and brought her down. The rifle bounced harmlessly off Mohammed's forearms. Leine covered Amira with her body to restrain her.

Amira fought ferociously, but Leine managed to keep her from breaking free.

"Amira..." Leine urged. "This isn't real. Calm yourself. It's a game."

Dani and Hassan joined Leine.

"Amira. Look at me. It's all right." Dani's soothing voice appeared to connect with the woman, and she stopped struggling. Wild-eyed, Amira latched on first to Leine's, then Dani's and Hassan's gazes, searching for something Leine couldn't identify.

"Shh, Amira," Dani cooed, drawing closer. "It's all right. You're safe. They can't hurt you anymore." Naza exited the SUV and joined them.

Amira's body relaxed. Leine slowly released her and sat back, adrenaline coursing through her system. Amira squeezed her eyes closed as tears escaped down her cheeks. Dani and Naza exchanged glances.

Leine nodded at Raheema, who had just joined them. "Raheema, can you help Amira into the SUV? The team needs a break." Raheema nodded and helped Amira to her feet. Hassan followed the two women back to the SUV.

"You all right, Mohammed?" Leine asked the recruit.

He nodded. He appeared shaken, but didn't display any injuries from Amira's attack. "I'm fine."

Leine turned to Dani and Naza. "Somebody needs to tell me what that was about." She searched their faces expectantly.

When none were forthcoming, she said, "I know something's going on with Amira. I've tried to find out from her, get her story, but she's been tightlipped. If I don't know her motivations, then I can't work to her strengths. I also can't trust her to act in accordance with our plan. She's compromised emotionally, which is obvious. Those emotions compromise her mentally and ultimately physically. This is an operation that cannot bear unpredictability in a team member."

The recruits exchanged glances. Naza nodded at Dani.

Dani sighed. A look of sadness enveloped her face. "Amira is Yazidi." She looked pointedly at Leine. "You know Yazidi?"

"I do. I worked to help several escape during multiple operations here in Libya." ISIS, as well as Izz al-Din, did their best to wipe out Yazidi men and the elderly, while kidnapping the younger women. They would then sell the younger women to each other and to outside traffickers. The conditions were horrendous, with many taking their own lives, fearing they would never survive to see their families again.

"Then you know the horrors of the women stolen from their families by the terrorists." Dani clenched her fists. "Amira was such a woman."

Finally, Amira's actions and attitude started to make sense. "How did she escape?" Leine asked. The terrorists kept the women under heavy guard, often locking them in cages to prevent escape. Leine couldn't imagine the hell these women went through, even though she'd heard firsthand experiences.

Dani gave Leine a weary smile. "She was one of the women my platoon liberated from a holding facility near Raqqa. She joined with us to show her gratitude, but also to exact revenge on her captors. She is one of the fiercest warriors I've ever seen on the battlefield. This...event was not surprising."

"We never expected her to lose it in training, though." Naza shook her head in disbelief.

Dani nodded. "Something set her off. Something she must equate with her experiences with the terrorists."

"And she saw America's withdrawal as a betrayal of everything she'd endured," Leine said. Amira's worldview leapt into sharp focus. "For her, Americans are not to be trusted."

Dani nodded. "Whether that is a fair assessment does not matter. It's how she views things."

"Thank you. You've helped me understand her so much better now," Leine replied.

"Are you going to remove her from the operation?" Dani's anxiety was obvious.

"Let me talk to her, see if we can come to some kind of understanding. Anger and rage, as long as it's directed, can be a potent force in battle, as it can be in life in general. I need to understand how best to direct her. Besides, it's possible this event may have soured her on the mission."

If Amira couldn't get her anger under control, she would be a detriment to the team. On the other hand, Leine meant what she'd said. Rage was an effective force multiplier, as long as the person experiencing it could control and direct their response. She'd offer Amira some psychological tools that she herself had found handy throughout her career to combat strong emotions.

But she'd also keep a close eye on her, just in case.

Dani gave Leine a relieved smile. "I believe in Amira. She has the ability to be a great soldier. I've seen her in action. But I also understand the nature of our current operation, how delicate the balance is between her quest for revenge, which I'm certain is always at the back of her mind, and succeeding in what we must do."

Leine nodded. "I'm glad you see the difference. I hope Amira does, too."

Amira looked out through the windshield at them, as

though she sensed her position on the team was being discussed. Leine nodded at her, but Amira looked away.

Leine would have to work to build trust between them. There were only a few more days until Yusuf and his entourage were scheduled to arrive.

She hoped there was enough time.

6

———

Tripoli, Libya

Paul Miller removed his headphones and handed them to Leine. "He hasn't said much since he checked in. One of my guys will relieve you in a few hours." He gestured toward a sandy-haired man wearing headphones working the monitor across from her. "This is Matt Price. He was recently reassigned."

Leine nodded at the agent. "Where from?"

"Syria."

"I'm sure that was interesting."

Matt grimaced. "It's a frigging mess over there. Oh, yeah. And Assad's a madman."

"Matt's acting as my second-in-command on this op," Paul continued, ignoring his comment. "If I'm not available, he's your guy."

"Good to meet you, Matt." Leine turned her attention to the monitor in front of her. With her eye on the video feed of Yusuf's hotel room, Leine took the headphones and checked the time. "He hasn't said anything to his bodyguards about going out?" When Miller shook his head, Leine added, "You mean he's going to pass up a chance to go to Excite?"

"It's invitation only. Maybe he couldn't get in."

Leine raised an eyebrow. "You really think the son of the head of Syrian intelligence couldn't get an invite to a pop-up sex club? Times must be rough."

Miller shrugged. "Maybe the handoff is tonight." He turned to leave. "I'm going for a bite to eat. Can I get you anything?"

"Thanks, I'm good."

The door closed behind him, and Leine put on the headphones. Matt monitored both audio and video of the hotel room and the hallway outside, ensuring uninterrupted access. Two other techs were busy on their laptops, monitoring visual feeds of the hotel grounds and the street beyond.

In Yusuf's hotel room, the flat-screen television was muted and turned to a Syrian news channel. Yusuf lay on his back on the bed, propped up by a stack of pillows and playing a hand-held video game, while a member of his security stood near the window, an assault rifle casually slung over his shoulder. Two more bodyguards with guns had taken positions outside the hotel room, while another roamed the grounds. A half-empty bottle of vodka and a glass sat on the nightstand.

"Don't worry, Jamal. No one knows I'm here." Yusuf took a break from his game to address the gunman next to the window. "My father took care of everything."

"I am paid to be thorough," answered Jamal. "I would have preferred we stayed in Benghazi. Your father instilled in us a commitment to your safety, which we take very seriously."

Yusuf waved his comment away. "Benghazi's accommodations leave a lot to be desired. Besides, you should trust my father to have done what was necessary to ensure that I will live to party another day." He tossed his gaming device to the side and reached for the vodka. "You're not going to be here all night, are you? Take a break, have something to eat."

Jamal stepped away from the window. "I will as soon as Farid checks in."

A moment later, Jamal touched his ear and listened. Then he said, "Farid's clear."

"And what did he say?" Yusuf said, boredom evident in his tone.

"Everything looks fine. Are you sure you don't want me to stay in the sitting room? I can use the couch."

Yusuf shook his head. "There is no need. Travel has made me quite tired. I'll most likely be in bed before you order your meal."

Jamal gave Yusuf a curt nod and left. The camera trained on the front door of the suite showed Jamal having a quiet word with the two guards. Then he disappeared into the elevator.

Inside the room, Yusuf remained on the bed, watching the news with no sound. After a few minutes, he took a business card from his pocket, picked up his mobile, and made a call. Leine motioned to Matt. "We have his mobile?" He nodded, and a moment later Leine heard Yusuf's phone ringing.

"This is Sarah. How may I help you this evening?" Leine's ears perked up at the woman's soothing tone and slightly breathless delivery.

"Yes, hello. I am in need of a babysitter tonight." Yusuf's voice faltered on the word babysitter. He cleared his throat.

"Yes, of course, sir. And would you prefer male or female?"

"Female, please. And I'd like her to be quite strict. My children are spirited."

"Yes, sir. I have the perfect person. May I ask, sir, are you a member of our network?"

"No. I am a visitor to your fine city."

"That's wonderful, sir. If I may, how did you hear of us?"

"Through a mutual acquaintance, Mr. Ali Zakaria. Your establishment comes highly recommended."

"Excellent, sir. May I have your access code?"

Yusuf read from the business card. "FRVNT007."

"Thank you."

"When can I expect her?"

"What is your location?"

Yusuf recited the hotel's address and his room number, then gave her his credit card.

There was a pause, then, "Aya will be there within the hour."

Leine picked up her phone and texted Dani over an encrypted app.

Text me. Urgent. Then she texted Miller to send a car for Dani, and briefly explained what happened.

Yusuf ended the call and walked through the sitting room to the door. He opened it a crack and stuck his head out.

"There's a young woman on her way here within the hour. She is my masseuse. We must not be disturbed." The gunmen both nodded.

Leine's cell phone vibrated. A text from Dani.

I'm here.

Leine texted: *You're on. Yusuf just requested a 'babysitter' named Aya to visit him within the hour.*

Tonight?

Yes.

Where do I go?

We're sending a car. Wear the long coat over the black outfit. Don't forget to accessorize.

Leine then alerted two of Miller's agents, who were conducting surveillance in a vehicle across from the hotel.

Woman named Aya coming to see our friend. Detain/detour.

Description? one of them wrote.

Strict.

Roger that.

Leine stood up and paced the floor. The group had gone over this type of scenario, one in which Yusuf would hire a call girl, although it was only one of many possibilities. *Did we spend enough time on what was expected from a dominatrix?* They'd reviewed several videos detailing what Yusuf would expect, but Dani told Leine privately that she had only been with one man, her boyfriend of several years, and had no experience with bondage or playing a dom.

"Will I be expected to have sex with him?" Dani had asked, clearly unhappy with the idea.

"Yusuf is into humiliation," Leine had answered, "so my guess is the more you reject his advances, the better." Her answer had appeared to calm any anxieties the young woman might have had.

Would Dani pass the test? Miller had argued that Leine should have sent Amira. Amira wasn't as attractive in a conventional sense, but she certainly had the domination thing down. The obvious problem being that the interaction with Yusuf could trigger an episode. Something Leine wasn't willing to risk.

Dani will be fine.

She had to be.

7

The SUV pulled to the curb of the upscale Hotel Tripoli and stopped. Dani drew a deep breath in and let it go, trying to calm her hammering heart.

What if Yusuf discovered her ruse? Dani had never done anything quite like what was depicted in the videos Leine had shown the team. She felt the smooth leather of the riding crop hidden beneath her long coat. What if he saw through her attempts at being a dominatrix? Would he believe her to be a spy? If he did, then she would most likely be killed, her body left to rot in the desert.

Or would he only think her inexperienced and complain to the company who provided Aya's services? At that point, she'd have to be gone, or she'd be discovered.

Don't think that way, Dani. You'll be fine. The pistol concealed under the false bottom of the case on the floor next to her gave her some small bit of confidence.

Very small.

Never in her life had she thought she'd be posing as the S in a sadomasochistic transaction. But neither had she believed she'd end up becoming a soldier and killing terrorists.

Remembering the horrific battle for Raqqa and the friends she'd lost, Dani steeled herself for the operation before her, just as she'd done throughout war. Often, during particularly difficult firefights when the soldiers she led could barely retain their fragile hold on the tiny advances they'd made, she'd been on the verge of despair, believing their cause to be futile. Then, she'd find it within herself to rally her troops. They pushed ISIS further back, and eventually out of Raqqa.

How was this any worse? The operation was different, that was all. Dani would have been much more comfortable leading the SDF into battle.

She opened the door of the SUV and stepped onto the drive, taking the case with her. Inside were several accoutrements common to the BDSM crowd. She'd marveled at their uses, shaking her head as Leine explained each one. Her limited exposure to implements of the sex trade caused a moment of panic—what if she froze, forgetting what a particular device was for?

Her spiked heels made her several inches taller, giving her some much-needed courage. Leine had regaled them with stories of female spies in World War II and the Cold War, and how, against all odds, they were able to help turn the tide of war. She would be one of those women.

She just wished she had an AK-47 instead of a ball gag.

Dani walked through the doors, held open for her by the doorman, and lowered her gaze as she passed. Her scarf covered much of her face, in the event that Yusuf demanded security tapes from hotel management. His father's power reached far into North Africa. She was certain that eventually someone would review the tapes of this evening, especially after the success of the operation.

Yusuf's room was on the top floor of the hotel. She had a brief moment of panic when she realized the elevator could only be accessed with a key card. As she stood in front of the elevator wondering what to do, a bulldog of a man dressed in a black suit appeared at her side.

"Aya?" he asked.

She nodded. He swiped his key card and the doors slid open.

"Thank you." She stepped onto the elevator, turned, and gave him what she hoped was a mysterious smile, but he'd already vanished.

When she reached the top floor, the doors slid open to reveal two gunmen stationed on either side of the entrance to the suite. As she exited the elevator, one of the gunmen motioned for her case. Blood pounding in her ears, she handed it to him, hoping her expression conveyed bemusement. The gunman opened it and pawed through the implements, his stoic expression unreadable. Finding nothing alarming, he closed the case. Relieved that he hadn't found the gun, she allowed herself a smile.

"Arms to the side," he commanded in Arabic. Dani unbelted her coat before she did as instructed so the gunman could frisk her. She half expected a clumsy groping attempt, and was surprised when it didn't happen. Strictly professional—the nostril flare and slight widening of his eyes were the only hints that her faux leather costume may have elicited a positive response.

Finished, the gunman stepped aside. The second gunman knocked twice, then opened the door to the suite. Dani picked up her case and strode into the room. The door closed behind her.

Test number one: passed.

The low lighting and soft colors of the entrance to the suite were meant to relax the occupants, but didn't do much for her.

She set down the case and waited, willing her heart rate to slow. A moment later, Yusuf Al Shami appeared, a drink in his hand.

"Aya." His gaze started at her feet and leisurely traveled up her body, pausing along the way.

When his gaze met hers, she smiled languidly and asked, "Do you like what you see?"

He nodded. "I do."

Dani dropped her coat on the floor and gave him a disparaging look. "Pick it up." She exposed the riding crop and slapped it against her thigh. "Now."

Yusuf's intake of breath was barely audible, but the speed with which he acquiesced told her she was on the right track. He set his drink on the hall table and walked over to the coat. As he bent to pick up the offending item, Dani placed her stilettoed heel against his backside and shoved him face-first onto the floor.

"On your knees, son of a dog."

Yusuf quickly climbed to all fours.

"What do you say when your mistress tells you to do something?"

"Yes, mistress."

"I didn't hear you."

Yusuf cleared his throat and repeated in a loud voice, "Yes, mistress."

Dani was absolutely certain she was having an out-of-body experience. Apparently, "Aya" relished having the upper hand. Dani wanted to giggle at the ridiculousness of a man paying good money to grovel in front of a strong woman, but realized that Aya needed to be the dominant force for now. *I would never have thought I had this particular talent.*

Something to tuck away for future analysis.

The idea of riding him like a horse occurred to her, and she almost smiled. *Why not?* She slapped the riding crop in her palm and moved toward him.

This was going to be more fun than she thought.

LEINE STUDIED THE MONITOR FROM THE ROOM ON THE FLOOR below Yusuf's suite, alert for signs they needed to intervene. A group of commandos stood ready to eliminate the two guards standing outside the room, although that was a last resort, as it would blow the operation. Plan B entailed taking Yusuf somewhere for interrogation, but then the trade likely wouldn't happen and they'd have to flip the son of a Syrian intelligence officer.

Not an easy task.

Dani seemed to be getting into her role as a dom, which helped sell the operation. Leine didn't know if having Dani on the inside would elicit any intel, but having someone Yusuf trusted, at least in theory, was a good idea. Yusuf had still proven to be tightlipped regarding the meet.

The door behind Leine opened and Miller walked in carrying a plate of couscous and a bottle of sweet tea. He closed the door behind him and joined Leine at the monitor.

"Anything?"

Leine shook her head. "Unless you're interested in Yusuf's capacity for humiliation. If that's the case, on a scale of one to ten, I'd give it a twenty-five."

Miller raised an eyebrow. "That good, eh?" He took the chair next to her. "No worries for Dani, though?"

"Not yet. She's performing well, considering."

He watched the action as he ate his dinner. "She appears to be enjoying the role."

"As is Yusuf, by the looks of things."

"Want some?" he asked, gesturing to the couscous. "That's some hungry work." She shook her head.

When they were finished, Dani untied Yusuf from the bed and removed the ball gag and other props they'd used. Yusuf poured himself another drink from the bottle of vodka, then walked to the dresser and opened one of the drawers.

"You have exceeded my expectations, Aya." He turned and held up a wad of bills. "I'd like to purchase your services for my short time here."

"That depends."

"On what?"

Dani busied herself putting the toys back into the case before answering. She straightened and glanced at him over her shoulder. "Are you certain you can afford me?"

Leine smiled. *Good girl.*

Yusuf walked over and clasped her hand over the money. "Oh, I'm certain of that, Mistress Aya. Shall we strike a deal?"

Dani opened her hand and glanced at the currency. "Twenty-four hours?"

"Let's say thirty-six. I'm leaving the morning after tomorrow."

"Then I will need a little more for my trouble. Shall we say half again?"

Yusuf went back to the dresser and counted out more money, which he handed to her. "Have you ever heard of Excite?"

"Of course."

"Have you been there?"

"It is by invitation only."

"Consider this your invitation."

"When?"

"Now."

Leine and Miller exchanged a glance, then picked up their phones.

8

Miller's contacts in Tripoli managed to swing Leine an invite to the exclusive nightclub for that evening. Although publicly denouncing anything to do with sex clubs as an aberration and affront to Allah, Libyan authorities looked the other way, since many of the patrons were wealthy.

Excite had become a phenomenon known to the international BDSM crowd, with attendees lured by the danger of going to such a club during Libya's civil unrest, not to mention the risk of ISIS and Izz al-Din threatening to invoke sharia law in their loosely held territories. Attendance was also largely thought to be a middle finger to the conservative religious sect from a younger clientele who believed that life was short.

Leine threw together a presentable costume for the evening, using hastily procured desert fatigues, and had almost talked Miller into accompanying her, when he balked.

"Do it for your country, Paul," Leine had insisted.

Miller rolled his eyes. "I do plenty for my country. Besides,

I'm much too old to be cavorting with you at a sex club, tempting as it may be."

Leine nudged him with her baton. "Seriously. Think of the stories."

Miller shook his head. "Yeah. Not something I want to regale my friends and family with around the Thanksgiving table. You go on and have fun."

She borrowed one of the women officers to help with her makeup and hair. Thick, smoky eyeliner combined with Leine's naturally dark lashes gave her eyes a dramatic appearance. She added a deep blush to her cheeks and a few different shades of eye shadow before she was satisfied.

"How do I look?" she asked the officer.

"Sexy. And dangerous."

"Perfect."

Leine borrowed an SUV and driver from Miller and followed the GPS beacon they'd slapped onto Yusuf's ride. Miller insisted on sending backup in the form of two officers in a nondescript SUV who would remain outside.

The club had popped up in a rundown warehouse on the outskirts of the city. The crumbling concrete walls covered in graffiti would look at home in any war-torn city in the Middle East.

Leine waited until Yusuf, Dani, and Yusuf's security entered the club before she and the driver, Talal, exited the SUV and walked to the entrance. A camera peered at them from above the door, its red light steady. Leine lowered her cap over her eyes and held up the business card given to her by the CIA officer who had secured the invite.

A girl never knew who might be watching, and Leine had done a fair amount of anti-trafficking work in Tripoli.

There was a loud click, followed by a buzzer, and the metal

door swung open. Leine slid the card back in her pocket and they walked inside.

Blue and purple lighting pulsed in time to throbbing electronic dance music blasting down a long hallway. Graffiti adorned the block walls of the corridor, matching the exterior.

Leine followed the music past heavily armed bodyguards to the main event: a cavernous space partially filled with people dancing, some dressed in the black leather of an old-school sex club, some in schoolgirl and harem outfits, both male and female, and all manner of interesting costumes in between, including a couple of younger men dressed in corsets and high heels, and sporting nipple rings. A large *Tyrannosaurus rex* roamed the crowd, attempting to frighten partiers. The cloying, chemical odor of methamphetamine vied for dominance with the tang of weed and hashish. People imbibed just about everything with abandon, as though betting the world might end tomorrow.

It was a fair bet in Libya.

Leine and Talal made their way through the attendees to the center of the room where Yusuf watched Dani as she ignored him and danced with two strangers. Yusuf's bodyguards stood at attention nearby. On the way, Leine and Talal passed dark alcoves with various accoutrements for patrons who preferred anonymity for their sexual escapades. She roped Talal into dancing with her, waiting until Dani gave her a slight nod.

"Follow my lead." Leine edged toward her recruit, with Talal in her wake. Using the other dancers for cover, Leine bumped into Dani.

"I'm so sorry," Dani said, leaning closer to Leine.

"My fault," Leine replied as she slipped a listening device into Dani's pocket. Then the two danced away—Dani toward Yusuf, Leine and Talal toward the crowd.

A man dressed like Zorro with a cloth mask and leather body harness stepped in front of Leine and swirled his cape around her shoulders. Concerned, Talal stepped toward her, but she shook her head.

"Would you be a dear and get us a drink?" she asked. Talal gave her a dubious look, but then stood down and disappeared into the crowd.

"I'll bet you like things rough," Zorro purred as he groped her thigh. "You look like special forces. Maybe you will perform enhanced interrogation on me, yes?"

Leine maneuvered her hand to his crotch and squeezed. "Actually, that's right up my alley. Wanna play?"

His face taut with pain, Zorro choked back his response.

Leine loosened her hold on his privates. "I take that as a no?" Zorro gasped in relief and staggered away, cupping his balls. *You'd think he'd get the picture.* She glanced down at the army fatigues, hiking boots, the baton. Maybe she hadn't given off enough of a dominatrix vibe.

Nah.

While the drama with Zorro played out, Yusuf and Dani had moved off the dance floor, headed for one of the dark alcoves. Leine followed, dancing her way behind them as she performed evasive maneuvers to fend off interested patrons. As she neared the alcove Yusuf had chosen, another man slipped in behind them. She snapped photographs using the baton, which Miller's techs had fitted with a digital camera, making sure to capture Yusuf and the mystery man before they moved too far into the shadows.

Leine reached in her pocket and brought out another gift from Miller: a pair of glasses with night vision capabilities, fresh from Defense Advanced Research Projects Agency, or DARPA. The NVGs had nanotechnology hidden in the bows, allowing for smaller components. Instead of the typical longer lenses, the glasses were much less noticeable.

Still moving to the music, Leine monitored the new addition to Yusuf's party, expecting to see a possible ménage a trois. What she got instead was a sit-down.

That must be his contact for the handoff. Leine held up the baton and pointed the camera lens at the alcove. She adjusted the camera to allow for low light and snapped several more pictures.

Leine exited the dance floor and took a seat at the bar with a view of the alcove. She spotted Talal at the other end, waiting for drinks. The man who had joined Yusuf and Dani emerged from the alcove and left the club. Leine texted their backup in the parking lot to alert them to the new addition, and suggested they follow him. Soon after, Dani emerged from the alcove and headed for the bathroom. One of the bodyguards who'd been lurking nearby trailed after her. Leine waited a beat before following.

The bodyguard had stationed himself outside the door to the bathroom. Leine ignored him and started inside.

"You must wait." He blocked her entrance.

She glanced at him with mock offense. "On whose authority?" she asked, indignant.

The man opened his jacket to show a machine pistol strapped to his torso. Leine lifted her chin in acknowledgement and backed away. She crossed her arms and leaned against the wall to wait.

A few minutes later, Dani walked out of the room. Her gaze flickered over Leine, but she didn't pause as she made her way past the man guarding the door. Leine gave the gunman a look. He ignored her and followed Dani into the main area of the club.

Leine moved into the bathroom and blocked the door. The stench indicated a poorly functioning toilet, if it was functioning at all. Breathing through her mouth, she went to work searching for whatever Dani left behind.

Cigarette butts littered the floor, and the sinks were stained and dirty. Burns from forgotten cigarettes or joints discolored the white porcelain, lending the space a gritty, urban feel, matching the graffiti on the walls. Leine checked every nook and cranny she could find, searching for something to let her know what Dani had found out, if anything.

They'd discussed dead drops during training, and Leine had emphasized using a hiding place out of visual range. The only possibilities here were the windowsills near the ceiling, which would have been difficult for the five-foot-six Dani to reach, or above one of the toilets, where a piece of tile had fallen out.

Neither place held anything. Someone pounded on the door and a woman's voice demanded entry.

"One moment," Leine yelled in Arabic. It had to be there. Finding a hastily written note or some other kind of message was difficult at best when the drop site was an unknown location.

She ran her fingers over the surfaces she might have used, but came up empty. She stood in the center of the room and scanned the walls, ignoring the insistent hammering on the door. Her gaze landed on the mirror. The glass was warped, like it hadn't been mounted correctly. Leine walked to one end where the mirror gapped away from the wall and ran her fingers along the edge.

There it is.

She withdrew a wadded up tissue and gently unfolded the message. Dani had used lipstick.

Tomorrow 07:30 the note read. She'd included a location

Leine wasn't familiar with, but she was damn sure going to find it.

Dani had done well. She would need to keep her head down and escape when the time was right.

9

Dani slipped out of bed and padded into the next room. It was early, a few hours before the meeting was to take place. She turned on the light next to the sofa and sat down. Although she'd resigned herself to sleeping with Yusuf, he hadn't made any moves toward her, which was a relief. The degradation itself seemed to do the trick. She decided he must have needed companionship as much as humiliation. Which seemed odd.

It wasn't as though she was an expert in such things.

Dani couldn't sleep from worrying about the handoff. The man who had met them at the club last night gave her a bad feeling. He'd watched her like a raptor with prey. She was certain Yusuf's assurances hadn't eased the stranger's suspicions about her. When she'd asked who he was, Yusuf shrugged it off, saying he was an old friend.

Had Leine found her message about the meeting? She'd feigned interest in a couple on the dance floor as the two men made their plans, and they ignored her as she'd hoped. Concerned that the bug Leine slid into her pocket wouldn't pick up their conversation over the loud music, she'd made the decision to leave the message for Leine in the bathroom.

Even though he paid for thirty-six hours, she assumed Yusuf would either let her go before the meeting or ask her to wait for him at the hotel. Either way, she'd make certain to rejoin her team as soon as possible. She doubted Yusuf would bring her along with him to the meeting. Operational protocol would surely require fewer people at the handoff, not more. And it wasn't as though he could run her name through a security check—he hadn't asked her for ID, so wouldn't know her "real" name. The son of an intelligence officer would never be so reckless as to bring unknown personnel to such a sensitive meeting.

She eased open the case, which she'd left by the couch the night before, and popped out the false bottom. Relieved to see the pistol where she stashed it, she replaced the bottom and closed the case.

"What are you doing?"

Dani froze at Yusuf's voice. Had he seen her? Forcing herself to relax, she smiled. "Just checking to make certain I didn't forget to put everything away last night." She stood and turned. He stared at her from the doorway to the bedroom, bare chested and wearing pajama bottoms. "Unless you'd like round two?"

He studied her a moment. "If only we had time." Frowning, he nodded at her. "We must find you different clothes."

"I can wear my coat home, if that's what you mean."

Yusuf smiled as he walked toward her. "You're not going home."

Dani's throat dried and she attempted to swallow. "What do you mean? Of course I am." She reached for her coat, but he grabbed her upper arm in a bruising grip.

"We have a deal, do we not? I paid for your time. I intend to get my money's worth."

Relief skittered through her and she moved closer. "Which I

intend to give you." She started to run her fingers along his chest, but he captured her hand and squeezed.

"I have a meeting out of town I must attend."

"Then I will await your return."

Yusuf shook his head. "You will accompany me." He brought her fingers to his mouth and kissed each one. "I want you to see what I do."

Dani's mind whirled, searching for an excuse that would keep her from having to go with him. "You want me with you at a business meeting? How will you explain my presence?"

"Who said anything about business?"

"I merely assumed."

"Don't." He pulled his phone from his pajama pocket and typed something into it, before sliding it back. "I have ordered a change of clothes for you. I expect you to be ready when I return."

"Of course."

Yusuf got dressed and left after telling her to order breakfast if she was hungry. She did, acutely aware that in addition to Leine and the CIA monitoring the suite, Yusuf's people were, too. Leine had briefed her on what to do and not do in that situation, so she went about her morning as though she were Aya, waiting for her client to return.

As the minutes ticked past, Dani's imagination got the better of her. Accompanying Yusuf to the meeting was too dangerous, especially with the addition of the "old friend." She'd have to work out a way to skip going.

If the mystery man was part of the handoff, she doubted she would survive. Not with how suspicious he'd been. He'd mentioned details to Yusuf about the fighting in Syria, leading her to believe she and he had fought on opposite sides. She shuddered at the thought of being murdered and left for the desert to claim her. Had she beaten the terrorists back from her city, proudly leading men and women into battle, only to lose her life at the hands of one of her own countrymen?

The impulse to contact Leine grew overwhelming, but she resisted. She didn't want to take the chance of being found out.

She would have to have faith that her team would be there when they arrived at the meeting site. And that Yusuf hadn't changed anything at the last minute out of paranoia.

Thirty minutes later, a knock at the door announced the arrival of her new clothes. Upon opening the package, her heart dropped. A bright yellow dress with matching spiked heels and scarf. She would be a hard target to miss if she tried to escape.

Which was most likely his plan.

What did she expect? Running shoes, cargo pants, and a T-shirt?

Not likely.

With a sigh, Dani finished her breakfast before rummaging in the toy case for something she could wear to hold the gun underneath the dress. The ball gag had possibilities. She could remove the ball and strap the gun to her thigh, tightening the buckles on the makeshift holster. Walking would be awkward, but she'd practice before Yusuf returned.

Her spirits somewhat lifted, with an ear toward the door Dani went into the bathroom and set to work rigging a holster.

AN HOUR LATER, YUSUF RETURNED. HIS MOOD HAD CHANGED. HE was curt, all business. When she asked him how he liked her dress, he waved her away.

"I don't pay you to ask my opinion. I pay you to be Aya."

Dani realized her mistake. He wanted her to be strong and domineering, not like every other subservient woman he'd most likely met. He was considered a powerful man. Women would try to please, not anger him. He'd hired her to abuse him. She spotted the riding crop on the couch and walked over to pick it up. He tracked her movements, his eyes showing a glimmer of interest.

"Come here. Now." She slapped the crop against her hand and glared at him.

Yusuf lowered his gaze. "Yes, mistress."

***

THANKFULLY, THE SESSION DIDN'T LAST AS LONG AS THE PREVIOUS one. Apparently his interest had waned, most likely because of the impending meeting. Dani put away her accoutrements before retiring to the bathroom with the case where she strapped the pistol to her inner thigh. Then she went back into the living room and turned on the television to catch the news. A few minutes later, there was a knock at the door.

Yusuf opened the door to let the man from last night into the room.

"Samir," Yusuf greeted him.

Samir's gaze flickered over Dani, before he turned to Yusuf.

"Is everything ready?"

Yusuf nodded. "Yes." He gestured toward a large bag next to the sofa. "It's all there."

"Good. Have you sent anyone ahead?"

"My team left an hour ago."

"Then we should go." Samir glanced at Dani. "What will you do with her?"

"She's coming with me. I paid for her until tomorrow."

"That's not a good idea."

"I don't care what you think." Yusuf's face flushed red. "She is coming."

Samir frowned, his anger matching Yusuf's. "Have you checked her for a wire?"

Yusuf rolled his eyes. "She works for a private company. Stop being so paranoid. My father has things under control."

"Then have her strip. I want to see for myself."

"Are you serious?" When the other man didn't answer, Yusuf sighed. "You heard him, Aya. Take off your dress."

Dani's blood froze. They would see the gun. Her mind scrambling for a good story, she smiled. "It'll cost you."

Samir narrowed his eyes. He strode to where she sat on the couch, seized her by the arm, and yanked her to her feet. "He said take off your dress."

Scowling to hide her fear, Dani wrenched her arm from his grasp and reached up to untie the halter. She let it drop, baring her breasts. "Satisfied?"

"All of it."

Dani bent to grab the hem of her skirt when Samir gave an impatient snort and snatched the fabric from her hands, revealing the pistol and makeshift holster.

Samir quickly removed the gun and stepped back, triumph plain on his face. "What did I tell you?"

Yusuf stared at the pistol in Samir's hand. "Why do you have a gun?" he asked in a quiet voice.

"Please. It's not what you think, Yusuf," Dani began.

"I asked you a question." The timbre of his voice had increased by several decibels. "Why do you have a gun?" Each word exited his mouth like a shotgun blast.

Samir grabbed her arm and squeezed. His cold expression brought a fresh wave of anxiety coursing through Dani.

Panic filled her, but she held on tight to the idea that Yusuf seemed to need her. "I was afraid. You didn't tell me anything about the meeting and I didn't want to be unarmed." She glanced at Samir, then back at Yusuf. "I always carry a gun. Ever since coming to Tripoli."

"And why is that?" Yusuf asked.

"I am Syrian. The Libyans in this part of the country think that we are all in league with the Russians. It's dangerous. As is my profession, which I'm sure you can understand."

"Release her," Yusuf said to Samir.

"You believe her?" Samir looked incredulous.

"I do. Release her, now." Yusuf moved toward them, his hand outstretched. "Give me the gun. I will keep it safe while we are at the meeting, and then return it to her once her time with me is finished."

Samir shook his head. "You are blinded by lust, Yusuf." He slid Dani's pistol into his waistband. "She doesn't need this while I'm here. I will keep it for now."

Dani almost fainted from the rush of blood from her head. She backed up until her calves met the sofa, giving her a modicum of support.

"Look what you've done." Scowling, Yusuf stepped forward and took her arm. "She's weak with fright."

"Better weak with fright than armed."

Yusuf studied Dani, his expression marred by disappointment. "Are you all right?" he asked in a low voice.

Dani nodded, stiffening her spine. It wouldn't do for Yusuf to lose interest in her. "Of course."

Yusuf stepped back. "Then we must go."

10

———

"Have you gotten any info back on those photographs I took at the club?" Leine sat with Paul Miller in front of the monitors in the room below Yusuf's suite. High resolution photos of the area where the handoff was to take place lay scattered on the desk before them. The coordinates turned out to be a village Izz al-Din destroyed during their retreat from battle three years prior.

Miller checked his phone. "Not yet. Don't worry. We'll have it soon."

"Let's hope so." Leine ran through several of the surveillance pictures. "My guess is that Yusuf and the Russians want to meet in the open to limit problems from either side." She pointed at a photograph depicting what was left of the upper floors of two buildings close to the village square. "I like this building and the one next to it for hides. We'll have to check for IEDs." Years before, she'd worked an operation in a similar village and had run into explosives left by retreating terrorists that were designed to blow up government forces.

"There's a handheld IED detector in your gear."

"Good. NVGs and body armor?"

"Of course."

Leine nodded her approval. "With the M2010s, we should be golden." Thanks to a last-minute shipment from Miller, the enhanced sniper rifle was a welcome addition to their arsenal.

"Just be aware the Russians will want to protect their investment."

"We'll be discreet. Until we aren't."

"That's what I mean. At the very least they'll deploy a drone to monitor the area."

"Weaponized, you think?"

Miller shook his head. "Doubtful. They don't want to take a chance on releasing whatever they're selling to the Syrians. There could be a ground team for backup in case shit goes sideways, although it would be a small contingent, since the two parties are allies and wouldn't expect trouble. There hasn't been any chatter in that regard."

"What about our guys?"

"I've got a team on standby, but they're fifteen minutes out. I don't want to spook either side."

"So, what you're telling me is we're on our own."

"Not exactly. I've requested a Predator for overwatch."

"No missiles, though, right?" Leine stacked the photos in a pile. When he didn't answer, she stopped what she was doing and glanced at him. "I said, no missiles, right?"

Paul sighed. "Leine."

"Paul?"

"I need to know obtaining the weapon is your priority one."

She frowned. "What else would it be?"

"A member of your team is involved."

"I'm going to make sure Dani gets out of there alive. Of course. But it won't compromise the op."

"You sure about that?"

She tamped down the angry retort that sprang to her lips.

"I'm sure." She wasn't about to tell him otherwise. An admission like that would make him doubt her understanding of the task ahead. Of course she understood. But getting Dani out of the line of fire was top of mind.

Miller nodded, crossed his arms. "Just so we're clear."

"We're clear." She crossed her arms, mirroring him.

"You realize if anything happens to undermine the objective of this mission, I'll do whatever's necessary. We can't allow the bioweapon to get into Syrian hands."

Leine leaned forward, narrowing her eyes. "You can't order a drone strike. First of all, you can't know for a fact that the strike wouldn't disperse the vector. And second, we're not going to endanger Dani's life any more than it already is."

Miller sighed. "Look, Leine. I get it. You bonded with your trainees, but you all knew the risks. You can't believe Yusuf will allow her to live, especially since he found a weapon on her."

When Samir had discovered the gun, Leine demanded they exfil Dani at once. Miller talked her down, arguing that the recruit had handled herself well, and that they'd blow the op if they did what Leine wanted.

"She's a witness, and a dangerous one," he continued. "You know as well as I do what happens to witnesses."

"That's awfully convenient." Leine took a deep breath and let it go, reining in another angry reply. "You don't get your way this time, Paul. You knew my rules when you and Scott brought me in, not to mention the fact that I have a crew who won't tolerate one of their own being collateral damage." Leine stood, her anger at a slow boil. This was one of the reasons she had avoided working for her old employer. The upper echelons referred to the practice of losing certain assets as "collateral damage," or "acceptable losses."

"Calm down, Leine. Look at what's at stake. Hit Yusuf and his entourage, there's a good chance you'll recover the weapon and save your girl. Win-win. Another win: we can eliminate one of the scientists who's been working on the bioweapon. Do that, and the Russians will realize somebody's onto them, putting their operation at risk. They'll go underground. It'll take years to recoup their losses."

"Why not allow the handoff to happen, then keep eyes on the scientist to see where he or she lands? You can take the lab offline with a direct action. That seems better than wholesale destruction. My team can grab Yusuf on his way back to Tripoli."

"Risky. I'd prefer to eliminate Yusuf and the Russians, recover the weapon, then locate the lab and take them offline with a cyber strike. More strategic."

"Which speaks to my suggestion of following the Russians back to their lab. Do we even know what kind of weapon they're selling? What if things go to shit, you order a strike, and it releases whatever the hell it is. What then?"

"We'll be tactical. Any possibility of hitting the bioweapon, I won't order the strike." He gave her a meaningful look. "Do you really think I want to chance that thing in the wild?"

"What about reverse-engineering the weapon? They're handing it off, so release is imminent, right? We grab the weapon, capture and interrogate both the scientist and Yusuf, find out what we're dealing with. That way we get out ahead of this thing. The Agency would be heroes."

"Look, I'm sorry your girl's in the mix. I really am. But some-times outcomes aren't optimal. Think of it this way—take out the group, grab the weapon, save Dani."

"If they don't kill her first." Leine sighed. This discussion wasn't getting them anywhere. She'd make sure to get Dani out in time.

She had to.

Time to change the subject. Her blood pressure would thank

her. "Let's talk about the lab. Successful or not, you know they'll try this again."

Miller rubbed his eyes. "Yeah. We're working on that. Once we know what they've got, we'll go from there."

He'd aged since their last op together. The lines around his eyes had deepened. "You look like you could use a vacation."

He gave her a tired smile. "After this is all over and we've got our hands on the weapon, I just might consider it."

***

DANI STARED THROUGH THE DIRTY WINDSHIELD OF SAMIR'S pickup, trying not to think about what he would do to her once they arrived at the meeting. Samir had insisted she ride with him for insurance, and now she was gagged and belted into the passenger seat, her wrists and ankles zip-tied so she couldn't escape. She'd tried everything she could to free her hands when Samir wasn't looking, but the ties were secure.

That wasn't going to help when Leine and the team made their assault. She'd have to lay low, hope she didn't get hit by a stray bullet. The problem was they'd expect her to be with Yusuf.

When Yusuf complained about her being tied up, Samir had told him he would hold her until he'd received what he came for, then let her go. Yusuf objected a second time, but thought better of it when Samir held his gun to her head and threatened to shoot her. He even tried backtracking, telling Samir he'd leave her behind, but at that point Samir had decided he needed her as a guarantee.

Why had Yusuf insisted she come along in the first place? It didn't make any sense. The more witnesses to the handoff, the more dangerous it would be for him. And for her. And now she'd made an enemy of Samir.

Worst of all, she had no gun. She eyed the AK-47 resting against the terrorist's leg near the door. She would try to get hold of a weapon. She'd wait until the firefight began, when Leine and her team attacked. If she could just get her hands free.

Dani felt Samir staring at her, and she met his gaze. His dark eyes held menace. A cold-blooded killer, she had no doubt. During the battle for Raqqa, she'd seen many eyes such as his. Eyes as dead as his housed no soul, no humanity.

It was then that she knew he had to die.

11

Leine and her team arrived at the meet well before dawn and did as thorough a reconnaissance as they could with the time they had. Their initial search didn't find any IEDs in the crumbling buildings they chose as hides, so they set up with a view of the ravaged village square.

Convincing Miller of the soundness of her plan had taken more work than Leine expected, which pissed her off. How could he not see the value of her argument? Fewer casualties meant more intel. Leine was not averse to eliminating terrorists, that much was obvious. But when it came to her team, she refused to allow the Agency to strong-arm her into acquiescing to Miller's "acceptable loss" policy.

Throughout history, soldiers on the ground acted as chess pieces to upper management. But the fighters in the trenches knew better, knew that no war, no matter what kind of technology dominated the battlefield now or in the future, would ever be won without boots on the ground, allies, and the relationships forged through common cause.

The overreliance on tech put her teeth on edge. She'd seen how its use took emotion out of decision-making, allowing those responsible to sleep at night. For Leine, making life and death decisions should never be easy. The disconnect between the human beings doing the killing via technology and the ones on the ground, caught in the crossfire of warring factions, set a bad precedent.

A persistent thought kept niggling at the back of her mind, having her second-guess the decisions being made in the upper echelons of the CIA. What was Miller keeping from her?

The team took their positions just before sunrise. She'd been right—the hide sites had excellent visibility of the rubble-filled center of the deserted village, but were far enough away to keep their cover intact. Raheema would act as spotter for Amira in the first building, and Mohammed would do the same for Hassan in the second. Naza and Leine would cover the remaining area from a third vantage point in the second building.

"Check in," Leine said into her mic.

"Alpha up," Raheema answered.

"Bravo up." Mohammed's quiet voice floated over the mic.

"Good. Now we wait."

Leine extended the bipod on her rifle, popped open the dust cover on her scope, stretched out on her stomach, and sighted in on the projected target area. "Wind?" she asked Naza.

"South-southeast, light and variable."

"Distance?"

Naza read off the numbers.

"Got it."

In addition to three M2010 sniper rifles, the group had a trio of AK-74s, fragmentation grenades, and five Makarov 9mm pistols. Each member carried several magazines worth of ammunition.

Leine was proud of her team. They'd worked hard and had come together as a solid fighting unit, even though half the group had been strangers before training. The men had no problem accepting commands from the women in the group, and the women hadn't balked at taking orders from someone who might have been lower in the military strata during the war.

Leine wondered if she'd get as much cohesion from the graduates of the SHEN Academy. Possibly, after a few missions where they had to rely on each other. That was the secret sauce in any successful fighting force—trust. Learning to depend on your team was paramount to gaining cohesion.

Interactions with Amira had been positive, with a sincere effort on the part of the recruit to work on her anger and regain her mental and emotional stability. Leine had shared tools she'd used herself to help Amira learn to compartmentalize. The recruit had been eager to demonstrate her willingness to use these tools, giving Leine a sense that perhaps the young woman might well work through her issues.

Leine settled in to wait.

"Two vehicles, three o'clock—" Hassan's voice filtered through Leine's earpiece.

She scanned the terrain through binoculars, settling on a cloud of dust to the north, coming from Tripoli. "Probably Yusuf's crew. They're early." Good. If they could get Dani out of harm's way before the Russians showed up, that would minimize the fallout. She continued to sweep the horizon but didn't see evidence of the Russians.

The two vehicles approached—a black Ford Expedition and a smaller white Toyota Hi-Lux pickup—and drove along the dirt road leading into the village. The black SUV slowed as it turned and headed into what was left of the city center. The pickup followed. Both vehicles had tinted windows, making it impossible to see inside.

"Wait for my signal." Leine followed both vehicles through

her scope as they circled the square. The SUV stopped, but the pickup rolled past and parked several yards from the Expedition. The driver's side door opened and a man in desert fatigues stepped out, holding an AK-74M. A second gunman exited the front passenger side, his head on a swivel. The pickup's occupants remained in the vehicle.

"Hold," Leine breathed into her mic.

"White SUV, two o'clock."

Leine pivoted to get a bead on the approaching vehicle. A rooster tail of dust trailed behind a GMC Yukon coming from the opposite direction as Yusuf and his crew. "Looks like the Russians are here."

That took care of Dani's immediate rescue attempt.

The driver of the black SUV knocked on the hood, and the back doors opened. Yusuf climbed out, followed by another gunman. There was no sign of Dani or the man they'd met with at the club.

The Yukon stopped a few yards away from the black Expedition. The rear doors opened and two men got out. The driver followed. Both the driver and one of the passengers carried assault rifles. They immediately flanked the third, an unarmed man carrying a metal case.

A scientist? Or merely a delivery man? The two men acting as close protection meant it was most likely the former.

"I've got eyes on the case," Leine said into her mic. "Amira, take the Expedition. Hassan, cover the Yukon. I've got the Hi-Lux." She glanced at the unendingly blue sky to see if she could spot the telltale flash of a drone. There was nothing. Smaller, low-flying drones could be seen, as long as one knew to look for them. The larger Reaper and Predator drones, however, operated at tens of thousands of feet, making them impossible to spot.

Where was Dani? Who was inside the Hi-Lux? She trained

her binoculars on the white pickup. The sun glinted off the glass, making it difficult to see through the windshield.

Yusuf walked over to the newcomers. The Russian opened the case for Yusuf's inspection. After a brief conversation, Yusuf returned to his vehicle and grabbed a duffel bag from the backseat. He walked back to the Russian and opened the bag to show him what was inside. The Russian nodded and handed the case to Yusuf.

"I don't have eyes on Dani." Leine's heart rate kicked up a notch. Where was she? Had Yusuf left her in the SUV under guard? Or had they already eliminated her?

The Russians started back to their vehicle. Yusuf did the same before he veered left and headed toward the white pickup.

What the hell is he doing?

"We've got company—two o'clock," Hassan said, his voice betraying his rising stress level. "Looks like a local."

Leine homed in on the approaching vehicle with her binoculars. An older Czech-made triple-axle utility truck trundled toward the burned-out village. More than a dozen head of sheep milled in the back under a canvas cover.

"What the hell?" Leine breathed into her mic. That's all they needed—some local shepherd to get caught in the crosshairs and end up in the news.

"What do you want to do?" Raheema asked.

"Hold. This doesn't feel right."

The truck slowed as it reached the entrance to the village, then stopped. Yusuf glanced at the truck, but continued toward the pickup without breaking stride. The Russian scientist had just deposited the duffel bag into the back of the Yukon. He glanced at the truck and said something to one of his bodyguards.

The driver exited the utility truck and walked to the tailgate, apparently intending to let the sheep out. Dressed in a knee-length tunic with a vest, long pants, and sandals, his sun- and wind-burned face gave him the look of a local. Yusuf's bodyguards approached the man and waved him off, while the Russians looked on with bemused expressions. The man appeared not to understand and released the gate. With a chorus of *baas*, the sheep poured out of the truck bed, some leaping to the ground, others falling on top of each other. Yelling at the driver, Yusuf's gunmen jumped clear, obviously angry.

Just then, three men in tactical gear carrying submachine guns materialized behind the last of the flock, throwing off sheepskins they'd been wearing for camouflage. They immediately fired on Yusuf's guards, mowing them down in an instant. At the same time, two more men exited the cab and strafed the Expedition and the Yukon, peppering the vehicles with rounds.

As Leine repositioned her rifle, the unarmed scientist and his bodyguards scrambled for cover. A barrage of rounds slammed into the scientist and one of the bodyguards. The surviving Russian dove behind the Yukon. Spooked by the gunfire the sheep scattered, as did the driver.

"Dani's in there," Amira cried.

"It's a strike team, and they're not Russian," Leine warned. "Take them out." She took aim at the newcomers and fired. The gunman on the right dropped where he stood. A pink mist appeared where his head had been, dissipating in the breeze. Leine worked the bolt, seating another round, acquired the next target, and took aim. Before she could squeeze the trigger, there was a volley of gunfire. Two more fell.

"Got him," Amira called over the mic.

"Same," Hassan said.

Naza started firing her AK, and was quickly joined by Mohammed and Raheema.

Realizing someone was picking them off from behind, the

last two gunmen took cover behind the big truck's engine block, out of the line of fire. The surviving Russian gunman popped up and shot at them, then ducked back behind the Yukon. They returned fire.

"Keep it up," Leine ordered as she turned her attention back to Yusuf. He was headed for the white pickup in a flat-out run, arms pumping, the case swinging wildly in his grip. She sighted on the drivers' side window, willing the occupant to show himself. The door to the pickup cracked open, and the driver popped his head out.

It was the man from the club. She still didn't know who he was or where he was from, but at that point it didn't matter. She'd take both him and Yusuf out to get the case.

Leine narrowed her eyes against the glare off the windshield, trying to see if there was anyone else in the pickup, but the mystery man wouldn't open the door any wider. Either way, she'd be sure the round didn't penetrate the passenger side. She took a deep breath and let it go as she pulled the slack from the trigger.

"Shit!" Hassan's voice ricocheted through Leine's earpiece.

Eyes steady on her target, she growled, "Report."

Naza sucked in a breath as she ejected her spent mag and slapped in a fresh one. "Oh, God. There's another—"

Before Naza could finish, a loud *hiss* erupted near the front of the utility truck. Leine swiveled in time to see the Yukon explode. The remaining Russian screamed. Automatic gunfire burst from Amira and Raheema's position, and the gunman who'd fired the RPG slumped to the ground, his rocket launcher slipping from his grasp. There was no return fire from the Russian.

"Where did *he* come from?" Leine scanned the area for more threats.

"Must have been hiding in the cab," Amira answered, breathless. "I didn't see him until just now."

"Amira, flush out the two behind the truck."

"Roger that."

"Mohammed, back her up."

"Wilco."

Leine swiveled back to the white pickup, but it was gone. "Dammit."

Yusuf was nowhere to be seen—a dozen sheep milled over the space she'd seen him last. Had he escaped with the driver? She reached for the sat phone to call Miller as a stream of gunfire erupted near the utility truck, the sound echoing through the empty square.

Amira had slipped behind the truck and was inching toward the two remaining gunmen. She was almost in position when an explosion rocked the second-floor hide site she'd just left. The already unstable walls blasted outward from the impact, raining pieces of concrete onto the road below.

"Raheema!" Naza yelled into her mic.

"What the—" Leine caught a flash of white in her periphery. A quadcopter the size of a microwave hovered a couple hundred yards above the building. Leine nodded at the AK in Naza's hands. "Bring that motherfucker down."

Naza swung the AK toward the drone and fired, hot brass pinging with each spent round. She scored a direct hit and the device dropped like an anvil, slamming to the ground next to the two-story building.

Freaked out by the latest blast, the sheep scattered, finally allowing Leine a clear view of the village square.

Yusuf sprawled face-down in the dirt, arms outstretched.

The case was gone.

12

"Raheema," Leine shouted into her mic. There was no answer.

Naza was already at the head of the stairs leading to the ground floor. "I'll check on her."

"There are still two combatants behind the truck."

"I'll be careful." Naza took the stairs two at a time and disappeared.

Leine returned to her scope and barked into her mic. "Where's the damn pickup?"

"We didn't have a clear shot." Hassan's anguished voice reverberated through her earpiece.

"Which direction did he go?"

"Southwest," he replied.

"Hassan, take the SUV. See if you can follow the tire tracks. Stay on it until I call you. Mohammed, keep covering Amira."

"Roger that," Hassan and Mohammed replied in unison.

The staccato hammer of automatic fire erupted from Amira's position at the back of the utility truck. Leine turned in time to see the two remaining gunmen collapse to the ground, their bodies riddled with bullets. Amira sprinted to the Expedition, cleared the front and back seats, then moved to the back and opened the door to the cargo area.

"She's not here," Amira said. She pivoted toward the center square, where Yusuf had fallen. Leine scanned the area through her binoculars to see what she was looking at. Yusuf was still alive, had managed to climb to all fours. Blood saturated the side of his neck and shoulder. Amira broke into a sprint, headed straight toward him.

"Amira—what are you doing?" Leine yelled into her mic.

No reply.

Leine went back to her scope to sight on Yusuf. By the look on Amira's face, if Leine didn't do something now, he'd be dead, or worse. She fired a warning shot. The round kicked up a spray of dirt in front of Amira and she skidded to a stop.

"Amira. Wait. Think about what you're doing." Leine seated another round. "The case—the bioweapon is gone. We need him."

Amira shook her head, staring at Yusuf. "Dani's dead." The torment in her voice was palpable.

"We don't know that. Amira, listen to me. Did you see a body?"

"Leine," Naza broke in over the mic, her breathing coming hard and fast from her sprint to the hide. "Raheema's hurt."

"How bad?"

"I've got pressure on the wound to stop the bleeding, but she needs a better medic than I am."

"We have another problem."

"What?"

"Give me a second."

Leine redirected her focus back to Amira. The Yazidi fighter hadn't moved, still watched Yusuf. He had his back to her with one knee up in an attempt to stand. In an even tone, Leine said into her mic, "Amira. Stand down. We need him alive."

There was a pause, then, "He killed Dani." Amira's voice cracked with emotion.

Leine lowered her head. She had to talk her down, or they'd never find the virus. Or Dani. "We don't know that. What if she was in the white pickup? He's our only chance to find her." She refocused on Amira through the scope. Amira shuddered, her body wracked by sobs.

Where the fuck was Miller's drone?

"It's Yusuf's fault for bringing her here, but you—us—this operation allowed her to be killed." Amira's anger reverberated through the mic. "We should never have come."

"Amira, wait. Think. You looked inside the SUV. Was anyone left in there?" Leine needed Yusuf alive. Needed to interrogate him to get insight into where the other man might be headed. Surely she could see that?

I should have dropped Amira from the team. What the hell was I thinking?

Second chances. That's what. Leine had been the recipient of multiple second chances in her life. And she'd continue to hand them out whenever she could.

Sometimes those choices turned out badly.

Amira wiped her eyes with her forearm and raised her gun, aiming at Yusuf.

"Amira, answer me."

"There was no one."

"Then you see? Dani didn't die in the assault."

"I don't care. She's not here. I'm going to kill him."

"Amira. Don't. We need him. He's the only one who can tell us where she might be." Leine sighted on Amira, ready to pull the trigger. She didn't want to fire, but she would if Amira was hell-bent on destroying any chance they had at recovering both the virus and Dani.

"Amira," she said again. "I don't want to shoot you."

"Then don't," Amira replied.

"If you attempt to kill Yusuf, I will have no choice." *C'mon, Amira. Think.* "If you kill him, there's no one left alive who can help us find Dani. She will be lost. Forever. Because of you."

Amira paused. She stared at the ground, her chest heaving as tears coursed down her cheeks.

"I know you're in pain, Amira," Leine went on. "And that pain makes you take chances you shouldn't. I get it. I've been there." Memories of her now-deleted Kill Wall crowded her mind. Her need for vengeance against the monsters who hurt so many innocents was still raw. "What Yusuf attempted to do was wrong. He deserves to pay. But we don't know that Dani is dead. Yusuf is here now. He's someone we can question to get an idea of where she might be."

The seconds ticked by like hours. They were running out of time. Yusuf had managed to stand, but appeared disoriented. He was wounded, but at least he was alive. He glanced behind him at Amira and stiffened.

She had to end this conversation, now. Leine took the slack out of the trigger, waiting. "It's now or never, Amira. Stand down, or I will shoot."

Amira turned and looked up toward Leine's hide site. The despair in her eyes took the former assassin's breath away. Still, Leine held steady. She would do what had to be done. There was too much at stake.

A moment later, Amira put down her rifle.

Once assured Amira was no longer a threat, Leine ordered her on perimeter check, while she secured Yusuf, and Mohammed rushed to help Naza carry Raheema out of the building. The cherubic recruit had lost a large amount of blood, and floated in and out of consciousness. Naza cleaned as many of the shrapnel wounds as she could and used clotting agent on the worst of them, but the damage was too great. Raheema needed a transfusion, now. Leine called Miller on the satellite phone and requested air support.

"What the hell happened out there?" Miller's voice had lowered several octaves, his concern obvious.

"First off, we have Yusuf. He's been shot, but he's stable." Leine brought him up to speed on the surprise strike team and the white pickup as she glanced at the general's son. The gunshot wound had been a through-and-through and he'd lost some blood, but he'd survive long enough to interrogate, at least.

"Somebody targeted one of the hides with an armed quad," Leine continued. "Raheema took shrapnel from the explosion. Naza shot it down and it exploded. The remnants look like an ISIS-style kamikaze drone equipped with a grenade."

"Any way to ID the maker?"

"Doubtful. It's toast. I'll collect what I can and bring it back for analysis." Leine picked her way through the bodies of the assault team, checking their pockets, trying to get a bead on who sent them. Their equipment was professional grade—there was money behind them.

"Then what?"

"The deal went down—Yusuf took control of the case, but he changed course midstream and headed over to the white Hi-Lux."

"And?"

"It was the guy from the club."

"Jesus."

By the tone of Miller's voice, he knew who the mystery man was.

"What did you find out about him?"

"We got a positive ID from the DOD." Miller blew out a breath. "His name's Samir Fakhri. He's a Syrian affiliated with Izz al-Din."

"That's not good."

"Understatement of the year."

"What the hell was he doing at the meeting?" Leine asked.

"The nearest we can tell, he and Yusuf are old school buddies."

"No. Seriously?" That explained why he was there. But why would Yusuf go to him with the case? Then the obvious hit her. "Yusuf had a side gig."

"He was going to sell part of the shipment to Samir." Miller's tone was matter-of-fact.

"That has to be it."

"And now you're telling me Samir has it all?"

Leine stopped what she was doing and studied one of the hi-tech suppressed submachine guns the strike team carried. Not Libyan military, that was certain. "Yes."

"Let me ask you again. What the hell happened out there?"

"Hold on a minute, Paul. Let me ask you first: what happened to the drone? I thought you were going to be our 'eye in the sky,' remember?"

"Somebody screwed up. The drone's somewhere over Chad."

"Wow. That's a big fucking screw up."

"You're telling me." Miller muttered. "For what it's worth, a surveillance drone is headed your way. Maybe we can pick up the Hi-Lux's tracks."

"Big maybe." Leine finished checking the assault team and the utility truck, and headed over to assess the dead Russians. "Looks like our unknown visitors were some kind of mercenary group. Professional tac gear, expensive guns, no IDs. I'll look at the Russians next, try to see who they belong to.

Maybe there's an angle we can use with our friends in the Kremlin."

"The chopper should be there in about five minutes. What are you going to do with Yusuf?"

"What I wanted to do in the first place—bring him back and interrogate him. He's our only lead right now."

"Did you at least get your girl out?"

"She wasn't in Yusuf's vehicle. If you haven't heard from her yet, then she's still out there somewhere." *Or dead,* Leine thought. "We think she might have been in the pickup with Samir."

Miller was silent. In a low voice he said, "I'm sorry, Leine. I know how much your team means to you."

"I'm not giving up on her yet. I'll get Yusuf to talk."

"I suggest you and your prisoner leave with air support. When Yusuf doesn't check in with Daddy, there'll be some pissed off Syrians headed your way."

"Don't forget the Russians. When they figure out the meet went sideways, they'll be swarming the place." Leine hesitated, not sure she wanted to broach a subject she'd been mulling over. *What the hell.* "Keep the fact that we've got Yusuf quiet, yeah?"

"What are you saying?" Miller's tone changed from professional to wary.

"The tac team, the missing drone. What do you think I'm saying?"

"Don't go there, Leine."

"I'm asking you to keep things on the down low—for now."

"You think we've got a leak."

"Sure seems like it." Leine let the words hang between them. He had to have thought the same thing.

Another long sigh. "Yeah. It's just you and me and your team. For now."

"What are you gonna tell your people? That he died?"

"Leave that to me. Call when you get to the hangar."

"Roger that." She glanced at the sky, wondering if someone was watching them now.

For all of their sakes, she hoped not.

13

———

Dani worked the zip tie circling her wrists until they were slippery with blood and sweat. The gag Samir had stuffed in her mouth tasted of diesel. She'd been right about the terrorist—she just didn't know how right until he took her hostage. When they'd rolled up to the meeting she surreptitiously scanned the places where she thought Leine and the team might be set up, waiting to ambush the meet. All she saw was dirt, and sand, and the bombed-out buildings of the village, but that just meant they were good at concealment.

She shouldn't have armed herself, should've known she'd be searched, but didn't like the idea of being out in the middle of nowhere with the likes of Yusuf and Samir and the Russians without a weapon. Had they not discovered the gun, they might not have restrained her.

Then again, she could have been inside the SUV when the strike team slaughtered everyone, and now she'd be dead.

What happened to support from the Americans? Surely the CIA knew she would be with Yusuf. Had they decided she was expendable? Leine would never have risked Dani's life, of that she was certain. And why had God spared her the quick death of a tac strike, only to exchange that for whatever Samir had planned?

She wondered when—and how—he would kill her. She eyed the silver case on the floor by his feet. The prize was so close. If she could only find a way to escape, then she would take her chances on her own in the desert. Anything would be better than to leave so much destruction in this man's hands.

Samir drove recklessly, his brows drawn together in a perpetual scowl. Every so often, he would reach down to touch the case, as if to make sure it was still there. He mostly ignored Dani.

Fine with her. That allowed her to attempt to free herself without him noticing.

They drove on through the day and into the night, only stopping for petrol at an outpost she assumed was owned and run by the terrorist network he belonged to. He let her out once to relieve herself after she'd repeatedly tried to communicate her need through the gag, and had offered her a tiny amount of water, but only when she insisted, each time replacing both the gag and the zip tie around her ankles. Other than that, he acted as though she didn't exist.

Later that evening, after hours of following what amounted to a camel track through the desert, they pulled into a camp of some kind. Small fires had been lit throughout, providing only enough illumination to see the silhouettes of several large tents. They drove through a metal gate topped with razor wire into the compound and were immediately surrounded by men carrying Kalashnikovs and dressed in the traditional tunics and loose trousers of the desert dweller. Two well-used all-terrain vehicles were parked nearby.

Samir parked near one of the tents, then came around the side of the pickup and hauled her out of her seat. He bent down and severed the zip tie binding her legs so she could walk. She flexed her ankles, trying to force feeling back into her feet. If he noticed the blood on her wrists from attempting to escape, he didn't show it. After a quick word to one of the gunmen, he dragged her to the entrance of the tent and shoved her inside.

The tent was spacious, its floors covered in richly textured rugs and floor cushions. A large, carpet-covered platform took up half of one side. Several propane lamps hung at intervals from the tent frame, casting dark shadows along the walls. A thin, bearded man dressed in desert camouflage sat in a chair at a desk to their left. He looked up as they entered.

"A new one, Samir?" A spark of interest flickered across his face as he put down the book he was reading and stood. He crossed the room to join them and studied Dani with narrowed eyes. He grabbed her by the arm and pulled her closer. A sneer of distaste curled his lip. "You've brought me Yazidi?"

Samir looked at her with renewed interest. "Why do you say that?"

The warlord lifted a section of her hair to his nose. "I can smell them."

Dani cleared her throat. "I am Syrian." She kept her intense dislike for the man on a simmer and lowered her eyes.

"Bah." The man waved the comment away. "My customers won't know the difference. Or care."

Dani bristled at his offhandedness, but kept her mouth shut. She had to remain vigilant, look for a way to escape.

"Same rate as last time?" The warlord walked to a large wooden chest and opened the lid.

Samir nodded, his scrutiny of her short-lived. "Yes, Beni. The same rate. As always."

Beni counted out a stack of currency and closed the chest. He returned and handed Samir the money. "I don't suppose you want to tell me where she came from?" He gestured toward her dress and shoes. "Do I need to be concerned about someone looking for her?"

Samir pocketed the cash. "Not any more than usual." He looked at Dani and smirked. "She's a dominatrix by profession."

"Oh?" The warlord looked at her with interest. "Then the tables have turned. I have several customers who would pay handsomely for the opportunity to bring such a one to heel."

The two men chuckled.

Beni turned his attention to Samir, his actions dismissive of his new acquisition, dominatrix or not. "Will you stay the night? Or must we say goodbye?"

Samir gave a slight shake of his head. "I should be on my way."

A look of disappointment crossed Beni's features. "Oh, come now. At least have a drink with me. I so rarely have interesting company."

"Isn't that why you chose this location?"

Beni chuckled. "Indeed. But please, indulge me."

"All right. But only one."

The warlord clapped his hands, startling Dani. "Fetch us some tea. Now."

Dani frowned in confusion. She was about to protest that she had no idea where the tea was when he backhanded her across the cheek. Reeling from the impact, Dani cupped her face with her bound hands, eyes watering from the assault.

"Now you are the slave." Beni pointed at a small table in a dark corner of the room. On it sat an ornate metal and glass teapot, surrounded by four colorful glasses.

Not knowing what else to do, Dani went to the table and, using her bound hands, lifted the pot. The exterior was warm and the pot full, as evidenced by the weight and the sloshing sound from inside. She inhaled a deep breath and let the sweet fragrance calm her as she poured first one glass, then two. She set the pot down and awkwardly picked up the glasses, which she delivered to the two men who had each taken a chair near the platform. As she did, she noticed a stack of rifles, machine guns, and ammunition in a pile next to the door.

Her heart quickened. She might stand a chance if she could get to one of the AKs. She averted her eyes, in case either of the men noticed her interest.

But how?

Beni gestured for her to sit on the platform. "Sit there. We may need your services."

Blood raced through Dani's ears at the thought of what the warlord meant by her "services." She eyed the weapons, trying to gauge how she could grab one of them, but discarded the idea. What if the magazines were empty? She'd never have time to load. She glanced at her shoes. She could inflict some damage with the spiked heels, but that would only get her so far. With nonchalance she didn't feel, she scanned the room, looking for something to use to enable her escape. A submachine gun leaned against the platform a couple of yards from her. Even with her wrists bound, she thought she might be able to fire it.

Dani waited until Beni turned his attention to his guest before she eased closer to the weapon using micro-movements so she wouldn't attract attention.

"So, Samir," Beni began, "Where are you off to now? Some seductress's bed, I presume?"

Samir shook his head and sipped his tea. "Nothing so exotic as that, I am afraid. I must join my brothers. They are in need of some good news for the fight."

"And you are the bearer of this good news?" Beni's transparent attempt to squeeze information from his guest was not lost on Samir.

The terrorist bared his teeth in what would never have been

mistaken for a smile. He wagged his finger in the warlord's face. "I see what you're doing, Beni. You must be careful of whom you ask these questions."

Beni smiled back and spread his arms wide. "I am always discreet, my friend. Forgive my directness. I am an old man in need of gossip."

"Old is not a word I would use to describe you." Samir finished his tea and set the glass back on the table. "I do have one favor to ask."

"Anything, my friend."

"I need a plane."

Beni nodded. "I know a man who can take you wherever you desire. His private airfield is but an hour from here."

"Excellent. I will pay him, of course."

"I would expect no less from my most honored guest. Simply tell him I have sent you and he will help you with whatever you need."

"Then I must go. Thank you for your hospitality."

Beni and Samir rose and clasped hands. Obviously the meeting was over.

It was now or never.

Dani lunged for the submachine gun. Hands curled around the stock, she jammed the gun under her arm and clamped down. Sliding her hands forward, she turned and swung the barrel in an arc, finger stretching for the trigger. Searing pain split her scalp as Samir yanked her back by the hair. He grabbed hold of the gun and wrenched the weapon from her grasp. She slammed her heel into his instep, but he wrapped her in a chokehold, weakening the attempt. Beni grabbed the gun from Samir, stepped back, and raised the barrel. Spots appeared before her eyes as she struggled to breathe. Samir let go and shoved her to the floor.

Dani landed on her hands and knees, choking and gasping

and angry with herself. She closed her eyes and bowed her head, trying to catch her breath.

"Spirited, this one. If she wasn't so valuable, I would not hesitate to kill her. Perhaps I should ask a ransom?" Beni glanced at Samir, who shook his head.

"She has no family. No one will pay for her return."

"Well, then, I'll have to sell her." Beni's whistle pierced the air, and a gunman appeared at the entrance. "Put her with the others."

"Don't worry," Samir said, humor lacing his words. "If she tries to escape, she won't get far."

14

____

The gunman seized Dani's arm and led her outside to one of the other tents. He shoved her through the darkened interior past several younger women huddled together on the ground, and into a curtained-off area. The gunman tossed her a piece of clothing similar to what the other women were wearing and indicated that she should put it on. When she showed him her bound wrists, he used a blade to cut her hands free. He then left her alone.

Samir was right. How would she ever escape? Kilometers of desert lay between her and any kind of safety. Now, because she failed to overpower both men, Samir would be set loose on the world with a deadly weapon and no one would know where he'd gone. He hadn't disclosed anything other than that he was headed to join his brothers and would need a plane to get there. Africa was a huge continent. He could mean anywhere.

Dani pulled the sky-blue abaya over her canary yellow dress and waited, sucking at the wounds on her wrists. The gunman returned and said something in a language she didn't understand. When she looked at him uncomprehendingly, he repeated what he'd said and pointed to her shoes. She reached down and slid off one of the spiked heels. When he nodded, she did the same with the other. He picked them up and motioned her back to the main section of the tent with the barrel of his gun.

He left her to find her way among the other women. The cloying scent of fear mixed with that of unwashed bodies added to the claustrophobic atmosphere. She found an empty spot on the floor next to a group of women. Two wore veils, making their ages difficult to determine. The rest were bare-faced. Dani guessed most were in their late teens or early twenties.

"May I sit?" she asked in Arabic.

One of the women nodded and motioned for her to join them. She leaned over and said in a low voice, "You must not speak. The guards don't like it."

Dani nodded that she understood and fell silent. A short while later curiosity got the better of her. She leaned in close and whispered, "What is this place?"

The woman put her finger to her lips and shook her head. At that moment, the guard walked by, a silent threat with a machine gun.

Once he'd moved out of earshot, she said in a low voice, "We are to be sold as slaves."

Dani's heart skipped a beat. Knowing it was one thing. Hearing it from another soon-to-be-victim made it much more real. "To whom?"

"The warlord Beni Haddad will sell us to the highest bidder."

The same guard walked past on the other side of their little group, making a circuit, and the woman fell silent. When he'd gone, she continued.

"In the morning, the guards round up a group of us and take us away. No one comes back. This happens at least two times each day."

"How many of us are there?" Surely there were many more women than guards. There had to be a way to overcome them and escape.

What then? She had no idea where they were, or even which country they were in. The all-terrain vehicles she'd seen near the entrance were a possibility, but again, only if she knew which direction to travel.

"More than I can count." The woman indicated the area around them. "You have seen the tents?"

Dani nodded.

"They are filled with women and girls."

"Where are we? Which country?"

"Southeastern Algeria. Near the border with Libya."

Dani's spirits plunged. Samir had driven them so far. There was no way Leine or her team would be able to find her.

She understood now why Samir had taken such a primitive route to the camp. He couldn't afford to have anyone follow him, leading to the discovery of either the warlord's outpost or the silver case.

She'd have to figure out a way to escape, get back to her team. The stash of firearms in Beni Haddad's tent gave her a spark of hope. She'd rather take her chances in the wilds of the desert with a machine gun than be a slave to any man.

15

———————

Abandoned airfield, Tripoli, Libya

Leine waited while Hassan took Amira to her room in the barracks at the airfield. She wouldn't participate in the interrogation, not after her actions during the op. Leine had remanded her to her quarters for the foreseeable future, hoping the time alone would reinforce the grave error she'd come close to making.

When they first arrived in Tripoli, they'd rushed Raheema to the hospital. Naza volunteered to stay with her as Leine and the rest of the team went to the training site to set up an interrogation room. Meanwhile, the surveillance drone Miller had requisitioned to look for Samir and the white pickup, scoured the desert for clues to where Samir had gone. So far, they'd had no luck spotting the Hi-Lux. Hassan arrived in the SUV not long after.

Unsure she could trust him, Leine sent Mahmoud on an errand, then had Mohammed and Hassan bring Yusuf into the hastily built interrogation room and tie him to a chair. His arm in a sling from a gunshot wound to his shoulder, Yusuf was tightlipped and didn't answer anything at first. After Hassan and Mohammed each had a turn, Leine deemed him sufficiently warmed up.

She walked into the room, pulled up a chair, and had a seat. Eyes hooded, he watched her, his expression impassive. She waited a few minutes, allowing the quiet to settle between them. Most guilty interviewees had a difficult time with silence, tending to jump in to fill the space. Not so for Yusuf. Leine studied him much like an entomologist would study a strange new insect. She sipped her bottled water, noting that his gaze followed her actions.

"Would you like some?" she asked in Arabic, indicating a case of bottled water on the floor nearby.

Yusuf looked away.

Leine shrugged. "Suit yourself." She settled in, deciding to wait him out a bit longer.

Several minutes ticked by before she started. "So, Yusuf," she began. He gave her a sharp look. "Yes, we know who you are. We know that your meeting earlier today was to purchase a biological weapon from the Russians. You were going to deliver the shipment to your father, who in turn would use it on the rebels fighting for freedom in your country."

He didn't respond verbally, although she could tell that his respiration had increased.

"We also know that before the strike team arrived in the covered truck you were about to hand the weapon to a known Izz al-Din terrorist." She leaned forward. "Does Daddy know about your little side hustle?" Leine stared him down. "I'm sure your terrorist buddy was more than happy to pay."

His lip curling, Yusuf lowered his gaze.

"But see, now he has all of the weapon, and that's just not acceptable. To me or to the people I work for." She paused to see if he had a reaction. Nothing. "I wonder what your father would say if I called to let him know? Hmmm? That Daddy's little boy thought he was smarter than your average bear, make a little extra coin? Certainly he'd never suspect his beloved son would allow a terrorist to have the bioweapon he so badly wanted." She pulled out the sat phone.

Yusuf's pupils dilated and he swallowed, indicating a dry mouth. She was getting somewhere.

"Look. I don't want to put you in a more difficult situation than you already are." She stood and walked over to the table to set the phone down. "But I need answers."

"I will never betray my country." His sneer was just short of believable.

"But you already have, haven't you?"

A scowl creased his face. "I don't know what you mean. I haven't done anything wrong."

Leine raised her eyebrows. "I'd have to argue the point. It looks like you allowed a member of Izz al-Din to acquire a weapon of mass destruction. Which, by the way, he could use to fight your president and father back home in Syria. Assad's been trying to get rid of ISIS for years, right? What happens when Izz al-Din joins forces with them? Tell me again how that isn't betraying your country?"

"Samir would never use it against Syria."

"Don't be naïve. Of course he would. Wouldn't you? According to my sources, the weapon he just acquired is most certainly capable of mass destruction. Bring-down-governments kind of huge. What do *you* think he's going to do?"

Doubt filtered across Yusuf's face.

"I have to tell you, after the strike team showed up, and Samir bolted with the case without checking to see if you were all right *after he put a bullet in you*, I knew he wasn't what you'd call a real *good* friend."

"He could have killed me. He didn't."

"That's a fair point. Although, perhaps he thought he had?" She nodded at his sling. "You could have died from those wounds. There was certainly enough blood to accommodate that assumption."

Yusuf closed his eyes and took a deep breath. *Got him.*

Leine walked back to her chair and sat down.

He opened his eyes and gave her a calculating look. "What do you want from me?"

"Let's start from the beginning."

SASHA FINISHED HER MESSAGE TO TONY AND HIT SEND ON THE encrypted app. She laid the burner phone on her coffee table and stared into space. Ilya, her only true friend at the lab, had given her an ominous warning that something very bad had happened, that the lab might be shut down with everyone sent home. When she'd asked what he knew, he shook his head.

"Someone from the lab has been killed. Rumor has it the higher-ups engineered a deal with the Syrians to sell the bioweapon. Apparently the deal went kaboom."

A frisson of fear skittered down Sasha's back. "That can't be good. What happened?"

"Just what I said. Kaboom. Someone leaked the meeting and they were attacked. Yanus is dead."

"No." Yanus had been one of the rising stars in their inclusive little scientific community. She'd been horrified by his willingness to create the super virus, but that didn't change the fact that he was a brilliant researcher. "If he's dead, then what's to become of the project?"

"The bigger question is what happened to the virus? The case he carried with him allegedly contained eighteen vials."

Sasha gasped. "Do they know where it is?"

He shook his head. "They've dispatched a security team to find out."

"What happens if they don't find it?"

"Use your imagination."

"But they won't shut us down. They can't." She wanted to add, *I've been working with the CIA.* The urge to tell Ilya about her idea to steal the vaccine to help keep the world safe bubbled to her lips, but she clamped her mouth shut. *Don't, Sasha. Tony said not to trust anyone.*

At least she could pass the instructions for the vaccine to Tony in case someone released the virus into the population. There was still hope. Tony had assured her his government would make the cure widely available, if and when it was needed. She couldn't say the same for hers.

Ilya gave her a rueful smile. "Dear, naïve Sasha." He tucked a loose strand of hair behind her ear. "Always the optimist."

She'd taken her break and gone out to her car to text Tony with the news. He hadn't replied before she had to go back inside and finish her shift. At the end of the day, she rushed home to her apartment and texted him again, demanding a reply. Several agonizing minutes later, he answered.

Remain calm. Events are in play.

Sasha wrote back: *When do I leave?* She was more than ready to go. Tony had promised to extract her if things changed.

Things had definitely changed.

Tony: *Soon. Monitor my messages. I'll be in touch.*

Sasha stood and began to pace. The urge to pack her things and leave was overwhelming. Why not just go? She would pack the phone, take off in the Saab, contact him when she'd made it to wherever she was going.

But where could she go? Her superior at the lab had her passport—a "precaution" he'd said. Against what, he hadn't specified. She figured it was to make sure employees didn't leave prematurely—once workers had a taste of what the project entailed, not to mention the setting in the middle of nowhere, many would opt to seek jobs elsewhere.

The extra perks offered when she signed up should have given her pause. Why else would a company need to bribe its workers? Sasha hadn't been put off by living and working in Libya, had thought that was the main reason for the generous bonus offered by her employers. She'd been vaguely aware that she'd be working for the government through a front company, but even that hadn't deterred her, though now that she thought about it, it should have.

Sleep on it, Sasha told herself. Throughout her life, whenever confronted with a major decision, she'd given her subconscious time to mull over her choice. More often than not, that extra bit of time would help clarify her position, allowing for an effortless choice.

After powering down the burner phone, she removed the battery, then grabbed the novel sitting on her coffee table. She opened the cover, revealing a cutout into which she placed the phone and battery. Closing the book, she buried it deep behind a set of romance novels in her bookcase.

16

———

The interrogation took longer than was optimal, but Leine had to give Yusuf props. The Syrian's cagey answers and delaying tactics worked against the clock, counting down the time it would take Yusuf's father to deploy a strike force to rescue his son—if and when they learned he was still alive.

According to Miller, the quadcopter strike to take out Amira and Raheema's hide had most likely been deployed to the meeting by the assault team in case there were complications. Since Amira hadn't been targeted when she left the hide, Miller said the device might have been an autonomous "Killer Drone," directed by artificial intelligence—a kind of "set it and forget it" weapon that could respond to various programmed actions. Once a target was hit, often the drones would turn kamikaze and destroy themselves by flying into the target and detonating.

Leine hadn't used force on the younger Al Shami, rightly guessing the more effective way of breaking him would be with psychological and emotional manipulation. He'd insisted that he hadn't meant for Samir to take the case. They'd struck a deal for one of the vials.

One. And now he had eighteen.

"There was a young woman with you at the meeting." Leine leaned forward in her chair. Sweat beaded on Yusuf's forehead, belying his feigned composure. "Where is she now?"

He didn't seem surprised that she knew about Dani, or, as he knew her, "Aya." Tapped phones and bugged rooms were standard operating procedure for the son of a Syrian intelligence officer. How Leine and her group had managed to evade his counter measures would be a question to which he'd never know the answer.

"She was inside the white pickup, with—"

"Samir," Leine finished for him. He nodded, looking miserable.

"He won't want Aya with him—he'll see her as dead weight." Yusuf avoided Leine's eyes.

"What about the weapon? She's at huge risk if the virus is released." Amping up his fear for Dani's safety was a calculated bluff, as was Leine's intentional use of the word virus, but Yusuf had already shown an attachment to Dani.

"What virus?" Yusuf eyed her warily.

"Stop playing me. What else could it be? The Russians have been working on a super virus for decades. What have they done? Something with smallpox? That's been their darling for ages."

The miniscule tightening of his facial muscles and narrowing of his pupils would have been invisible to the untrained eye, but Leine picked up his tell immediately. "What are we talking here, designer virus? Recombinant? Chimera?"

The last word brought a more noticeable reaction. *Shit.* She moved closer so she was up in his face. "The name Yusuf Al Shami will go down in infamy if you don't tell me what it is we're looking for. You'll bring shame on your family and death and destruction to your country. Is that what you want?" A fleeting look of despair crossed his face. Leine leaned in closer. "You'll be responsible for the deaths of thousands of your countrymen and women if you don't answer me," she growled. "Tell me what we're dealing with."

The faint release of his shoulders told her she'd won. She pushed away from him and crossed her arms.

"They call it a chimera."

Her hope for a lesser threat vaporized. A hybrid virus. Not good, but at least now they were getting somewhere. "What are the components?" If she could relay the information to Miller, they might be able to get out in front of it before Samir or Izz al-Din deployed the virus.

Defeat showed plain on his face. He closed his eyes. "Smallpox and Ebola."

"Jesus." It was as if a lead weight dropped in Leine's gut. With smallpox's ease of transmission and no known cure for Ebola, the combination would be much more deadly. The Russians had been working on that particular combination for years. Apparently, they'd succeeded in weaponizing it. But there was still the possibility that the World Health Organization could get out in front of it by deploying smallpox vaccines and Ebola protocols as soon as it surfaced.

"How were they able to keep the Ebola viable? Transmission is generally through bodily fluids." Oxygen and UV light lessened the virus's effects considerably.

"There's more to it."

The weight in Leine's stomach grew heavier. "Tell me."

"Only if you promise to let me go."

"That can be arranged." It could be, but she sure as hell wasn't going to be the one doing the arranging.

Yusuf studied her for a moment before he responded. "The scientists spliced a synthetic agent they created into the virus's DNA. They call it Doomsday."

Leine rubbed her eyes, trying to wrap her head around what he'd just said. Clichéd moniker or not, combining smallpox and Ebola in a viable, transmittable super virus was horrific enough. Adding a lab-created agent of unknown origin would be next to impossible to stop. CRISPr technology had made splicing and modifying DNA much easier. All a person needed was a few hundred dollars and a little knowledge, which could be easily found on the internet. But this was entirely new territory.

"Do we know what this added agent is?"

"All I know is that it makes the combination virtually indestructible. And one hundred times more transmissible."

Transmissible equaled deadly. Leine took a deep breath and let it go. "And your father wants to use this against his own people."

Yusuf glared sullenly at the far wall.

Leine resisted the urge to grab Yusuf by the neck and choke the information out of him. *Patience, Leine. You've almost got what you need.*

"Aya is in grave danger, Yusuf. Depending on where your friend releases the virus, millions of innocent people will be, too. You have to tell me everything you know about Samir. Where he might be going, where his contacts are, anything."

"He spoke of an Algerian warlord."

"And what does this warlord do? Would Samir go there if he's on the run?"

"He buys and sells women. Some he ransoms, depending on the family's wealth. Whenever Samir needs cash, he kidnaps women and sells them to this man."

"Kind of like an ATM for terrorism. Good to know." Once she'd tracked down Samir and the virus, Leine would make sure she reconnected with this warlord to give him some extra special attention. "How does the warlord find the women otherwise?"

"He raids schools, mostly. Younger women bring a higher price."

"Charming. Where can I find him?"

She brought up a map on her tablet, and he indicated an area near the Algerian-Libyan border, east of the Ahaggar Mountains.

"Samir mentioned that he could see Mount Tahat from the camp, although he didn't say how close it was. He kidnaps the women in Libya, then transports them to the camp. The location makes it easy to outrun the army if they come for him. He's never been caught."

Yusuf's information could be verified by the CIA using satellite photos. A solid lead. Samir would be several hours ahead of them. She called Miller to give him the news.

"A fucking chimera? So the Russians finally did it." He paused, took a deep breath, let it go. "I'd hoped we wouldn't have to deal with this in my lifetime. If the virus is released, the fallout will continue well after we're both gone." Another sigh. "We'll identify the location, send in a team, see if Samir's still at the camp."

"I have a better idea. Why don't you let me be your eyes on the ground? That way, once my team IDs Samir, yours can swoop in and save the day."

"What's in it for you?"

"I rescue Dani if we find her. Then you can send in the cavalry."

"I'm not planning to destroy the camp, Leine. Not with the possibility of so many civilian casualties."

"Why don't I believe you?"

"You don't have to. For what it's worth, you have my word."

Leine suppressed the sarcastic remark that bubbled to her lips. There was no need to antagonize him. "I still think having a smaller, agile scouting force is the better play." She paused a moment before she added, "And you owe me."

"You have six hours."

"Make it twelve and we've got a deal."

"That may be too long."

"Samir's going to have to rest sometime. Even if he powers through and keeps going after he drops Dani off, he'll make mistakes. Exhaustion affects everyone—even terrorists. If we can get to the camp before daybreak, I think we have a good possibility of finding him."

"Unless he's eating uppers or chewing khat." Miller sighed again. "Fine. Twelve hours. But keep us in the loop. Wear the mics, keep my team apprised. If we don't hear from you, my guys go in hard."

Nothing like a little added pressure. "Twelve hours, no less."

"Twelve." His annoyance was palpable. "What are you going to do with Yusuf?"

"We need to keep him off the grid for the time being. I want a member of my team with me at the camp. With Dani captured and Raheema in the hospital, that leaves two to guard him. I'd feel a whole lot better with a few more pulling security."

"I count three."

"Long story. There's two." Leine didn't feel like getting into a discussion with Miller about Amira. She'd address the recruit's state of mind when she got back.

"Deal. I've got just the place to put him."

"It better be a fortress. You can bet his father's already mobilized a rescue team."

"Don't worry. We'll be ready."

"What are you going to do about the lab that created this monster?"

"We've got it handled."

"Are you sure?"

"Of course I'm sure. You might want to keep your eyes on your own paper, Basso."

"Huh. Does this mean you don't think you have a leak?"

"I didn't say that. I said I've got the lab handled."

"Let's hope so."

17

———

Damascus, Syria

General Mustafa Al Shami's mobile lit up as it vibrated on his desk, indicating a call from his top security man, Sayed.

"When?" was all he said.

"Within the hour, sir."

"Good. We must strike quickly, before they know we're coming."

"Yes, General."

"You have called upon the best we have? The rescue of my son must be carried out with absolute meticulousness."

"Only the best, General. I sent the roster as you requested."

"Good. Good. I expect regular updates as the operation commences."

"Of course, General. I will update you myself. God willing, your son will be returned home by morning."

"I expect nothing less, Sayed."

"Yes, General. Of course."

"May God protect you."

"And you, sir."

General Al Shami ended the call and leaned back in his chair, thinking of the phone call from his contact at the Russian lab in Libya just hours before. The contact verified that their scientist and two bodyguards had been killed, along with at least two of Yusuf's security and several unknown assailants. To Al Shami's intense relief, his son's remains had not been found at the scene.

The scientist and Yusuf's bodyguards had been the victims of what appeared to be a direct action by a group of mercenaries, who were then killed by another unknown force. No one seemed to know who'd ordered the strike by the mercenaries, as there had been no chatter intercepted on frequencies monitored by the Russians, and no one had yet claimed to be the perpetrator. The consensus was that this strike team had been supplied either by the United States or Turkey, since neither the Russians nor Al Shami had sent them. But the mercenaries had all been shot by snipers, which begged another question—who did the snipers belong to? Obviously, they had prior knowledge of the meeting and had infiltrated the meeting site before anyone else.

After sifting through the rubble of the gun battle, the remnants of an armed drone had been found, but there were no identifying marks. As of yet, the Russians hadn't found the case with the virus, or his son.

When Yusuf didn't call, General Al Shami knew he'd been captured. A bit of digging and a message to his contact in the Libyan security forces suggested one possibility: CIA operatives were in Libya. The evidence pointed to a team of American snipers.

But how had they known?

The answer was starkly obvious. Yusuf.

I should never have sent him.

Al Shami's son hadn't been ready, but Yusuf's insistence that he be given more responsibility to prove his worth had won Mustafa over. He knew all too well the pressure the son of a famous father was under to prove himself. Al Shami's own father had been the revered spy master for the senior Assad, before Bashar had inherited the office. When Al Shami's father died of old age, the younger Mustafa stepped into his place with Assad's blessings, eager to bring Syrian intelligence into the new century.

He'd made some missteps, but nothing he couldn't correct.

Until now.

What had become of the virus? He assumed there would be a ransom request, both for his son and for the weapon. When none occurred, dread painted the general's heart.

Part of him hoped the Americans had retrieved the case. At least he could be sure they wouldn't deploy such wanton destruction against his country. The possibility that it could be in the wrong hands sent a shiver of anxiety through him. His Russian contact had assured him the case held enough virus to destroy Syria's enemies several times over. But if it had fallen into their enemies' hands, it would require a strong response. One that Al Shami had hoped to avoid.

Once his men returned Yusuf, he would know the fate of the weapon, giving him the information he needed to plan his response.

He swallowed his anger at his son's gross misstep. Only when and if Yusuf had been shown to be reckless would Al Shami entertain his anger. Before that, he would do whatever was necessary to recover the virus, and his son, no matter who had them.

18

Samir followed Beni Haddad's directions to the private airfield and parked near the entrance. Although it was dark, he could see that calling the place an airfield was a stretch—in addition to a dirt runway flanked by burn barrels for night landings and takeoffs, the rusted corrugated metal "office" looked as though a stiff breeze would demolish the structure. Light spilled through cracks in the building and the one and only window. An old motorcycle leaned against the outside wall.

A smuggler's airport. Perfect.

Further investigation revealed a lone Beechcraft sitting on the runway. From what Samir could tell it looked airworthy.

He exited the truck with the AK-47 and his duffel bag, which contained the money from selling the woman and some other cash, the vials, both his and the woman's semiautomatic pistols, and ammunition for both the pistols and the AK. He'd removed the vials from their original case, had carefully rewrapped them, and transferred them to a wooden box after he realized the Russians would track the bioweapon to ensure it didn't fall into the wrong hands. He'd felt an uncharacteristic pang of regret as he slipped the empty case into Beni's trunk when the warlord wasn't looking.

Beni had been a reliable source of income. Now that he'd stolen the virus, Samir didn't need him. His contact in al-Shabaab would make sure of that.

Samir had been intentionally vague when Beni asked where he was going. Most likely the warlord assumed he'd be able to get the information out of his pilot friend once he'd returned from wherever Samir asked him to go. Unfortunately for Beni, it wouldn't be long before the Russians converged on the trafficker's camp looking for the case with the beacon.

Better Beni than me.

The only places Beni could tie him to were the old Izz al-Din training camps scattered throughout Africa. As long as he avoided those, Samir would be difficult to find. He would visit his al-Shabaab brothers at their new training facility in Kenya. They would be ecstatic when he showed them the vials. Soon, he would be known the world over for having brought down the infidels. They would write songs about him. Stories would be passed down through the generations telling of his exploits, that he alone had destroyed the Great Satan and its allies, and avenged his family. He would make sure to save a few vials for his brothers in Syria, as he had promised in the last conversation with his contact. They would decimate the Assad regime and rebuild the caliphate, setting in motion the prophecies.

Samir slung the AK over his shoulder, walked to the metal building, and knocked on the rust-covered door.

"Hello," he called. When he didn't hear a response, he added, "My name is Samir. I am a friend of Beni Haddad's."

Inside, a chair scraped the floor, and moments later the door screeched open, revealing a tall, thin man about Beni's age. He was dressed in an ankle-length tunic and pants, and held a hand-rolled cigarette between two skeletal fingers. An older model AK was slung casually over one shoulder. Deep wrinkles formed a map of his features, speaking to years of exposure to sun, wind, and hardship. Samir suppressed an urge to turn up his nose at the smell of the burning tobacco. Instead, he smiled.

The older man didn't return the smile. "My services are not free."

Samir nodded obsequiously, attempting to get on his good side. "I have cash." He lifted the duffel bag as if to prove it.

"Come in." The man stood aside, allowing Samir to enter.

Inside was a makeshift desk, an oil lamp, and an open Koran, as well as a large container of water and some tinned food. A stack of aeronautical charts sat on a shelf behind the desk. A set of keys hung from a nail on the wall.

"Cozy." Samir set his bag on a plastic crate near the door.

"Where do you want to go?" the man asked.

"Kenya."

He shook his head. "That is too long a journey. I can take you part of the way. You will find other transportation for the rest."

Samir lifted the barrel of the AK and aimed at his chest. "I'm afraid that's the wrong answer. Drop your weapon."

The old man shrugged off his AK and slowly raised his hands.

"You're not afraid."

The man shrugged. "I'm old and have no family. If you shoot me, I will go to paradise and you will not get to where you need to go. If you don't, I will fly you as far as I can, and make a little money. Then, when I return, I will visit my old friend Beni Haddad and drink tea. Either way, I win."

Samir smiled. "There's just one thing wrong with your reasoning."

"What?"

"I know how to fly. After I kill you, I'm going to steal your plane."

19

Abandoned airfield, Tripoli, Libya

Leine finished stowing weapons and provisions inside the helicopter that would ferry them to the landing zone, a few klicks east of the warlord's desert camp. From the LZ, they would hike on foot the rest of the way, carrying what they could. She was about to head back to the hangar when Amira appeared.

"You were remanded to quarters for the night." Amira had objected when told to go to quarters, but Leine would hear none of her protestations. She could have locked her in her room, but hated coming down that hard on a recruit. Especially one with Amira's issues.

Amira lifted her chin and squared her shoulders. "I want to come with you to find Dani."

"We already talked about this." Leine crossed her arms. "Your emotional responses are a liability. Unless and until you're able to control your anger, you have no place on this team."

Amira nodded. "But I need to do this. Dani was the one who...rescued me. I must pay this back."

"Look, I understand your need to balance things out, but you've shown that you're unable to compartmentalize." At the look on the young woman's face, Leine added, "That's not a criticism, it's an observation. You need to find someone to talk to about what you experienced. That's the way you're going to get past this."

"Then I will talk to you." Amira sat on the tailgate and fixed Leine with a determined stare.

Leine glanced at the time. They were set to leave within the hour. "I'm listening."

"I wasn't the only person in my family captured by ISIS. The night they came to my city, my mother, my sisters, and my niece were all made to stand outside in the square with our neighbors, barefoot and in our nightclothes, as they rounded up the men. They beat them, including my father and brothers, and then shot them in cold blood. This happened in front of me, my mother, and my sisters." She closed her eyes for a moment before she went on. "Then they dragged my mother from my arms, beat her until she couldn't walk, and left her for dead. The man responsible said he wouldn't waste one more bullet on a Yazidi. Then he spit on her."

Tears streamed down Amira's face, but her measured voice didn't change. "Then they came for my niece." She glanced at Leine, but quickly looked at the ground. "She was seven."

"I'm so sorry, Amira." It was all she could say. Amira had lived through a nightmare. Leine had heard the horror stories from the Yazidi women she'd rescued. ISIS believed them to be less than human because of their religious beliefs, and treated them as such. But Amira wasn't through.

"When they finished with her, they came for my sisters and me. They treated dogs better than they did us. I was bought and sold and assaulted so many times, I lost track. I also lost track of my sisters. To this day, I don't know if any of them are alive." Amira took a shaky breath as she wiped angrily at her tears. "Then Dani and her troops arrived. It felt like a light turned on and there was hope and possibility instead of death and despair. Dani took an interest in helping me—she refused to give up, no matter what I did. I acted out, I admit it. I have such rage inside me, sometimes I can't bear it. It's like a monster, trying to break free." Her voice softened. "When Dani and the others are nearby, life becomes brighter. I forget for a moment the darkness."

Leine didn't say anything, allowing Amira's story to settle between them.

"Thank you for trusting me." Leine sat next to her on the tailgate. "I can't imagine how difficult it's been to come back from that."

A sad smile played at the corners of her mouth. "That's the thing, though, isn't it? I haven't come back, not really." She shook her head. "That's why I must be with you when you rescue Dani. I *must*. Please give me another chance. Don't give me a weapon. Let me be your support. *Please*."

Leine sighed. Amira's main problem was being near guns or explosives when events triggered her. She could be an asset, as long as Leine didn't have to worry about her losing her shit and killing every man in sight. Not supplying her with a weapon took care of the main component, at least temporarily.

"Other than my past actions, what's holding you back from giving me another chance?" Amira asked. "You're going to need a woman to infiltrate the camp to find Dani, right? Why not me? Mohammed won't be able to do it, and Naza wants to remain with Raheema as she recovers. You need me."

She had a point, although the idea still didn't sit well. If something triggered Amira while inside the camp, she wouldn't only be a danger to herself, but to Dani as well as the other women there.

Teach her what you do to keep the monsters at bay.

The thought popped into Leine's head, unbidden. It had merit. Perhaps another crash course in compartmentalization would help. Amira had such potential as a sniper, she hated to see her skills go to waste. But she had to commit to a solid course of action.

"Say I give you another chance, you'll be putting yourself in harm's way—the same kind of situation that you endured at the hands of ISIS. What makes you think you'll be able to handle yourself? You'll be killed if you try to fight your way out of the camp."

"Better dead than captured again."

Leine narrowed her eyes. "If I allow it, you're going to have to prove your ability to compartmentalize, to overcome your emotions. Any more erratic behavior and I'll take active measures to keep the team safe. Is that clear?"

"I swear I will not endanger the lives of our team."

Give her another chance. She's good, really good. Leine sighed. "Fine."

Amira's face lit up. "This means I can go? Thank you, Leine. Thank you. I won't let you down."

"Go get your things."

Amira sprinted off as Mohammed arrived carrying his pack. He stowed it in the helicopter and, nodding toward his team-mate, asked, "She's coming with us?"

"Would you be all right with that?"

He was silent for a moment, then said, "She deserves another chance. I fought alongside her in the siege of Raqqa. I would trust her with my life."

Leine studied Mohammed. He had every reason to not want

Amira along on the op after she'd attacked him during training. That he vouched for her spoke to his respect for his teammate, giving Leine a modicum of relief.

"I'm giving her another chance." Leine sighed.

She hoped she hadn't just made a huge mistake.

20

Southeastern Algeria, near the Libyan border

Leine stopped at the crest of a slight rise on the dirt track they'd been following on foot and held up her fist, signaling to Mohammed and Amira to do the same. The crisp, moonless night brought the stars into sharp relief against the blue-black sky. Undulating shadows of distant sand dunes stretched in every direction.

"Got some activity over there," Amira said, nodding toward several fires glowing in the distance.

Leine scanned the terrain through binoculars. "According to Miller, that's where we'll find the Marlboro Man." Miller had sent Leine high res satellite images of the camp to help map their recon.

"Why do they call him that?" Mohammed asked. "Seems like a strange nickname for a warlord."

"He made the bulk of his money smuggling cigarettes. The name stuck, apparently." From the photographs Miller provided of Beni Haddad, the Algerian warlord hadn't garnered the moniker because of his rugged good looks.

Leine trained her focus on the camp. The fires had been placed between several large tents. A metal fence topped with concertina wire surrounded the compound.

"Do you think those tents are full of soldiers or women?" Amira asked, peering through her own binoculars.

"Most likely women. Miller's intel would have identified the presence of a small army. There's no way a large group of gunmen could stay hidden from CIA surveillance." The drone video and satellite photographs Miller shared with her showed one or two gunmen posted outside each of a dozen tents. One structure was positioned away from the others. Photographs placed the warlord going in and out of it numerous times. There was no evidence of a large number of armed combatants anywhere nearby.

"But the photographs only show one or two guards at each station," Mohammed said. "Some have none at all. What's to stop the captives from joining together and trying to escape? Surely there are more women than guards."

"They wouldn't make it far," Amira said.

"She's right," Leine said. "Hundreds of kilometers of desert stand between the detainees and the nearest village. Unless they stole one of the vehicles, which has its own set of problems, without a compass, food, and water, escapees would be hard-pressed to make a successful bid for freedom." Leine shrugged. "That, and a surplus of machine guns tends to sour even the most determined escapee."

She pointed to a darker section of camp to the east. "Doesn't look like there's a perimeter watch, just gunmen guarding the tents. We'll cut through the fence and enter the camp there. Stay low and out of sight when you search for Dani and Samir. Mohammed and I will find Haddad and take out his security— once he's captured we'll hopefully get a good idea where to find Samir if he's not in camp. If and when you locate Dani," she said to Amira, "key the mic three times and bring her back to the rally point. We'll join you as soon as we can."

"Roger that."

"Remember, if you come across Samir, we need him alive. He's the only one who knows where the virus is. Let us know you've found him and we'll extract."

"Understood."

"You're sure?"

Amira nodded. "Yes."

As Amira and Mohammed reapplied camouflage to their faces, Leine called Miller's second in command, Matthew Price, on her sat phone to relay their position and let him know what they had planned. He informed her that a ground force of six elite commandos were at the LZ, waiting for a positive ID of either Samir, the case, or Beni Haddad, before taking the camp. If the case or Samir weren't there, Leine would take the lead interrogating combatants who might have information on either's location.

The group continued along a set of faint tracks in the sand visible through night vision goggles. In the vast, dark space of the desert, lights, including flashlights or the like, would be seen far ahead of their arrival. They'd painted or taped over shiny or noisy items, and kept their weapons hugged tight to their bodies.

They regrouped fifty yards shy of the camp. Staying low and keeping to the shadows, the three of them sprinted the remaining distance to the fence. Leine set her pack on the ground and pulled out a pair of bolt cutters, which she handed to Mohammed. A few minutes later, he pried apart a section of the fence large enough for them to squeeze through.

Once they were inside, Amira disappeared into camp, in search of Dani.

Leine turned to Mohammed. "Ready?" He nodded. "We

think Haddad's quarters are at the front of the compound. Look for a full security contingent." Warlords didn't sleep without armed guards nearby. "Feeling good about the knife?"

Mohammed nodded. "Yes."

Leine made sure the recruits trained with combat knives, but Mohammed had been reticent to use his, citing an aversion to up close and personal execution. When Leine gave him real-world examples of its efficacy from her time as an assassin, he'd seemed to come around.

"Good. Silent is how we live to see daylight." Stealth was the only way to infiltrate an enemy camp filled with gunmen who would be all too happy to hunt down intruders. Although Leine and Mohammed both had AKs, a couple of frag grenades, and a sidearm, they'd be much better served by getting to the head guy without raising the alarm. Once Leine identified the warlord and Amira had checked the compound for Dani, Matt Price would send in his group and lock down the camp.

Leine led the way, following the fence, with Mohammed close behind. Insects buzzed in the night air, partially masking the sound of their approach. A goat bleated somewhere in the darkness, followed by the distant clank of a bell.

They entered through the center of camp and stopped near one of the tents. Leine eased around the edge to get a visual on the guards at the entrance, then pulled back. She held up two fingers, indicating two guards, and nodded at the hemp ropes used to stabilize the tent. The ropes kept the structure in place in case of a windstorm, but were also dangerous and could trip an unwary intruder. Mohammed signaled that he understood.

Leine dropped to her stomach. Using her knife, she sliced the woven camel- and goat-hair tent enough so that she could get a peek inside. The scent of the dusty fabric brought back memories of an op from an earlier lifetime when she'd taken out a particularly ruthless Somali warlord.

Leine snapped back to the present and scanned the dark interior. Several bodies lay huddled together on the ground. They were dressed in identical, light-colored abayas, and all appeared to be women. Thankfully, there didn't appear to be any small children.

She climbed to her feet and briefly described to Mohammed what she'd seen. Then she motioned for him to follow her around the rear of the tent onto the next. They ghosted across the camp, keeping to the shadows. Leine pushed aside her anger at the warlord and his compatriots, choosing instead to focus on the mission at hand rather than what the captives in those tents likely had to endure.

For now.

They skirted the fires to avoid the armed guards, and made it to the entrance. Leine stopped short of the larger tent and raised her fist, signaling Mohammed to hold. Two gunmen with AKs stood at the entrance with two additional guards near the sides—the only structure they'd come across with more than two guards.

It had to be Haddad.

She motioned for Mohammed to circle around back, signaling him to neutralize the gunmen guarding each side. With a determined expression, he slid his knife free and slipped around the tent.

The seconds ticked by. There was a brief scuffle followed by a quiet thud. She winced at the sound and waited for the second, but it didn't come.

Mohammed reappeared at her side, a smear of blood across his face. He gave her a curt nod and held up two fingers, then wiped his knife across his sleeve and slid it back into the sheath on his tactical vest. Leine gestured to him to stand watch in case either of the two forward guards became curious.

Leine dropped to her stomach and sliced through the tent to

get a look inside, but something heavy blocked her view. She moved several feet to the right and lifted the edge. This time, a portion of the interior was visible. Rich carpets covered the floor. In the far corner near the entrance was a large cache of weapons. A few pieces of furniture, including the chest that had blocked her view, gave it a permanent feel. Someone lay on a raised platform on the far side of the room, covered in blankets, obviously asleep.

She eased the fabric down and motioned for Mohammed to lean in as she dug through her pack. "One combatant," she whispered. She closed her fingers around the item she was looking for: a pre-filled syringe containing a strong sedative. "I didn't see anyone else. A pile of weapons is stacked at the far end, near the entrance. I'll neutralize the occupant and make a positive ID. You watch the forward guard. If you see movement, use our signal to let me know."

Mohammed nodded.

Knife in one hand and syringe in the other, Leine slipped underneath the tent wall and crept toward the gently snoring figure. As she neared the platform, the man's face resolved in the NVGs. It was the warlord, Beni Haddad. She readied the syringe and moved closer. Before she got close enough, there was a commotion outside. Haddad stirred and Leine froze, then slowly backed away. The warlord mumbled and sat up. Shouting erupted outside the tent. Leine covered the rest of the space in two strides and slipped behind the wooden chest.

Grumbling, Beni Haddad climbed off the platform and grabbed a jacket hanging on a peg nearby. As he shrugged it on, the front flap of the tent flew open and Mohammed catapulted inside onto his knees, followed by one of the guards.

Haddad paused for a moment to collect himself. He gestured to his guard, who grabbed Mohammed's arms and pulled him up to face the warlord.

"Who is he?" he asked his guard.

"He was hiding behind your tent."

Haddad studied his captive. "Where are the others?"

Mohammed shook his head. "What others?"

The warlord slammed his fist into Mohammed's stomach. Mohammed jackknifed forward and let out a groan. "How did you get inside the camp?"

Obviously winded, Mohammed just shook his head.

Out of the guard's line of sight, Leine carefully aimed her pistol at the warlord's back, calculating the fallout from killing both Haddad and his guard.

It wasn't good. Haddad was their only link to Samir. The mission would be exponentially more difficult if she killed him. Leine stood down, deciding to wait. As long as Haddad wanted information from Mohammed, he'd keep him alive.

The sporadic sound of automatic gunfire erupted in the distance. Shouting followed. Had Matt Price ordered his men to breach the camp already? Leine hadn't given them the signal. They'd been instructed to wait.

Haddad backhanded Mohammed across the face. He loomed over him, hands clenched into fists. "Answer me."

The guard closed in and rammed the muzzle of his rifle into the side of Mohammed's head.

Leine keyed her mic, using Morse code to send an S.O.S. to Price.

Time for Plan B.

21

Felix Andreyev ordered the driver of the armored truck to stop. The flare from the fires lit by the warlord known as the Marlboro Man shone like a beacon to Felix's contingent of operatives.

Correction: group of untrained, inexperienced thugs. Ever since his employers had ordered the doubling and tripling of "independent operators" to deploy to Libya, qualified fighters had been harder and harder to come by. Especially after the Jordanians put the kibosh on a shipment of US-made Cobra helicopters and gunboats from the UAE two years before. It had been difficult to get good equipment.

To handle the increasing demand for fighters, Felix's bosses had started accepting every piece of shit who called himself a mercenary. Much like the Spartans had done centuries before, after the Battle of Leuctra. Of course, that was just the beginning of the great warrior state's demise.

"We kill everyone who tries to stop us, yes?" asked Azim, a newer recruit from the UAE. His eyes glowed with the light of a zealot, a sure sign of his eagerness to wreak havoc wherever he directed his AK.

Felix sighed as he scanned the men, wondering if the extra money was worth the headache of trying to lead this band of murderous misfits. It wasn't like he'd receive a commendation from his government for a job well done, or even a payout for his family in the event of his death. Not as a member of a group of mercs easily disavowed by the Kremlin.

And the oligarchs who funded them certainly wouldn't part with any portion of their precious wealth.

The outcome of most of the ops he was assigned to had been predictable, and this one was no different. He'd direct his men to quietly infiltrate the camp, taking out whichever guards put up a fight as they searched for the case.

A river of blood would be spilled tonight. He just hoped he could rein in his men before they slaughtered Beni Haddad.

Once they secured Beni, Felix would interrogate the warlord. The offer of money would probably be enough of an enticement, but Felix had been feeling bored and could use a bit of entertainment to break the monotony. Perhaps staking the man out on a sand dune with multiple cuts would be entertaining.

He keyed his mic. "Everybody out."

The sound of doors opening and closing from the two vehicles lined up behind them grated on his ears. There went any possibility of stealth. With a sigh, he exited the truck and walked to the head of the group, waiting until they were in formation.

That they could do.

Felix retrieved a pack of cigarettes from his tactical vest, shook one out, and lit it with a cheap plastic lighter. He exhaled a cloud of smoke and sized up his team, remembering the old days when most of the fighters were former Spetsnaz, men who had actually experienced battle: veterans from Chechnya, from Ukraine, commanders from Syria. These new recruits were undisciplined, uninspired soldiers of fortune who only cared for money and bloodlust. He feared for the outcome if they were ever called to perform a precision military strike.

This is what happens when leaders become desperate.

Felix took another drag off his cigarette and dropped it on the ground, crushing it with the heel of his boot. It was those damned recruitment videos. The oligarch who funded Felix's group, in league with the Kremlin, had hired a slick videographer who made the group's mission look almost glamorous against a backdrop of international intrigue, exciting operations, and fervent patriotism. Felix had even been pulled in by them. He couldn't blame the poor bastards for believing the lies. A combination of kompromat and propaganda worked wonders when deploying such fantasies.

He nodded toward the compound. "The camp beyond is our target. This is a surprise attack. You are to approach quietly." He studied the faces of his men—some expressed excitement and eagerness, others bored indifference mixed with contempt. A paycheck was a paycheck. They would do whatever they wished, and Felix would let them. He couldn't be everywhere at once and had to focus on his objective: find the case. The signal from the beacon had led them here.

Needless to say, he hadn't told his men what the true objective was. He didn't trust them to turn the case over, and would only allow a select few to be present at the interrogation. Once they found the container, he would transport it back to the lab. No one needed to know what was inside. Hell, he didn't even know exactly what was inside, only that the case and its contents were to be recovered at all cost.

When he'd asked his contact if his men needed to wear protective suits during transport, he'd been told not to worry, that the box was virtually indestructible.

It was the word "virtually" that gave him pause.

Maybe he'd give it to one of his men to carry.

22

Dani woke with a start. The soft snores told her that many of the women captives were catching what sleep they could. Fear and intimidation were exhausting, and Dani's last twenty-four hours had been as tense as any she'd experienced in war. She may not have had to dodge rocket-propelled grenades from the enemy, but keeping up the ruse of the woman named Aya and then being held captive by both a terrorist and now a slaver ranked with any battle she'd endured.

The only difference was that she'd failed at her objective. The thought of Samir in possession of the virus gave her heart palpitations. The only bright point was that she'd heard Beni Haddad tell Samir about his friend's plane. The information wasn't much, but it was something.

She had to escape. Not only to give the CIA information on Samir, but the idea of being sold as a piece of property was horrifying. Once the initial buyer grew tired of her, he could resell her to another, albeit at a reduced price for wear and tear, continuing in a never-ending cycle until there was nothing left to sell.

Her thoughts turned to Amira and the horror she'd endured at the hands of ISIS. She'd always tried to understand the other woman's pain, knew she could only scratch the surface. If she didn't find a way to escape, she'd soon have firsthand knowledge.

She scanned the room for the guard, but didn't see him. Most likely he'd stepped outside for a cigarette. The cloying smell of spent tobacco followed him whenever he walked past. Careful not to wake any of the other women, she made her way to the back of the tent. On her knees, she hefted the bottom edge of the tent and peered outside. She gulped in the cool desert air and studied what she could of the terrain. A row of tents rose from the desert floor behind them. She tried to get a glimpse beyond, but it was too dark.

What will you do if you make it past the guards and the metal fence? She lowered the thick material back into place. She had no water, no food, no shoes, and no idea where they were. Trying to escape would be suicide.

She would have to wait until an opportunity presented itself. Perhaps when the guards came for her she could seize one of their guns and turn it on them.

Probably not. The obvious outcome of that maneuver would be a different form of suicide.

Perhaps when she was sold? Could she lure her new owner into a false sense of complacency, then make her escape? She would have to endure whatever they had planned for her. Dani swallowed her fear. Other women throughout the ages had survived capture—and worse. She would, too.

The guard appeared at the entrance and began his rounds. Dani waited until his back was to her before she quietly returned to her spot and lay down. The woman who'd spoken to her when she first arrived stirred, but remained asleep. Several minutes later, the guard walked by and she closed her eyes.

Having completed his loop, the guard exited the tent again, probably for another cigarette. She couldn't blame him. The air inside was stifling. The tiny amount of fresh air she'd been able to breathe when she lifted the section of the tent had reminded her of freedom, and how rank the air had become inside. She sat up and stretched her back, too keyed up to sleep.

At that moment, something moved in her periphery and she turned. A dark shape skirted the first group of women and headed toward her. Alarmed, Dani curled her hands into fists and moved to a crouch, ready to fight off anyone who might seek to hurt or otherwise accost the women. As the shape drew closer, she mustered her courage and her pent-up anger at Yusuf, at Samir, at Beni Haddad, at any man who thought they had the right to buy and sell a human being, let alone a woman.

The shape stopped short and dropped to its knees. A dark hooded sweatshirt obscured the person's features. The intruder pulled the hood back and a jolt of recognition shot through her.

Amira?

Heart soaring, Dani crawled toward her friend and whispered, "How is it you are here?"

Amira glanced left and right, scanning for the guard. "Leine and Mohammed are in camp, looking for Samir and the case. I'm to bring you to the rally point and wait for their return."

"Samir left hours ago. He'd never leave the case here."

"Do you have an idea where he might have gone?"

"I heard Samir and the warlord talk of an airfield an hour's drive from here."

Two of the women nearby had awoken and were watching them, their eyes wide.

"We should go." Amira turned to leave but Dani stopped her.

"Where is your gun?"

"I only have this." Amira pulled her pant leg up to reveal a small pistol.

They wouldn't be blasting their way out, which would probably work to their advantage, as long as they weren't seen. Dani nodded toward the women. "What about them?"

"Miller's men will be here soon. They'll be taken care of then."

Dani nodded and followed Amira, zigzagging through the sleeping women, careful not to disturb anyone who might voice concern. As they reached the back wall of the tent, the guard walked in. The two women froze.

One of the women who had watched them leave called out, apparently attempting to draw his attention. The guard started toward her. Amira grabbed Dani's hand and pulled her down so they wouldn't be seen. They crawled along the back wall of the tent, staying low in case the guard looked their way.

Amira reached the far corner and stopped. She waited for Dani to join her before lifting a section of the wall, revealing a jagged slice through the fabric. Amira gestured for Dani to go first, then squeezed through, following her out. She slid the fabric back into place.

"Follow me."

Dani sucked in the fresh desert air as they sprinted to the metal perimeter fence. They didn't see anyone. Pausing long enough to catch their breath, they then followed the fence line for several yards. Amira stopped and pulled on a section of the enclosure, creating a gap wide enough for them to squeeze through. As Dani stepped toward the opening, shouting and automatic gunfire erupted near the entrance to the camp. The two women exchanged looks.

"We need to follow the plan." Amira nodded toward the opening.

Dani shook her head. "What if Leine and Mohammed need our help? We should go."

Indecision flashed across Amira's features. A moment later determination took its place.

"You're right. Follow me."

23

———————

CIA Safe House, Tripoli

Naza made her second perimeter check of the evening, worry for Raheema tugging at the back of her mind. The doctor had assured her she would survive her wounds, but she'd lost so much blood. Naza had seen similar injuries during intense fighting against ISIS. Many didn't survive. True, in those instances they hadn't been able to get the victims to the hospital in time, but worry ate at her nevertheless. She hadn't the skills to keep her teammate safe. Yes, Raheema was alive, but what if she didn't make it? Naza vowed to learn advanced field medicine once she returned home—perhaps even become a doctor. Anything to help her soldiers.

She checked the time on her phone. In two hours she would return to Raheema. Her colleague would be out of surgery by then, although Naza doubted she'd be coherent. It didn't matter. Raheema needed a familiar face when she woke up. Whenever possible, Naza had been there for every one of her soldiers after surgery. Sometimes a friendly face meant the difference between survival and death. She knew the depression many of the injured endured—wondering how they could have prevented the attack, if they should have been somewhere else, if they could have saved someone.

Survivor guilt was pervasive in the ones who lived, and they often took their own lives. Living while their comrades had not weighed on their souls. This, mixed with the horrors of war, ultimately became too much to bear.

Raheema would be one of the lucky ones. Naza vowed to do everything in her power to help her rehabilitate so that she could resume a normal life.

Worry for her other teammates gnawed at her and she picked at her nails, tearing the jagged pieces. *Stop it. Worrying isn't going to help anything.*

She breathed in the cool night air, grateful for the brilliant stars. Libya reminded her of Syria, and she felt a kinship with the land and the people here. She studied the CIA safe house, glad to be away from the decrepit old hangar where they'd done their training.

In its prime, the villa was owned by a favorite of Muammar Gaddafi's. The once magnificent house was rundown and threadbare, although remnants of its former glory shone through. Two stories surrounded a courtyard with a now-defunct fountain. The walls were solid, with vestiges of colorful tiles. The perimeter had been outfitted with cameras and pressure and motion sensors, in addition to the armed guards stationed at various points on the property.

Besides her and Hassan, close to a dozen gunmen were on loan from the CIA. When she asked Miller if the Agency had been using the safe house for long, he replied that they changed it up often enough that no one would know where they had secured Yusuf.

Although that had relieved some of her anxiety, Naza still remained on alert. She passed Hassan once in her circuit of the property, and he'd expressed his concern regarding security. Naza had assured him that Miller and the CIA were professionals. They were prepared for whatever General Al Shami might attempt.

Just then, Naza's radio chirped and Hassan's voice came over the mic.

"I think I saw something out near the street. I'm going to check."

Naza keyed her mic. "Be careful, Hassan. Don't let anyone see you."

"Roger that."

The minutes ticked by. Naza was beginning to get worried when his voice came back over the radio. "Everything's fine. It was only—"

The sound of automatic gunfire came over both the radio and from outside.

"Hassan—Hassan!" she shouted into her mic. "Report." There was no answer. Heart racing, Naza sprinted for the front of the house, yelling as she ran, "Shots fired. Near the entrance to the villa. I'm heading there now."

As though the flames of hell were licking at her feet, Naza flew around a corner into a straight hallway and launched into a flat-out run for the front door.

Please let him live, please let him live, she prayed silently. Her father's voice intruded on her thoughts. "Insha'Allah," he'd always said. *If God wills it.*

The sound of gunfire grew louder, amplified by the plaster and tile walls. Men shouted in both English and Arabic, adding to the chaos. Naza reached the hallway that led to the front entrance and stopped. The sound of breaking glass and bullets ricocheting off the walls told her there were multiple shooters.

Naza moved along the wall in a crouch until she came to the corner of the entryway. She took a knee, pulled in a deep breath, and glanced around the corner, then immediately fell back. A body lay on the floor. Several CIA officers were locked in a gun battle with an unknown number of assailants dressed in black and wearing balaclavas. Steeling herself, she sucked in another deep breath, then rounded the corner and let loose with the AK-74, hitting one of the black-clad gunmen. He collapsed to the floor, his weapon clattering on the marble. Too soon, she was out of ammunition, and she fell back behind the wall to reload.

Her foray into the gunfight had garnered the attention of one of the gunmen in black. Rounds pinged near her position, the assailant trying to gain an advantage. Naza ejected the spent magazine and slapped in another, waiting for a pause in her opponent's gunfire. It came quickly. She rounded the corner, spraying bullets as she did. She hit another of the intruders, this time in the stomach. He grunted and collapsed.

Not stopping to check whether he was dead, Naza continued shooting, laying down cover fire, buying the others time. When her ammunition ran out again, she ducked into an open doorway to reload. She had one more magazine. Judging by the firepower of the attackers, it wouldn't be enough.

The echo of gunfire receded, and she stuck her head out to gauge what was going on. Eight bodies lay on the bloody marble floor. Three were CIA. In addition to the two gunmen she'd killed, two others wore the dark clothing of the attackers. To Naza's dismay, the eighth body was Hassan. She ran to him, checked his pulse. There was none. His eyes stared sightlessly at the ceiling.

Years of training kicked in and she ignored her anguish at seeing yet another fallen comrade. Naza raised her weapon and moved toward the section of the house where they were holding Yusuf, stepping over bodies as she went. As she grew closer, she heard more gunfire, followed by a large explosion. Heart in her throat, Naza raced the rest of the way.

She rounded the corner and stopped.

She was too late.

Bodies lay scattered along the hallway, like a lineup of grotesque mannequins pointing to the fortified room where they'd been keeping Yusuf. A jagged hole stood in place of the reinforced door, presenting a clear view inside. She found two more dead bodies in the room near the bed.

Yusuf was gone.

In shock, Naza stepped around the bodies—once living, breathing human beings with whom she'd exchanged few words—but comrades in the effort to stop a deadly weapon of mass destruction.

She keyed her mic. "Is anyone here?" Her voice echoed against the tile and plaster walls.

There was no answer.

Naza closed her eyes. She couldn't be the only survivor.

"Please. Come in, *anybody.*"

Silence.

Naza picked her way through the bodies and returned to the entrance. She knelt beside Hassan and wiped a trickle of blood from his lifeless cheek. Tears rolled down her face as the adrenaline rush she'd experienced during the gunfight receded. In its place was the realization that the entire CIA team had just been slaughtered, and yet she'd been left alive.

How could that be?

As she found her mobile and hit speed dial to call Miller, her father's voice echoed again in her ears.

Insha'Allah.

24

Beni Haddad's Camp, Algeria

"What the hell is that?" Beni Haddad glared at Mohammed as the sound of gunfire erupted outside. "Who's out there? How many?"

"I don't know." Mohammed shook his head, despair from failing his mission plain on his face.

Leine sighted on the guard, finger caressing the trigger. Hopefully, the shock of the guard's death would buy her enough time to capture Haddad without further bloodshed. Before she could fire, Haddad seized a submachine gun leaning against the platform and shoved past Mohammed and his gunman to the entrance of the tent. Leine stood down.

"What should I do with him?" The gunman nodded toward Mohammed.

"Keep him here. I may want to interrogate him later." Without another word, Haddad disappeared through the door.

Leine unsheathed her knife and eased from her hiding place behind the chest. She ran her thumb over the blade, testing its sharpness. Even after cutting through the tent wall, the knife held its edge.

Mohammed's gaze flickered to her and immediately snapped back to the guard. "May I sit?" he asked the gunman, drawing his attention.

The guard mumbled something and Mohammed turned toward the platform.

Without a sound, Leine moved behind the guard, reached up, and sliced through his carotid artery. Blood spurted across the tent, painting the wall red as Leine lowered the dying man to the ground. Mohammed sprang to his feet and helped her lay the man out.

"Praise Allah. I hoped you were still here."

"We need to find Haddad before he gets himself killed." As if to emphasize her words, more gunfire broke out near the tent. "Do you have any idea who's out there?"

Mohammed shook his head. "I saw only the warlord's gunmen."

"I sent an S.O.S. to Price's ground force. They should be here soon." Leine strode to the stash of weapons in the corner to see if there was anything usable. More AKs, a couple of man-portable rocket launchers, a sniper rifle that had seen better days, and several pistols of various origins. Boxes of ammunition were stacked nearby. Leine pocketed several rounds as she checked an older model H&K to see if the machine pistol was serviceable. It would do. She loaded a magazine and snapped it home before she tossed a Ruger to Mohammed.

"Can't have too many guns."

Felix Andreyev shot another of the warlord's gunmen point blank and turned to see what was happening with his team.

The carnage wrought by the undisciplined band of operators didn't surprise him. His men's pent-up need to fight had turned out to be very bad for Haddad's contingent. He counted twelve dead just in the section of the camp he could see. Following the blinking light on his phone that signaled the location of the case, he strode toward the front of the camp. One of Haddad's gunmen appeared, weapon raised to fire, but a member of Felix's team cut him down before he could get off a shot.

The blinking dot led him to a larger tent near the entrance. Obviously Haddad's quarters. The rest of the tents had held women. Young women. He'd cautioned his team not to partake, but his warning had fallen on deaf ears.

Felix waited a moment, deciding how he wanted to proceed. Should he go in shooting, kill anything that moved, and rip through the tent to find the case? Or should he be more tactical and figure out a way to keep the warlord and the terrorist alive in case things didn't turn out the way Felix assumed they would?

Tactics won out, and Felix sidled up to the entrance. He was about to enter when the tent flap opened and Haddad strode out. Their eyes met. Felix moved first, crouching low as the warlord raised his weapon. Felix's rifle connected with Haddad's knee with a *crack* and the warlord crumpled to the ground. He had to hand it to the guy—he didn't utter anything more than a grunt of pain.

Felix kicked the warlord's gun to the side and yanked Haddad to his feet.

"You and I need to have a little talk."

Pop-pop-pop. Felix swiveled toward the sound of automatic

gunfire. Who did his team miss? Azim sprinted around the corner of the tent, breathing heavily.

"What's happening?" Felix growled.

"Soldiers." He glanced behind him. "We're being attacked."

"Haddad's men?"

Azim shook his head. "I don't know who they are. They look like pros." He moved aside so that Felix could see.

Several meters farther inside the camp, men in tactical gear with submachine guns mowed down his team. The difference between his fighters and the unidentified insurgents was stark —the former used brute force but were no match for the efficiency, control, and firepower of the latter.

Who are these men? Judging by their weapons, Felix and his mercs were woefully outgunned. Then, as if to prove his point, two women appeared, both wielding Kalashnikovs. One wore a tactical vest and a hoodie, while the other had on a bright yellow dress and walked barefoot. The woman in the vest fired on one of his men and he dropped where he stood.

Felix said to Azim, "Let them go." The man she just killed hadn't been a particularly good mercenary, so no great loss. He nodded at Haddad. "We have bigger concerns." He guessed they were two of Haddad's captives who had decided to take advantage of the chaos. They'd most likely commandeered the guns from Haddad's dead guards and were looking for revenge. He decided not to find out if his observation was correct and shoved Haddad back into the tent before anyone saw them.

LEINE AND MOHAMMED WERE ABOUT TO WALK OUT THE DOOR when Haddad stumbled through the entrance. They immediately aimed their weapons at the warlord, although Haddad was unarmed. Leine registered the scowl on Haddad's face, but before she could react a blond man with a buzz cut followed him inside.

Buzz-cut's eyes narrowed. He ducked behind Haddad, using him as a shield, and aimed his weapon at Leine.

"Put your gun down. Now." Leine's voice cut through the muffled shouts and gunfire outside the tent. She gestured toward Mohammed. "You're outnumbered."

The tent flap opened and a slender, dark-haired man with a gun walked in behind Buzz Cut. A look of surprise registered on his face before he raised his gun to cover Leine and Mohammed.

Buzz-cut gave her a sardonic grin. "Not anymore."

"Who are you?" she demanded.

"Felix Andreyev. And you are?"

"Leine Basso. Your accent. Russian?"

Felix nodded. "And you are American."

"Yes." She glanced at the new addition to their group. "Who are you?"

With a quick look at Felix, he answered, "Azim."

"I believe you would call this a stalemate, yes?" Felix studied her, his gaze predatory.

"Not exactly. How many of you are there?" Leine nodded toward the sound of the ongoing gunfight.

"Over fifty."

It was Leine's turn to smile. "Try again."

Felix shrugged. "A dozen."

"And how many of Haddad's men have yours killed?" The Russian's fighters showing up just might turn out to be a good thing.

Felix appeared to think for a moment. Then his gaze caught Leine's. "All of them."

Leine nodded. "Then that takes care of my biggest problem. Thank you."

The look on Felix's face told her he hadn't quite caught on to what was happening.

"That means the gunfire we hear right now would be my men subduing yours," Leine said helpfully.

Felix narrowed his eyes again and frowned. "Who are your men?"

"Is that really important?" Her gun still raised, she stepped back, getting into a better tactical position. Mohammed followed suit. "What is important is why you're here. Although I'm pretty sure I can guess."

Felix grinned, reminding Leine of a lunatic who didn't understand reality, perhaps didn't much care. "If what you say is true about your men, then my comrade and I have no chance to make it out of here alive. Why shouldn't I just kill you and your friend?"

"Because those men out there will be less than lenient if they find that you have killed two of their own."

Felix raised his chin, acknowledging the impasse. "Then I would like to make deal."

The sound of automatic gunfire was now directly outside the tent. Someone shouted in English.

Leine shook her head. "I'm afraid that ship has sailed. You're out of time."

Felix glanced at the man beside him and shrugged. "Then we give ourselves up." He placed his weapon on the ground and stepped back. Azim did the same.

The entrance opened again and two men from Price's group stepped inside. In the lead was Verdun King, the commander of the operation. Tall and square-jawed with a piercing stare, his gaze swept over the five of them and the two machine guns on the ground before he looked at Leine. "Everything all right here?"

Leine nodded. "This is Felix, and the other guy is Azim. I believe they're part of a Russian mercenary group, am I right?"

"You are well informed." Felix considered the new additions to their little party and nodded. "Obviously I have made right move." He turned to Leine. "You will show leniency when the time comes, yes?"

Verdun and the other gunman zip-tied the two captive's hands behind them, then their ankles, and had them sit on the platform. Mohammed tied Haddad's wrists together and shoved him away from the mercenaries.

"Have you seen Amira or Dani?" Leine asked Verdun.

He nodded. "Two women with AKs were doing a good job backing us up. I assume that would be them?"

Relieved to know both recruits were alive, but wary at the mention that Amira was now armed, Leine nodded.

"Good to know." Verdun eyed the warlord with an impassive stare. "Most of the tents have female captives in them. I've instructed my team to liberate the camp. We've got a call in to one of the NGOs in the area. They'll house the women until they find other quarters for them." He checked his watch. "They should be here within the hour."

Haddad grumbled and shook his head.

Leine glanced at the warlord. "You have a problem with that, Mr. Haddad?"

A look of indignation crossed his features. "Of course I have a problem with that. I paid good money for those women. They are my property. You have no right to confiscate my property."

Leine raised her eyebrows at his outburst. "Wow. You seriously think this ends well for you?" She moved closer to the warlord and said, "Now is when you tell me where Samir is headed."

Haddad scowled but didn't reply. Leine allowed herself a little smile. "I think I'm going to enjoy asking you questions."

25

Leine was preparing for Haddad's interrogation when one of Verdun's men ushered Dani and Amira into the tent. She gave both women a bear hug.

"I'm so glad to see you two." She eyed the Kalashnikov slung over Amira's shoulder. The sniper appeared calm and in control of herself, so Leine let it slide. "You both did a great job out there." She glanced at Dani's feet. She wore a pair of oversized hiking boots. Apparently she'd taken them off one of the dead gunmen. "Can we find this woman some shoes that fit?" Verdun's guy nodded and exited the tent.

Leine turned back to the two women. "Are you both all right? Anything happen that I should be aware of? Were you mistreated?" She was going to ask Amira if she experienced any PTSD while she was fighting, but thought better of it and decided to save the question for later.

"Nothing to report." Amira glanced at Dani, who shook her head.

"I overheard Samir and Beni Haddad talking about an airport an hour's drive from here," Dani offered.

"When did Samir leave?"

"Hours ago."

Leine nodded. "I was afraid of that." She turned to Verdun's man. "Tell Verdun to contact Miller for satellite photos of the area. Tell him we're looking for landing strips or airfields." He nodded and left.

She led the two women outside. She gestured toward the large group of former captives milling near the front of the camp. "A group that's expected to help these women return to their homes should be here within the hour. I need you two to organize them so it goes smoothly."

Amira and Dani made their way over to the group. Leine instructed Mohammed to guard Felix and Azim, who turned out to be from the UAE. Another of Verdun's men stayed behind to help him. Verdun's forces had neutralized the remaining mercenaries, so neither Felix nor Azim were seen as much of a threat.

They moved Haddad to one of the empty tents for privacy. Only a select few could be present depending on what kind of information they might be able to drag out of him. Verdun insisted that he be one, especially while Leine conducted her interrogation. She didn't have a problem with that, although his insistence gave her pause.

It didn't take long to break Beni Haddad. The warlord caved at the mere mention of a bribe for information on Samir. Well, that and evidence of the tools Leine said she was eager to use on him. Curiously, Verdun had suggested she not use anything on him, but rather soften her interrogation.

Sure.

"Tell me about your meeting with Samir." Leine paced in front of the warlord. Moving helped to focus her thoughts.

"Of course," Haddad said, nodding, his gaze riveted to the pliers in Leine's hand. His arms were stretched tight and zip-tied behind him. "I had a conversation with him before he left."

"And when did he leave?" Leine sat on a chair across from Haddad.

"I don't remember."

"Don't remember, or don't want to tell me?" Leine leaned forward, her elbows on her knees.

He shrugged. "I am an old man. My memory is not what it used to be."

"I'm sorry to hear that." Leine sat back and crossed her arms. "Since you have nothing of substance to tell us about your friend, then I assume you don't want the reward my employers are willing to pay."

"You know as well as I do if I say anything and he finds out he will not hesitate to kill me."

"Then your information must lead us to where he is so that doesn't happen. If not, then you aren't of use to us. What do you think happens to informants who don't inform?"

At that moment, one of Verdun's men came into the tent. He and Verdun had a hushed conversation before the man nodded and left.

Verdun walked over to Beni Haddad. "Your so-called buddy Samir killed your pilot friend and stole his plane."

Haddad's face paled as sorrow washed over his features at the news. He closed his eyes for a moment, then opened them. Anger burned in their depths, giving Leine a glimpse of the force he had once been.

The warlord glanced at Verdun, then back to Leine. "I must be assured that I will have safe passage."

Verdun cleared his throat. "That can be arranged."

That was when the penny dropped. The CIA had some kind of prior arrangement with Haddad.

Beni Haddad sighed, pausing for dramatic effect. He raised his eyes to the ceiling and said, "Allah forgive me," before he lowered his gaze to Leine's. "He is headed to join his brothers in the fight."

Leine frowned. "Could you be more specific?"

Haddad shrugged. "I'm afraid not."

She was about to comment on the inadequacy of his answer when the warlord shot her a conspiratorial look.

"Although, I've heard from certain other traders who have passed this way that Izz al-Din has a training camp near the city of Khartoum. But you didn't hear it from me." He cocked his head to the side and studied Leine. "Surely the information is worth something, yes?"

"Maybe. Did he leave anything here for safekeeping?"

It was Haddad's turn to frown. "I'm not sure what you are referring to."

"A metal case."

"I'm unaware of him leaving anything." Haddad's gaze flickered, but not enough to register as a tell. Could be he knew something, could be Samir had kept the virus's existence a secret. Leine presumed the latter. Why tell an Algerian criminal about a priceless weapon of mass destruction?

Leaving Verdun with Haddad, she exited the tent and walked to the warlord's quarters. As she pushed through the entrance Mohammed and Verdun's guy looked up from a card game they were playing around the tea table. Mohammed stood when he saw her.

"Anything?" he asked.

Leine shook her head. "Not much. We may know the direction he's headed. Where are Amira and Dani?"

"They're still helping the people from the agency."

"Good. I don't think we're going to get much more out of Haddad." As she spoke, she noticed that Felix had moved closer to the large wooden chest. He now appeared to be dozing. Azim was still sitting where she'd left him.

She walked over to where Felix sat on the floor, stopping just short of his bound ankles. She prodded his foot. "And what are we doing?"

Felix feigned waking up but it was a poor attempt.

She rolled her eyes. "Seriously? Can't you do better than that?"

He gave her a disarming grin and shrugged. "Just want to know how much I can get away with."

Leine studied the Russian. He was obviously up to something. Her gaze shifted to the wooden chest, then back to Felix. He watched her, unblinking.

She moved to the chest and lifted the lid. A folded blanket and clothing lay on top, along with a cash box. She opened the box, revealing a stash of dinars and euros. She flipped through them, mentally calculating the total. Had Felix been working his way to the chest to grab the money? Curious, she dug deeper. Her fingers brushed something hard. She lifted clothes out of the way to reveal a metal case. Her heart skipped a beat. She checked the electronic lock. It was broken.

She'd open it later, away from Felix. Replacing the clothes, she closed the trunk lid and looked at Felix. She couldn't be sure, but the muscles around his eyes appeared to relax.

Leine took a step back. "Nothing inside there. I wonder why you're so curious?"

"What makes you think that? I was just looking for something to lean against."

"Sure you were. Why don't you slide on back to where your friend is?"

Felix grumbled, but did as she asked.

"We're almost finished with Haddad," Verdun said as he entered the tent. Leine joined him, far enough away from the Russian to hold a private conversation.

"Did he say anything else?"

"Only that he wishes Samir would have paid him more for his trouble." Verdun nodded at Felix and the other man. "What would you like to do with them?"

Leine considered the two. "Pretty sure they're looking for the same thing we are. Let them go, but keep tabs on them. It might keep the Russian government off our asses."

Verdun nodded. "You're the boss."

"Oh yeah?" Not that Leine minded, but Verdun's abrupt shift in deference gave her pause. Was Miller setting her up to take the fall if things went sideways?

"Matt Price told me to take orders from you while we're here. Is there a problem?"

"No. No problem." She walked back to Felix and Azim and cut their ties, then gave them both a hand up. "You're free to go." She stifled a chuckle at the wary look on Felix's face.

He looked at his friend, who appeared as mystified as he did, then back at Leine.

"I don't understand."

"Since there's only two of you left, we don't believe you're much of a threat." She nodded toward the entrance. "Go on. The lead commando has your phone." They'd already cloned Felix's iPhone knockoff and sent the results to a CIA lab to break his password. Leine doubted the merc left anything incriminating on his device—most used burners with no identifiers. Better safe than sorry, though.

Felix's raised eyebrows showed his surprise. "What about our weapons?"

Leine shook her head. "Nice try. Time to go."

Galvanized into action, Felix and his sidekick headed for the door. Azim hesitated near Haddad's weapons stash. He pointed to one of the Kalashnikovs. "May I?"

"The offer isn't permanent, gentlemen." She crossed her arms.

Felix lifted his chin. "Can't blame him for trying."

Leine sighed. "Just go already, will you?"

She and Verdun watched as the two men exited the tent.

"Think that was a good idea?" Verdun asked.

"I'll let you know. Make sure we've got eyes on them both."

"Roger." Verdun motioned to his guy to follow him and walked out. She moved to the wooden chest and lifted the top, then pulled out the metal box. Mohammed joined her.

Leine opened the case. Gray foam lined the interior with several cutouts large enough for a number of vials. Eighteen of them, to be exact.

All empty.

"Did those all hold vials?" When Leine answered in the affirmative, Mohammed's eyes widened as the consequences became clear.

Leine studied the empty case, her mind whirling at the implications. A terrorist was on the loose with eighteen weapons of mass destruction. All they knew at this point was that he was supposedly going to meet his brothers, maybe in Sudan, in an airplane he'd stolen. Those were weak suppositions, but it was all they had. He could be headed anywhere in the vast African continent.

How did Felix know to look inside the chest? He hadn't been allowed to speak to anyone since he'd been caught, and he didn't have enough time with Haddad to get the information out of him. Besides, the warlord didn't seem to know what Leine was talking about when she mentioned the case.

Felix had found the camp, which pointed to a tracking device planted by the Russians. Made sense. So much could go wrong with the handoff. They'd ensure a way to track the vials if the deal went sideways.

Leine felt along the lid's underside, searching for a mechanism. Finding nothing, she removed the foam and examined the interior but still came up empty. Then she studied the lock.

Bingo.

The electronic keypad included a tiny tracking device with a pinpoint of red light to indicate it was still active. She'd seen the same type of tracker incorporated in other Russian-made locks powered by a micro battery. She removed the wire connected to the tracker and the light blinked off. She reconnected the wire, completing the circuit between the micro battery and the tracker, and the light came back on.

Leine turned to Mohammed. "Go get Amira and Dani. We're leaving."

Mohammed nodded and exited the tent. Leine pulled out her burner phone and checked how much juice she had left. The battery icon showed fifty-three percent. She opened the back of the phone and removed the battery. Then she eased the tracker free of the case and jury-rigged the battery to power the device. She put the tracker into the wooden chest, closed the lid, then grabbed the case.

It would give them a good head start.

26

"They're on the move." Felix studied the camp through binoculars as Leine and three others boarded a helicopter and lifted off. The leader of the ground force remained with a group of his men, along with the do-gooders who were helping the trafficked women. Little did they know the item they were looking for was still inside the camp.

Felix checked the tracking app for the case on his phone, but the dot remained in the same place it had when he and his group breached the camp: inside Haddad's tent. He glanced at the lightening horizon. They had less than an hour before sunrise.

"Stay here," he said to Azim, and handed him the binoculars. "Watch the soldiers and signal me if any come too close."

Felix stepped over the dead soldier the Americans had sent to follow him and Azim, before he sprinted to the far end of the camp where his team had breached the metal fence. He had a narrow window of time before the remaining ground force figured out they had a man down, and he intended to use it. Careful to stay in the shadows as he moved, he made his way forward to Haddad's tent.

He'd almost gotten as far as Haddad's quarters when the entrance to one of the other tents opened and a man wearing the tactical gear of the American group appeared. Inside, Felix caught a glimpse of Haddad, tied to a chair with three of the invading force surrounding him.

Felix froze, waiting to see what the other man would do. The man reached in his pocket for a pack of cigarettes and lit one, exhaling a cloud of white smoke as he did. After he'd taken a few drags, he shouldered his submachine gun and walked toward the perimeter.

He hadn't seen Felix lurking in the shadows.

The Russian let out his breath slowly, then resumed his mission. He eased up to the rear of Haddad's tent and waited, listening for movement inside. There was nothing.

Quietly, Felix got down on his stomach and lifted the bottom of the tent. Surprisingly, the material gapped open without much force. After a quick investigation, he found a section had been sliced vertically, allowing for easy entry.

Must be how the Basso woman gained access.

Lanterns illuminated the interior, leaving large areas in shadow. There didn't appear to be anyone inside, so Felix slid under the edge of the tent. He stopped to listen, but there was no sound. The rest of the gunmen must have been either interrogating the warlord or were out on patrol.

Lucky for him.

He moved to the large wooden chest and opened the lid. Tossing the blanket and clothing aside, he dug to the bottom. There was no case. Puzzled, he continued his search. His fingers closed around something hard. Instead of the expected case, he found a cell phone battery. That wasn't all. Attached to the battery was a tiny tracking device. The kind that would have been on the case his employers wanted back.

"Fuck." Felix checked his impulse to throw the battery to the ground, which could alert the gunmen outside. Basso must have taken the case.

Think, Felix. If the weapon had been inside the case, why were they still interrogating Beni Haddad?

The answer was obvious. They hadn't yet found the weapon. If they had, Felix was pretty sure they would have all left, the operation complete.

So, a mixture of good and bad news. The good news was that the weapon was still in play and all Felix had to do was locate the terrorist who had stolen it from the Syrians.

The bad news was that the weapon was still in play and he had to locate the terrorist who had stolen it from the Syrians. And Leine Basso had a good head start. He eyed the stack of weapons in the corner.

At least he would be well armed.

LEINE ENDED THE CALL AND POCKETED THE SAT PHONE. THE sound of the helicopter engine made it difficult to hear what Miller was trying to tell her, but she got the gist. Somehow, Al Shami's forces had found the CIA safe house and shot their way in, rescuing Yusuf and murdering everyone except Naza. Not only had Yusuf, their Syrian bargaining chip, escaped, but now she had to tell her team that Hassan was dead.

Her expression must have telegraphed her anger because Dani put her hand on her arm and asked, "Is everything all right?"

Leine shook her head. "They came for Yusuf."

Mohammed and Amira looked at Leine with alarm, having heard her over their headsets.

"Are Naza and Hassan all right?" Mohammed asked.

"Naza was the only survivor. I'm sorry."

Amira blinked, hard, obviously stunned by the news. Dani bit her knuckles and looked away. Mohammed closed his eyes and hung his head.

Leine hated to lose even one member of her team. She was responsible for them. Now one was in the hospital, and one was dead.

How did Al Shami find the safe house? Paul Miller had assured her that only a few people knew of that particular building. When she'd pressed him for names of those who knew, he balked, citing security concerns.

Obviously, Miller had a traitor problem, had finally agreed to as much in the phone call. Miller notified Leine that he was putting her in charge of their search for Samir.

"You're on point, at least until I figure out who the leak is. Think you can handle it?"

"We've trained for this, Paul," she'd replied. "We know as much about Samir and the contents of the case as any of your operators. I've worked in Khartoum before and have a few contacts left." She'd wanted to remind him that she tried to tell him his team had been compromised, but held back. It would do no good to antagonize him. He'd lost a lot of his people in the safe house attack. He knew full well there was a leak. Whether that leak was Libyan or within the CIA was another story.

The idea that Miller might be involved danced across her mind.

"Fine. But keep control of your team."

"What's that supposed to mean?"

"Matt Price told me Amira was part of the op."

"I gave her another chance, yes." Obviously, Verdun had reported back to Matt about the two members of Leine's team he'd encountered.

"We talked about this, Leine. She doesn't have the requisite temperament."

Leine rolled her eyes. "Just say it in English, Paul. Amira's a loose cannon. I get it. But she's also damn good with a sniper rifle, and she infiltrated Haddad's camp with no problem. She would have gotten Dani out if the Russian and his mercs hadn't made an appearance. As it was, Amira and Dani helped take out several of them."

"Be that as it may, she's unstable. I wouldn't feel comfortable having her participate in any aspect of the operation."

"If I had a dollar for every unstable operative I've worked with..." Leine let the sentence hang between them. His argument didn't cut it with her. Miller was the king of working with unstable operators, having been stationed in Tripoli for so long. He understood what she meant.

He sighed. "Fine. It's your funeral."

"Nice vote of confidence, Paul. Thanks."

"You're welcome. And Leine? Just so we're clear, I don't advocate that."

"What?"

"Your funeral."

"You're a peach, Miller."

Leine ended the call and studied what was left of her team. Amira stared silently out the window at the slowly brightening horizon. It would be dawn soon. Dani folded into herself, her face a study in grief. The stormy look on Mohammed's face told Leine she'd need to watch him. Hassan's death would take a larger toll on Mohammed than the others. As the only men on the team, he and Hassan had forged a close bond, forming a united front when the women sought to divide and conquer them with practical jokes or teasing.

Leine leaned her head back and closed her eyes. The helicopter would drop her and her team near Khartoum, where they would try to pick up Samir's trail. She didn't have high hopes. Trying to find the terrorist with the sketchy intel Haddad gave them was like looking for a blade of grass in a meadow. Still, if Miller confirmed the Izz al-Din training camp was still active, they'd at least have somewhere to start the search.

A slim possibility.

27

Nairobi, Kenya

Samir sipped his tea as he waited for his friend Ali to arrive. The open air café boasted several picnic tables with benches, with plenty of shade and distance between them. The day was beginning to warm. The temperature was pleasant enough for now, although soon the afternoon heat would drive pedestrians inside to cooler environs.

He'd been in Nairobi less than six hours and already felt familiar with the streets and the people. Traffic laws were suggestions, and he'd determined a motorbike would be the best mode of transportation in the gridlocked city center. So, he'd stolen a red Honda 125cc being used to deliver food. He switched plates on the bike in case the previous owner called in the stolen vehicle, but otherwise left it as it was.

His flight to Sudan in the stolen Beechcraft had been uneventful. Using a fake passport provided by his contact, he'd taken a commercial flight from Khartoum to Nairobi. The passport worked perfectly, and, although he'd sweated discovery, thanks to lax security the duffel bag and virus sailed through.

Once he landed in Nairobi, he purchased two thermoses to transport the virus. He'd surrounded the vials with cotton gauze to keep them from hitting against each other, then put the thermoses inside his duffel bag, although he assumed the glass wasn't exactly fragile. Only an imbecile would transport a deadly pathogen in breakable vials.

He'd examined the glass with the clear liquid inside and marveled at being able to hold the potential death of millions in his hands. The glass appeared sturdy, their caps secured with a thin metal covering.

And he had all of it. His contact had become upset when Samir told him he wasn't going back to Syria straight away. Samir resisted the man's reasoning that the sooner he brought the virus back to his home country, the sooner he'd be able to avenge his father's and brother's deaths.

But Samir had another stop before Syria.

The only unfortunate part of the plan was that he'd had to kill Yusuf. But that was a small price to pay for immortality. Once Samir released the pathogen, he'd be known everywhere as the man who singlehandedly saved Syria and the world.

His friend Ali showed up fifteen minutes late, with company. Similar to Ali, the unexpected arrival sported a full beard and wore a black T-shirt and black cargo pants. Wary, Samir made room on the bench for his friend, with the surprise guest taking the seat across the table from them. Samir kept the shoulder strap of his duffle bag over his knee, with the bag itself on the ground between his feet.

"How are you, Samir?" Ali grinned as he clasped Samir's hand.

"Peace be unto you, my friend." Samir nodded at the man across from him. "Who is this?"

Ali's grin stretched wider. "Meet Abdul. A very important man. One who will help us make the most of your windfall."

Samir eyed Abdul guardedly, then turned to Ali. "You didn't mention bringing anyone else."

Ali's grin faltered as he looked from Abdul to Samir. "But he is an operational genius. I thought you'd want to hear what he has to say."

Abdul cocked his head to the side, his lips twitching in a smile. "It's clear that I make you nervous. This is not my intent, Brother Samir. I only wanted to meet the man whom Allah has chosen to change the world."

"And it is not my intent to insult you, as we have just met. But I'm sure you can understand my wariness." Samir cut his gaze to the side. "The fewer people who know about this, the better."

Ali cut in, obviously eager to make amends for his blunder. "This is known to only the three of us, I swear."

Partially mollified, Samir shrugged off the tension in his shoulders and leaned forward, his forearms on the table. He caught Abdul's gaze and held it. "Tell me what you envision."

"This depends on several factors," Abdul began. "One, how much of the agent you possess. Two, the best way to disperse it. And three, the most effective targets. Answer these questions, and I will compose a plan to make the most efficient use of this amazing gift from God."

"In answer to your first question, there is enough." Samir wasn't about to tell either of them that he had eighteen vials. His other contact, the one he was keeping on the line in case al-Shabaab proved stingy, had assured him he could do what he wanted with the virus, that they would help him in his endeavors as long as he kept his promise to return to Syria. But he'd decided on the flight to Khartoum that he would hold several vials back from both that contact and his brothers in al-Shabaab so that he might have them in reserve in case anything went wrong.

"As for question two, I have no idea, although I've been assured it's easily transmissible, even more so than the deadly variants of the coronavirus. And three, I wish to use this weapon on our greatest enemy."

Abdul nodded. "As I assume that by enough you mean a sufficient amount, may I suggest testing it on a small population —a control group, if you will. This way we can be assured of maximum exposure when we take it to the enemy."

"I'm listening."

Abdul took out his phone and brought up a map of Nairobi. "There are several areas where we might test its effectiveness. We must avoid the suburb of Eastleigh, as that is the base of operations for many of our brothers. There are plenty of other possibilities that we can explore. First, we must determine how best to deploy it, and when." His smile sent chills down Samir's back. He narrowed his eyes. "I trust you have it in a safe place?"

Samir closed his legs protectively around the duffel bag. "It's safe enough. I am not such a fool as to bring it with me."

Abdul raised an eyebrow. "Oh? Then where is it?"

"Like I told you. Safe." Samir checked the time on his phone. "I will conduct the test. Once we have the data, then we can determine where and when to deploy it." He rose from the bench.

Ali scrambled to his feet, casting a worried glance at Abdul, who remained seated.

Samir slung his duffel bag over his shoulder. "I have Ali's mobile number. I will contact him when I've completed the test, although you'll most likely know before then." It wouldn't take long for the news to report on a mysterious outbreak.

Ali moved next to Samir and pressed something hard in his side. Samir stiffened and narrowed his eyes at his friend.

"I'm sorry to have to do this, brother," Ali murmured. "You must take us to where you have hidden your gift."

Abdul slowly climbed to his feet, never taking his eyes from Samir. His gaze hardened, transforming his bland expression to one of malevolence. "You will do as Ali says, and keep your life."

Samir frowned. "But if you kill me, how will you find it?"

Abdul nodded at the duffel bag. "Because you're not stupid enough to leave it anywhere unattended."

Samir dropped his shoulders and lowered his chin, signaling to the two men his defeat. Ali relaxed and withdrew his gun.

"I told you he would listen to reason—"

At that moment, Samir pivoted and punched Ali in the throat. His eyes wide, the younger man gurgled and clawed at his neck as he fought for air. Samir moved his foot behind Ali's leg and threw him to his back on the ground. Abdul leapt across the table but lost his footing and fell to his hands and knees.

Samir sprinted to his bike, latched onto the handlebars, and rolled into traffic, starting the Honda as he leapt onto the seat. He gunned the engine and glanced in the rearview mirror in time to see the two men race to a white pickup and climb inside.

With the strap around his neck and the bag itself resting on the gas tank in front of him, he weaved in and out of traffic, narrowly missing pedestrians and coming close to getting wiped out from an open car door. Several blocks up from the café, he turned right, unsure where to go, but certain he needed to keep moving to stop Ali and Abdul from catching up to him. He had no doubt they would shoot him if they did.

He came to a roundabout and followed the traffic, his head swiveling, looking for the white pickup. He'd made it to the last spoke in the road and was about to veer left when he caught a flash of white in his periphery.

Pop! Pop! Gunfire exploded behind him. Samir ducked. A round pinged off his back fender, and he gunned the engine again, hoping to put enough distance between him and the shooters.

Samir raced through busy neighborhoods and shopping areas, unsure where he was or where he was going, but determined to lose the deadly terrorists on his tail. He should never have trusted Ali. He'd assumed al-Shabaab and Izz al-Din were in alignment, that they would work well together. Philosophically they had the same objective. It was apparent that Abdul had corrupted Ali, had schemed to steal the virus as soon as Ali had told him about its existence. Ali was weak, and couldn't be trusted.

He checked behind him once more for the white pickup but didn't see it. He was close to the Ngong River, remembered the area from his earlier forays that morning through Nairobi. Steel foot bridges spanned the polluted river bed from the slums of Kibera, giving residents a way across for work. He slowed, searching for a place to park the bike and hide from his pursuers.

He spied an open garage on the shady side of the street and started moving toward it, when the sound of squealing tires brought him up short. He turned in time to see the white pickup barreling toward him along the sidewalk, Ali hanging out of the passenger side window, his AK propped on the roof of the cab.

Samir jerked the bike to the right and headed for a nearby footbridge, scattering pedestrians as he flew past. A glance in the rearview told him Abdul had no qualms in following him across a bridge that was not intended for vehicular traffic.

Samir juiced the throttle and the bike shot forward, becoming airborne off the end of the bridge. A barrage of gunshots from Ali's automatic weapon filled the air as people screamed and ran for cover. The bike's back tire landed at an odd angle in the mud, skidding to one side, but Samir kept control and straightened, then resumed his flight. Heart thudding in his ears, he wove in and out of the warren of alleyways, ducking under laundry hung out to dry, screeching to a halt to avoid a collision with first a rusted building, then a passerby.

Several turns in, he hit a dead end. He stopped, dismounted the bike, and turned off the engine. The throbbing beat of African music could be heard in the distance as he attempted to slow his heart rate. He glanced behind him down the narrow corridor he'd just used. There was no way the pickup would be able to make it through the same path. He was safe.

For now.

28

Outside of Nairobi, Kenya

The helicopter carrying Leine and her team landed in an empty field outside of Nairobi. According to satellite photos provided by the Department of Defense, there was a possible al-Shabaab training camp nearby. They'd been to two other camps: one in Chad rumored to be Izz al-Din's that turned out to be abandoned, and one in Somalia, which was part of al-Shabaab's terror network. That one had promise, except that US Africa Command was in the process of conducting an air strike, which ultimately destroyed the camp and scattered the survivors.

The day prior, Miller received reports of an abandoned Beechcraft outside of Khartoum, Sudan, with a call sign matching the one used by Beni Haddad's friend. He'd at first thought to redirect Leine and her team to Khartoum. But facial recognition footage provided by the airport suggested Samir had continued on to Nairobi on a commercial flight. Once Verdun and his team finished with Beni Haddad, they deployed to Khartoum to investigate. Leine and her team headed for Nairobi.

A fuel truck was already there, waiting to refuel the chopper. Leine, Amira, and Dani made their way to a white Land Cruiser parked at the edge of the field. Mohammed remained in the chopper, having decided to return to Libya, then eventually travel back home to Syria. He was going to rejoin the SDF and fight against the ISIS resurgence happening there. Leine was sorry to see him go, but understood. Hassan's death had hit him hard. Grief affected people differently. Often, the one left behind needed something to distract them from their loss.

Fighting terrorists in your home country wasn't a bad way to do that. They'd all wished him luck and promised to keep in touch.

The three women stowed their packs in the Toyota's cargo area and piled in. Leine took the front passenger seat while the other two sat in the back. She extended her hand to the driver, a wiry twenty-something with a serious demeanor.

He shook her hand and said his name was Henry.

Leine and the other two women introduced themselves.

"My orders are to take you directly to the embassy," Henry said. "The chief of station would like to have a word."

"Is it far?" Leine asked.

"About an hour."

"And how far to the training camp?"

"From the embassy, at least two hours."

"And from here?"

"Maybe one hour."

"Then I would like to go the camp. But first, I need to make a stop."

"I am to take you to the embassy."

The firm set of Henry's jaw told Leine he was a rules

follower. She nodded. "Of course. But I'm sure the chief understands that time is of the essence here."

"Of course."

"I assume you are aware of our mission? Where we're going, who we're surveilling?"

Henry nodded, a wary look replacing the obstinate one.

"Well, then, why don't you brief the team, and bring us within spitting distance of the camp?"

Henry's brows pulled together. Her request was not part of the plan. "I'm not authorized to deviate from my orders." He put both hands on the wheel and stared straight ahead. "We are to report to the embassy."

Leine sighed and held out her hand. "May I have your phone?" At his puzzled look, she added, "I'd like to call your chief, Joe Darwin, if that's all right."

Henry held his finger up as he dug in his pocket. "I will make the call."

Leine exchanged looks with Dani and Amira, who both shook their heads at the man's devotion to protocol. Leine shrugged. He'd certainly been trained. She assumed he was new to his position.

"Hello, Mr. Darwin? It is Henry." Henry paused for a moment, then said, "Yes, they are here. Miss Basso insists she will go to the camp, but I told her—" He grew silent, listening to the voice on the other end of the call. "But my orders were to bring them to the embassy." More listening, followed by nods. "Yes. Yes, I understand." He ended the call and put the phone back in his pocket.

"Well?" Leine asked.

Henry blinked once and swallowed, his Adam's apple bobbing. "I am to take you wherever you wish to go, and brief you on the way."

Leine patted him on the shoulder. "That's perfect, Henry. I

have every faith in your abilities." Without a word, Henry put the car in gear and drove away.

By the look on his face, he didn't.

TWENTY MINUTES LATER, THEY ARRIVED AT AN OUTDOOR CAFÉ ON the outskirts of an upper-middle-class section of Nairobi. Leine smiled at the familiar sight of the person sitting at one of the outside tables, drinking a beer and watching the people pass by.

"Come and meet a good friend of mine, ladies." She turned to Henry. "If you can't find a parking space, just drive around and come back to pick us up in about fifteen minutes, all right?" Henry nodded. He'd gone all in once he tasted the forbidden nectar of skirting the rules. Leine had to admit, bending protocol could be a gateway drug, might even lead to actual rule breaking. She'd be interested to see how far Henry decided to go before he pulled himself back from the brink.

The three women waited for a break in traffic before heading across the busy boulevard to the café. A speeding motorcycle almost took Amira out. She let loose with a stream of what Leine assumed were Kurmanji curse words, before Leine grabbed her arm and pulled her onto the sidewalk. The man at the table looked up and grinned as they approached.

"Derek," Leine said with an answering grin of her own. "Good to see you." The two embraced. Leine broke away first and nodded at the two women with her. "Derek, I'd like you to meet Amira and Dani. Some of the best fighters I've ever had the chance to work with."

Derek flashed a boyish grin and extended his hand. "Good to meet you. Any friend of Leine's is a friend of mine."

The three women took a seat and ordered iced tea.

Dani asked, "Where did you two meet?"

"Derek and I have known each other for a few years," Leine said. "We met on a cargo ship headed to Tanzania."

"What were you doing on a cargo ship?" Dani leaned forward, obviously intrigued. Amira drank her tea, an expectant look on her face.

"It wasn't by choice," Leine offered. "I was looking for a backpacker who'd been trafficked by a man named Wang. He found out and decided to teach me a lesson. Derek had done some things Wang didn't exactly approve of, and was headed for an early death."

"Sounds like a nice guy," Amira said.

"Yeh." Derek shook his head. "You didn't want to get on his bad side, that's for sure."

"So what happened?" Dani urged.

Derek took another sip of his beer. "We got on his bad side."

"What do you do?" Amira studied Derek.

"I used to be the guy who helped hunters bag trophy animals, then got into a bit of illegal smuggling. Now, I do the opposite."

Leine added, "He travels all over the world, tracking poachers. The last time we saw each other was a couple of years back when he was following some guy in the States who trafficked in bear gall bladders, right?"

"North Dakota." Derek feigned a shiver. "Colder than a witch's tit." He grew pensive and stared at his beer. "Let's talk about something else, yeh?"

He's thinking about Chloe. "You doing all right?" Leine asked in a low voice.

Derek waved away her concern. "Never better. So what's this all about? Why couldn't you tell me anything over the phone?"

"I'm not comfortable talking over an open line."

"What about the sat phone? Isn't that safe?" Amira asked.

Leine shook her head. "I'm not in a trusting mood."

"Even the CIA?" Dani asked.

"Especially not them."

Derek raised an eyebrow. "Trouble with the overlords?"

"I think there's a leak."

"Something go sideways?"

"You could say that, yes. Our op was compromised by what looked like a private security contractor. And someone redirected surveillance support from the operation. We lost something important. And someone."

"Ah. Let me guess. The CIA considered whoever it was an acceptable loss?" he said, using air quotes.

"Pretty much."

"But isn't that the way they handle things? Their methods aren't normally subtle."

Leine tore her napkin into little pieces, then brushed them toward the center of the table. "There's also the compromised safe house. One that my contact at the Agency assured me wouldn't be compromised."

"Okay," Derek said. "The evidence is building toward your assumption. How many casualties with the safe house?"

"At least a dozen. And they lost the asset."

Derek whistled. "Yeh. That's compromised, all right. Why don't you tell me what you're looking for that got so many people killed?"

"Bioweapon." The word fell between them like an anvil.

Derek frowned and leaned forward, looking left and right before he asked in a low voice, "You mean like anthrax?"

Leine shook her head. "Worse. Lab-created super virus. Enough to kill tens of thousands, maybe millions."

"So who are we looking for?" Derek threw back the rest of his beer and set the glass decisively on the table.

"A lone terrorist named Samir, although it's possible he's headed for an al-Shabaab training camp near here."

"Al-Shabaab. Of course." Derek grimaced. "So this is like a nuclear bomb in the hands of Al Qaeda."

"Kind of, yeah. We've got to find this guy before he deploys the virus."

"Why here?"

"There is one known camp currently in use by al-Shabaab that's just outside of Nairobi. Our latest intel suggests the target flew to Sudan, abandoned his plane outside of Khartoum, then hopped on a commercial flight to Nairobi. A different team is checking more leads in Sudan. We're hoping to get the jump on him here."

Derek studied the throngs of people passing by, going about their business. "Nairobi's an international city of millions. Think he'd shit where he sleeps? I mean, if he releases a deadly virus here, doesn't that put himself and his mates at risk?"

"Most certainly, yes. But that's what we don't know—whether he'd test it here or try to move it someplace else. We need to stop him before he does either one."

"Any other leads?"

Dani, who'd been listening avidly, replied, "The training camp is all we have."

"That's why I called you. I figured we'd need all the help we could get. Why not a master tracker?"

Derek gave her a look. "Flattery will usually get you everywhere." He sat for a moment, thinking. "How much virus did you say he had?"

"Eighteen vials."

"Christ." He shook his head in disbelief. "If I were Samir, I'd want to test it out first. How does it spread?"

"According to the guy who was supposed to take delivery, it's easily transmitted. Whether that means through the air or some other way, we're not sure. One of the components is smallpox, though, so there's a clue."

"Yeh, airborne. Not good. What else is in this thing? Ebola?" Derek's tone dripped sarcasm.

"Actually, yes."

Derek's eyes widened. "Fuck." A couple sitting at a table a few feet from them turned to look. He lowered his voice. "Are you fucking kidding me?"

"I'm dead serious." Leine gave him a grave look. "I was tapped by my old boss at the Agency to train a group of fighters to stop the exchange before it happened. Amira and Dani are two of the recruits from Syria—they fought in Raqqa and Kobani. We were set up to intercept the case with the virus when a strike team arrived. We think they were there to create a diversion for the terrorist to escape with the entire shipment."

"How did a member of al-Shabaab end up with the virus?"

"He's actually a member of the Syrian faction of Izz al-Din. The Russians and Syrians set up a meeting to make the exchange. But the guy we were watching, Yusuf, had a side deal to sell Samir one of the vials. When the strike team showed up, Yusuf was halfway to Samir's truck to deliver one of the vials. Then all hell broke loose. Samir used the chaos to his advantage, shot Yusuf, stole the case, and escaped."

"He took me as collateral, in case Yusuf reneged on the deal to sell him the virus," Dani added.

"We tracked Dani and Samir to a warlord's camp in Algeria," Leine continued. "We found the empty case, but not Samir. Eventually the warlord told us he was traveling to be with his brothers. That's why we're here now."

Derek sat quietly for a few moments, absorbing the information. "I think I have an idea."

29

———

Café in Nairobi

S amir eyed the waitress and shifted in his seat.

She knows.

He checked the time on his phone. His contact was late. Was this a set up? Luckily, he learned from his meeting with al-Shabaab and didn't bring the vials. Although somewhat risky, he'd left the thermoses in a cardboard box in a pile of trash off the beaten path in Kibera. No one would give the garbage a second look, much less find the thermoses and the vials inside them, as long as he retrieved them before too long.

He glanced out the picture window at the bright sunlight. The chaotic traffic and crush of pedestrians played into his strategy. He'd chosen the restaurant for the meeting because of the crowded neighborhood, but also because the window seat gave him a commanding view of the street outside, allowing him to see if and when Ali or Abdul drove by looking for him.

He had no doubt they were.

A tall, dark-haired man with a day's stubble on his chin walked through the front door. His gaze swept the room, landing on Samir. The waitress walked over and said something to him. The man nodded at Samir and headed his way. Samir wiped the perspiration off his face with a napkin as he studied the man. He was taller than he expected. Younger, too. In his mind's eye he'd envisioned a sandy-haired American man of about forty, who was slightly overweight. But this man looked fit. And lethal.

The contact stopped at his table and asked, "Is this seat taken?"

Samir tensed, shooting a look at the door. He nodded at the chair across from him. The voice was different than the one on the phone. "Who are you?"

The man pulled out the chair and sat. "You look nervous," he said, ignoring the question. "Were you followed?"

"I don't think so." Samir glanced through the window at the street, then back at his contact. "Who sent you?"

The other man smiled. "Don't worry. Your dealings with the CIA are safe with me."

Samir cupped his hands around his tea. "Where is my original contact?"

"He couldn't make it. I'm here instead."

Samir shook his head. "I only work with him."

The other man rose to leave. "Then I'm afraid you're shit out of luck, Mr. Samir."

"Fine. Fine. Get to the point. I met you here at great risk to myself."

The man glanced under the table as he sat back down. "Did you bring the shipment?"

Samir smiled, triumph at second-guessing the American's intentions. "Do you think I'm stupid?"

His contact shook his head, smiled. "Of course not. It's just that I'm concerned someone else may find it."

"There's no need to worry," Samir snapped. "It's safe."

The man leaned across the table and said in a low voice, "I'm concerned that you're reneging on the deal you made with my employer. You agreed to bring the shipment to Syria, to use against Assad and his regime. Now it appears you have made another plan." He held his gaze. "We need to know what that plan is, before we help you again."

"We? I thought my contact acted alone."

"Who do you think gave you cover to escape with the entire shipment?"

"So that *was* you." Samir had suspected as much, but wasn't sure. The armed group at the handoff could have been some other faction—perhaps whomever the dominatrix had been working for, or someone else who'd found out about the sale.

"A lot of good men died helping you."

The bitterness of the man's tone told Samir to tread lightly. "But it will be worth it."

The dark-haired man nodded. "I can help you now. But you need to trust me and do as I say. Otherwise, what's the point?"

"What makes you think I need help?"

"You called me, remember?"

That was true. "I need to leave Africa. It's too dangerous here."

"And return to Syria?"

"Eventually, yes. Get me to Europe and I'll find my way."

"Europe? What's there?"

"That's none of your concern. I will do as you wish—I will bring the shipment to Syria with me and do as agreed. But I have something else I must attend to first."

"Tell me about Europe. I assume you're going to release some of the...product there?" When Samir didn't respond, he continued. "That would be unwise. Our original agreement was that we would help you transport the shipment to Syria, where you would use it against Assad."

"I know what the original agreement was," Samir snapped. "I've changed my mind."

"Why?"

"Because of my family, why else?" Samir hissed.

A thoughtful look came over his contact's face. "You got it all wrong, *hombre*. I saw the report. Assad killed your father and brother."

Samir narrowed his eyes. "You lie. It was the West."

"You've been misinformed. Shit, I thought that was why you agreed to go back to Syria. Assad's regime ordered the air strike on Aleppo. The Europeans—or the United States, for that matter—had nothing to do with it."

This man was lying. He had to be. But how did he know Samir had vowed to avenge his father's and brother's deaths? Samir's mind went numb. He'd process the new information later. If what this man said was true, then Samir's plan to use the virus against the Great Satan and his allies would not be condoned by Allah, nor by his brother or father.

"Help me leave Kenya. You can tell your boss the original plan still stands."

"All right. But I need time to set things up. Give me twenty-four hours. I'll have something ready by then."

30

———

Kibera slum, Nairobi, Evening

Samir watched the woman he'd picked up as she moved to the makeshift dresser for her clothes. Her lithe body had been a distraction, taking him out of his head. She'd been alluring, her large, dark eyes, graceful manner, and submissive attitude were attractions even he couldn't ignore. He'd made sure they weren't followed, that she wasn't some honeypot sent to delay him or take the weapon, but there'd been no suspicious activity and he'd relaxed.

As much as he could.

The woman turned and gave him a shy smile. He couldn't remember her name, or even if he'd asked. His disastrous meeting with al-Shabaab had produced one fortunate result. He'd given more thought to Abdul's suggestion that he try the virus out on a smaller scale first. Of course he should find out how it spread and how fast people succumbed to it. Would they die right away? Or would they become sick and take days to expire? Thanks to his American contact, he'd be a continent away before they figured out who was responsible.

The slums of Kibera would do nicely. No police presence, no security cameras, no streetlights. Best of all, there were several unsecured water sources.

Yusuf had assured him that part of the virus was the dreaded Ebola, which caused hemorrhaging and a horrible death, combined with the easy transmissibility of smallpox. But the virus was also mixed with a synthetic agent that had never been used before. The Russians had tested the product via air transmission and water, but only on a small group. Once infected, the victims bled through every orifice and through pustules that formed on their skin, then were seized by convulsions until they died.

It was time the viral combination was tested on a larger subset.

"Would you like something to eat?" the woman asked. He'd insisted that she bring him to her home instead of a hotel, assuring her he needed a break from city life. She'd been understandably reticent but agreed when he offered more money. He wondered if her neighbors knew exactly what she did to put food on the table, although even if they did, they would most likely look the other way.

Although Kibera's population was considered the poorest of the poor, the area was known for its entrepreneurial fervor. In between the mountains of trash and raw sewage running down the middle of the alleys, it seemed that everyone lived behind some kind of storefront, whether selling food, clothing, or plastic trinkets. If there was a market for the item, there was a store selling it.

He supposed prostitution could be considered a business enterprise. Money exchanged hands and a service was performed. He'd been sure to use a condom. HIV was still a problem, especially in Kibera.

He climbed from the mattress on the floor and got dressed,

then double-checked the bag to make sure all eighteen vials were still inside the thermoses. They were. Then he checked to make sure there was a bullet in the chamber of his semiauto. He'd picked up extra ammunition for the dominatrix's gun from a contact in Nairobi, having pawned his Kalashnikov and other pistol when he abandoned the Beechcraft near Khartoum.

In addition to the virus and his gun, the bag contained an extra set of clothes, a used gasmask, and elbow-length rubber gloves. He zipped the bag closed and left it on the mattress before joining the woman in what passed for a kitchen.

They sat on plastic crates at a makeshift, two-person table to share a simple meal of flatbread with beans and tea. She kept her gaze lowered, answering his questions about Kibera with one-word replies. Afterward, she made noises about needing to get back to work, but that he was welcome to stay as long as he liked. He offered to drive her back to the tavern where she worked. She accepted. Before he dropped her off, he got her mobile number, and told her he wanted to see her again.

Hoping to throw Ali and Abdul off his tail, he'd dumped the motorbike that afternoon and boosted an older-model Toyota Fortuner, switching the plates in another neighborhood far from where he'd stolen the SUV.

Samir drove back to Kibera and parked away from the entrance to the slum. He grabbed the duffel bag and continued on foot, having to retrace his footsteps when he became lost in the warren of passageways. The flashlight on his phone was a poor substitute for a regular torch, but it was all he had. It took the better part of an hour before he was able to find her place again.

He moved quietly past the metal shacks that passed for homes and storefronts, the heavy beat of recorded music thumping somewhere in the distance. The prostitute's section of the slum was quiet. Dozens of rats scurried about, rooting through the accumulated piles of trash, accompanied by the occasional bone-thin dog.

Near a patchwork fence of rusted metal and wire, Samir stopped to listen, to make certain no one was awake at that late hour. Satisfied that no one was, he made his way to the large black tank he'd noticed earlier, the one where the prostitute had indicated residents of the neighborhood retrieved their water.

Bats careened by him, capturing insects for their late-night meal. He unzipped the bag to get to his protective gear, then climbed the rungs on the side of the tank. At the top was a large cap, which he unscrewed. Removing one of the vials from the case, he peeled off the metal seal. He then donned the mask and rubber gloves.

Sweat dripped down his face as he wiggled the cap loose, and he had to blink away the perspiration that fell into his eyes. His breath sounded loud and heavy through the mask, reminding him of Darth Vader, the Star Wars character.

He had no idea what would happen to the virus, much less to the people of Kibera, when he emptied the vial's contents into the tank. Yusuf had assured him that the virus was highly transmissible through the air and in a glass of water. Surely it would survive in a water tank.

Samir held his breath as he removed the vial's cap and poured half the contents into the tank. Would that be enough? He hesitated a moment, then upended the vial, emptying the rest into the water. Then he quickly replaced the tank cap, and wrapped the vial in a length of gauze. He peeled off the gloves, turning them inside out, and shoved the gasmask up off his face. He'd change at his car, then toss his clothing, the empty vial, and the rubber gloves into a pile of trash. No one would ever find them.

Now he just had to wait.

31

———

Outdoor café, Nairobi

Leine flagged Henry down and invited him to the table. He briefed them on what was known about the al-Shabaab training camp and provided the coordinates. Although Henry argued that he was supposed to drive them, when Derek explained that he was familiar with the terrain and with the terrorists, Henry called once again to speak to Joe Darwin to confirm it was all right to let them go, and he capitulated.

Derek drove the three women in his own well-used and fully outfitted Land Cruiser. Eventually, he pulled up a gravel drive and parked near a green-painted concrete building. Leine got out first, followed by the rest. The day had grown warm, with a clear blue, never-ending sky particular to that area of the world. White, fluffy cumulus clouds cast sweeping shadows across the ground. Savannah stretched in every direction, with golden brown, green, and rust-colored grasses waving in the light breeze.

Derek approached the building, which turned out to be a

ranger station. A large emblem of a spotted leopard with two crossed rifles below it graced the front in bright yellow. A woman carrying a rifle slung over her shoulder walked out to greet him. She was dressed in jungle fatigues, lace-up boots, a green T-shirt, and a boonie hat. A shoulder patch identified her as a ranger. They exchanged a few words, then Derek gestured for Leine to join them.

"This is Leine—the woman I told you about," he said. "Leine, this is Eunice. She's one of the rangers here."

Leine offered her hand and the two women shook. "Derek's told me what you and your team have been doing for the wildlife here in Kenya. I'm impressed."

Eunice smiled, her pride obvious. "Thank you. We have trained hard. We're known to track as well as any man."

Derek snorted. "Better, if you ask me. The men can't hold a candle to the Leopards."

Leine glanced at Derek, then at Eunice. "You call yourselves the Leopards?"

"Yes. We are quiet and stealthy, but also fierce." Eunice's eyes sparkled as she spoke.

Leine smiled. "That's a great name." She didn't mention her old nickname when she worked as an assassin. Known as "The Leopard," Leine was rumored to have the same qualities as the big cat. She immediately felt an affinity for the anti-poaching ranger.

"Derek mentioned on the phone that you might need our services?"

"We are looking for a man who goes by the name of Samir. He's a member of Izz al-Din who is looking to work with al-Shabaab."

"And he's been seen in this area?"

"Not exactly," Derek replied. "Rumor has it he's visiting an al-Shabaab training camp not far from here."

Eunice nodded. "We've made occasional surveillance sweeps of this camp."

"Have you had interactions with any of the members?" Leine asked.

"No. Once we determined they weren't poachers, we informed the anti-terrorism police unit and left them alone."

"Probably wise. Did they investigate?"

She shrugged. "They wouldn't tell us if they did. Who are your other friends?" Eunice nodded at Dani and Amira, who were sitting in the shade of an acacia a few yards away.

"The woman on the left is Amira, and the other is Dani. They're both veterans of the Syrian civil war who have come to help find Samir."

Eunice's gaze lasered into Leine's. "You mean they've come to help *stop* Samir."

"Yes."

The ranger nodded. "My team is scheduled to go on patrol this evening. We can take you to the camp if you'd like. It's not far from our regular rounds."

"That would be great. Thank you."

"Are your friends comfortable walking great distances?"

"They're ready to do whatever is needed to catch this man."

Eunice nodded. "Good. Because we cover many kilometers each night. We've found it's one of the most effective methods for catching poachers. Daylight works better for locating their traps. Tell me, are your friends also ready to assist us if we run into trouble?"

"I can't speak for them, but I think you'll find the three of us willing to help you should the need arise." Leine waved Amira and Dani over. The two women joined them, interest sparking their eyes as they took in Eunice's uniform.

Leine introduced them. "Eunice has offered to take us to the training camp. In return, we'll back up their team on patrol."

Amira broke into a wide smile. "I would enjoy that very much." Then she sobered. "Do you shoot them? Or only capture them?"

Eunice gave her a startled look. "We try very hard not to hurt anyone. Our mission is to bring them to justice, not kill them." Seeing the dejected expression on Amira's face, Eunice quickly added, "but if they resist, then they are fair game, so to speak."

Amira brightened. "Then I'm in."

"And you?" Eunice looked at Dani.

Dani nodded. "Of course. It would be my honor."

"Are there many predators in Syria?" Eunice asked. "I've never been."

Dani and Amira exchanged glances. "That depends on your definition of predator," Amira replied. "ISIS and Izz al-Din would certainly be considered that. As well as Assad's troops."

"What of wildlife?"

"Syria used to have big cats like tigers, and cheetahs, and leopards, but now only the smaller species survive," Dani said. "We still hear of occasional bear and wolf sightings, and we have fox, and badger, and hyena."

"What happened to the larger cats?"

"I blame Assad's never-ending war." Amira scowled as she spoke.

Dani nodded. "My country has lost so much since the war started. Will there be anything left once Assad has finished?"

"Which is why we're going back to Syria after we find Samir." Amira put her arm around her friend's shoulders. "Assad will pay for what he's done. He has to."

Leine hoped she was right.

32

L ater that evening, the Leopards on duty created a bonfire and invited Derek, Leine, Amira, and Dani to share their meal before heading out on patrol.

The team of eight rangers ran the gamut in age from early twenties to mid-thirties. All had a fierce pride in their organization, and each had a story to tell. One woman regaled Leine and the others with the harrowing tale of coming face-to-face with a poacher who was stalking a bull elephant. The elephant spooked and trampled the poacher.

"African justice," she quipped with a grin.

Many of the women had heart-pounding encounters with both poachers and wildlife. They all agreed that knowing how their adversary thought, along with animal behavior, made a huge difference in the outcome of those encounters.

After dinner, the rangers organized themselves in a circle and bowed their heads. Eunice said some encouraging words, much like a coach giving their team a pep talk. The group broke apart and each went to retrieve their weapons for the patrol. All carried rifles with scopes, and most had a sidearm. Everyone had hi-tech night vision gear and radios. When Leine asked about the NVGs, Eunice smiled and mentioned a wealthy donor who supplied them with cutting-edge tools to fight poaching.

"You'd be surprised who is on our side," she said. "Many of the anti-poaching groups throughout Africa do not carry weapons, but we believe having the ability to shoot back keeps us safe. The weapons scare off armed poachers who would otherwise see us as an irritation rather than a deterrent."

The evening was cool with a pleasant breeze to keep them comfortable as they walked. The night sounds of insects were interrupted by the occasional roar of a distant lion, or the manic laugh of a hyena. Amira was unfazed by the presence of wildlife. Dani, not so much.

Her eyes wide, she whispered to Leine, "What do we do if a lion or an elephant charges?"

Leine shrugged. "Follow the rangers' lead. If your life or the life of another is in danger, shoot."

Dani swallowed and nodded. "I have waited in the dark for an ambush by ISIS. That wasn't as scary as this."

"You'll be fine," Leine assured her. "Just think what you'll tell your kids."

"If I live to have any," Dani muttered.

They continued walking in silence, fanning out at various points. Derek assisted the rangers, while Leine, Amira, and Dani brought up the rear. Eunice stayed back with them to watch her team.

Dani moved up to where Leine and Eunice were talking in low tones. They acknowledged the younger woman and continued their conversation.

"Derek has been a great help with our training," Eunice explained.

"How did the Leopards start?" Leine asked.

"It all began with a village. A woman named Kaya had been abused by her husband and feared for her children, so she took them and started her own village with her sisters, who also had bad luck with their men."

"Like Umoja?" Umoja was an all-female village founded by women for women who had either been victims of violence and were homeless, or were being forced into marriage. They earned income by creating jewelry and renting out campsites.

Eunice nodded. "Exactly, yes. Kaya got the idea from Umoja's founder. Our village grew to over one hundred women and children, and came to the attention of a retired military commander named Howard Lennox. I was living there at the time he visited. He was impressed with what we had created, and asked to put forth a proposal at the weekly meeting."

"And his proposal was to form the Leopards?" Dani asked.

Eunice nodded. "We did not call ourselves the Leopards then. The name came later. He proposed an anti-poaching unit much like the Black Mambas of South Africa, or the Akashingas of Zimbabwe. I was one of the first to join. He found funding for the group, and trained us in hand-to-hand combat and weapons." She sighed. "It was very difficult, that training."

"What kind of schedule do you work?" Dani asked.

"Twenty days on, ten days off."

"That must be hard on your family."

"It is, but they are proud of the work that I do. I am helping to save the earth's creatures. If I don't do it, who will?" Eunice shrugged. "Women are perfect for this role. We already care for our families. It's a natural extension for us to care for wildlife."

"Where is Commander Lennox now?" Leine asked.

"He returned to England. His family needed him."

"I'm glad Derek was able to help fill in. Where did you two meet?"

Eunice smiled. "He was tracking the same poacher as my team. A man from a nearby village had been paid to kill a local family of elephants for their ivory. He'd already killed a bull. Derek joined us and we were able to apprehend the poacher."

"What happened to him?"

Eunice was silent for a moment before she replied. "Derek took him, so I am not sure. He came back to share the reward he received. He offered to train us further, and we agreed."

"Derek's as good a tracker as I've ever known." Leine smiled at the memories of when he taught her the fine art of tracking, whether human or animal. Humans were much easier than animals—they left so many more clues.

"How do you treat those who have killed to feed their family?" Dani asked. "Do you differentiate between hunters and poachers?"

"Sometimes it is hard to do this. We used to. But poachers understand that we would spare hunters who needed the food, and would pretend to be such. Of course, if we caught them killing something like an elephant, then of course we knew they were poachers. But sometimes poachers supplement their income with bush meat. Their ability to slaughter so many and then sell the meat at market is destructive to the ecosystem. So now we do not differentiate."

"That makes sense." Dani fell quiet, lost in thought.

Eunice stopped abruptly, signaling to the group to do the same. Leine stilled, listening for what had brought the anti-poacher up short. The faint sound of a vehicle idling could be heard in the distance.

Eunice put her finger to her lips, then gestured to her team to spread out and move forward. She joined Leine and the other two women, and said in a low voice, "We will come up behind the vehicle to overwhelm whoever is out here at this late hour. They are most likely poachers."

Leine, Dani, and Amira raised their weapons and followed the others at a distance. Derek went with Eunice.

The idling engine grew more distinct. The group slowed their approach. The Leopards were stealth personified—each walked slowly through the brush, careful not to make a sound that would alert their prey to their presence. The air was electric, signifying the peculiar focus that comes from a group experiencing an adrenaline surge. Amira and Dani imitated the anti-poachers, their training both during the war and for this op kicking in, helping them to be effective in the moment.

Leine brought up the rear, watching the group's six, making sure no one was circling around behind them. Satisfied no one was, she skirted the larger group to move closer.

Eunice held up her fist and the advance stopped. Leine caught up to her and stilled, wondering what the anti-poacher's next move would be. The distinct odor of exhaust filled the air, telling her they were close. The idling engine abruptly stopped, filling the night with a profound silence. A woman nearby dropped to her haunches, getting into position. Soon, the night sounds resumed in earnest, insects and nocturnal creatures filling the void left by the idling motor.

Eunice leaned to the woman next to her and whispered something. That woman whispered to the next woman, and so on. Eunice gestured to Leine to follow her forward. Derek joined them.

A trio of male voices floated toward them as they approached. Headlights illuminated the dirt track in front of the idling truck, spilling light to the sides and partially to the back. A group of four men, two of them armed, surrounded a small utility truck, a canvas cover over the open bed. The back flap of the cover was open, displaying a dark interior.

Eunice whispered, "Poachers, although I'm not sure what they're transporting. See the guns? I've instructed my crew to surround them. We'll show ourselves first. If they allow us to look inside the truck, there will be no problem." She didn't elaborate on what would happen if they refused her request.

Guns first, Leine, Eunice, and Derek moved through the brush toward the truck. Four other women joined them.

They broke cover and Eunice shouted in Swahili, "Hands in the air where we can see them."

Startled, the four men spun to face their visitors. The two with automatic rifles slung over their shoulders scrambled for them now.

"Drop your weapons," Eunice growled. The rest of the Leopards, including Dani and Amira, materialized from the shadows, guns drawn.

Realizing they were outnumbered, the two armed poachers put down their weapons and raised their hands. At first glance, the other two appeared unarmed. Leine moved toward them. The man to Leine's right took off at a full-on sprint into the bush. Her chase reflex triggered, Leine followed him.

He was easy to track. The noise of him crashing through the brush signaled his trajectory. Focused only on the chase, Leine continued her pursuit, gaining on him in less than a minute. She caught sight of him and slowed, before firing into the air.

"Stop now, or I'll shoot." The sound of the gunshot had the desired effect. The poacher ran a few steps but then stopped, raising his hands in surrender. Leine walked over and ordered him to turn around. He did. He looked like he might be in his late teens, although the night was too dark to be sure.

His eyes narrowed. "What are you," he asked in Swahili. "One of them?"

Leine ignored him and checked his pockets. They were empty. She pulled his jacket off and tied his wrists behind his back, then prodded him back the way they came.

When they returned, his compatriots were all sitting on the ground, guarded by three of the Leopards. Eunice and Derek stood on the truck's bumper, peering with flashlights into the box. Leine deposited her captive with the others and walked over to join them.

"What did you find?" She climbed onto the truck and looked inside. At first she didn't understand what she was looking at—there appeared to be several dozen small knobby tires crowded inside the box. Upon closer inspection, she realized they weren't tires but animals. Animals that looked like round pinecones.

None of them were moving. Leine turned to Eunice. "Pangolins?"

Eunice nodded. "Yes."

Leine used her flashlight to get a better look. She'd seen photographs, but had never seen one in real life. She mentally recalculated her first guess from dozens to most likely over one hundred of the poor things. Most were curled into a ball, their heads tucked in to protect themselves. A few of them moved.

Amira and Dani climbed up to see what they were looking at.

"What are they?" Dani asked.

"They're called pangolins. Currently the most poached animal in the world." Eunice pointed at the animal closest to her. "They're hunted for their scales, mainly, but also for their meat and blood."

"Why?" Dani gently touched one of their scales. The pangolin curled tighter. "What are they made of?"

"The scales are keratin—like our fingernails and hair." Derek scowled. "The same as a rhinoceros horn. They're believed to have healing properties, like the horn, but the scientific evidence tells us otherwise. Those beliefs are untrue. And deadly."

"The poor babies," Dani cooed. "They look so sweet."

"They are," Derek replied. "Transporting them is very stressful. They're nocturnal, and not easy to hunt." He nodded at the number of pangolins inside the truck bed. "This amount would be quite valuable."

"What will you do with the poachers?" Amira asked Eunice.

"I have called for backup. Once they arrive, they will transport the poachers back to headquarters where they will be taken into custody."

"And the pangolins?" Leine asked.

"There is a conservation group out of South Africa dedicated to helping them. I will contact this group as soon as we return to base. They will instruct us in how to care for the ones that survive until they can arrange for transport."

A short time later, Eunice's backup arrived. Two women from headquarters secured the poachers in the back of their truck, while one from Eunice's team climbed into the drivers' side of the truck holding the pangolins. Several of the rangers joined them, and both vehicles pulled out, headed back to the Leopards' base camp. Eunice, Leine, Derek, Amira, and Dani joined three of Eunice's team to continue patrolling.

Not long afterward, a series of dark shapes materialized in the distance. "Is that the al-Shabaab camp?" Leine asked.

Eunice peered through her binoculars and nodded. "Yes. They don't run electricity past twenty-one hundred hours. The camp itself gets its power from solar panels."

"Is there somewhere my team and I can remain hidden and still surveil the camp during daylight? The only way we're going to know if Samir is there is to get a visual."

Eunice nodded. "There is a rise just past the camp. If you climb to the top and lay flat, you will not be seen. There are bushes you can use for cover."

As they approached the camp, Eunice stopped and motioned for Derek and Leine to join her. "This is as far as we can take you. We must resume our patrol."

"I understand. Thank you for your help."

Derek shook Eunice's hand. "I'll take them the rest of the way, Eunice. Good luck tonight."

"The same to you. If you need us, don't hesitate to call. We're as invested in finding this Samir as you are. We would like for these people to leave our area. They're most unwelcome."

"I can't promise anything, but we'll do our best." Leine motioned for Amira to join them. She finished talking with one of the rangers and jogged over to where they were standing.

"Eunice says there's a rise on the other end of the camp that we can use for cover. We'll set up our surveillance there, see if we can spot Samir. If not, then we'll have to do some more leg work."

Eunice added, "My team and I will go village to village during the day, to find out if anyone has seen any strangers. These are tight-knit communities. If anyone new has been there, someone will know."

"Perfect. Thank you." Leine turned to Derek. "Ready for some recon?"

He smiled, teeth gleaming white in the inky darkness. "Always."

33

———

Acme Bar, Nairobi

Samir walked into the tavern and took a seat at the bar. The room was open to the outdoors, with palms, bougainvillea, and fragrant jasmine surrounding the patio's perimeter. The woman he'd been with the night before was sitting at a table with another woman under a big screen television. She was crying. Samir ordered tea and tipped the bartender.

He sipped his drink for a time, waiting for the other woman to leave so he could approach, but that didn't happen. His curiosity got the better of him and he made his way to their table. Had the virus already ripped through the slum? Did it work that fast? He checked the television on the wall as he walked, which was tuned to the local news. There'd been nothing about an outbreak yet, but it had been less than a day since he poured the virus into the water tank.

Excitement spiraled through him. If there was already evidence that the virus had spread, his plan would work well. So well that no one would be able to stop him.

The woman looked up, her eyes red and puffy, diminishing her earlier beauty. He hid his annoyance and tried to look concerned. "Why are you crying?"

Fresh tears tracked down her face as she shook her head. The woman sitting with her had a grave expression. "Joan's father is very ill. She can't go to see him because her mother is afraid he might be contagious."

Samir sat near Joan and placed his hand on her back, as he'd seen the other woman do. "I'm so sorry. Do they know what has caused this terrible thing?"

Joan shook her head. "That's just it. He was healthy. He didn't even get colds. All of a sudden, he could not get out of bed. He developed a fever and there are blisters all over his body. The doctor thinks it might be related to smallpox, but they haven't gotten the test results back yet."

Samir's heart beat happily in his chest. He alone knew what was happening. He felt god-like.

"Has anyone else in your neighborhood taken ill?"

Joan shook her head.

Samir's heart froze. The virus had to be easily transmissible or his plan wouldn't work.

"I don't know," she answered. Samir's heart took flight once more.

A man came into the establishment and had a seat at the bar. The other woman climbed to her feet. "I'd better start work or I won't eat this week. Will you be all right, Joan?"

Joan nodded through her tears. "Yes, thank you, Maude."

With a nod, the other woman sidled up to the man at the bar and engaged him in conversation.

Samir leaned in closer, eager for more information. "When did he fall ill? What were his first symptoms?"

Joan dabbed at her eyes with a tissue. "Earlier today. It was so fast..." Her voice trailed off.

"What were his symptoms?" Samir pressed.

Joan frowned, obviously annoyed by his questions. "I already told you. My mother said he was so exhausted he couldn't get out of bed, which is unusual for him. A little while later, dozens of horrible blisters started to form on his body. That's when she called for the doctor." A sob bubbled up from deep inside her and she let the tears fall. "They think he might die."

Perfect. "Maybe we should go see him."

She looked at him in horror. "We can't. What if he's contagious?"

"But you might never see him again."

At that, a fresh set of tears cascaded down her cheeks.

Joan's mobile buzzed, rattling the table. She looked at the screen and snatched it up. "Mama?" She grew silent, then her eyes widened. "No."

Samir strained to hear her murmured conversation, but it was difficult to differentiate the words between Joan's sobs. She ended the call and slowly set the phone back on the table.

"Is it your father?" Samir's growing impatience was starting to get the better of him. Why couldn't she just tell him what was happening?

"He...died. Less than one hour ago."

The finality of the words landed between them. Joan sat in stunned silence. Samir had to keep himself from shouting from the rooftops. The virus was incredibly fast acting—even more than he'd been led to believe. Her father had died several hours after he'd ingested the virus, which told him it worked in a large amount of water, but also that it might well infect more than those who came into contact with the liquid carrier. This was the best news he could have hoped for. With as much control as he could muster, he kept his voice gentle and asked, "What happened?"

She took a shaky breath and let it go. Tears leaked from the corners of her eyes. "Mama said he began bleeding—" She closed her eyes and shuddered. "He began bleeding from his eyes and his ears, his nose. She...she couldn't stop it. She tried... but now she's beginning to have the same symptoms." At this she dissolved into more tears, leaning her forehead on the table as though her head was too heavy to hold up.

Samir patted her back and made sympathetic noises, but inside he rejoiced. This was happening from one vial diluted in however many hundreds of liters of water in the tank. How would it perform in its pure form? Or atomized? Samir's brain whirled with possibilities. He himself hadn't developed any symptoms, so the gasmask and rubber gloves had evidently protected him.

Allah be praised. I will soon bring the world back to its rightful state. With this kind of power, once the information about the virus's efficacy was publicized, he'd be able to threaten any nation with certain death unless they bowed to his demands. The populations of the countries who failed to take him seriously would die a gruesome death, their economies ruined because of crushing medical emergencies and the lack of a cure. If the pandemic of 2020 had taught Samir one thing, it was the power of a virus no one had prepared for.

He'd have preferred a longer illness, though. Better optics with more suffering.

No matter. If the contents of one vial produced this kind of reaction, what would several doses do?

Samir fought the euphoria threatening to spill from him as he patted Joan's back in mock sympathy. He'd have to figure out his next steps soon. But first, he wanted a full account of what his virus had done.

34

───────

Al-Shabaab training camp, outside of Nairobi

The morning dawned bright and clear with a blood red sunrise. Leine, Amira, and Dani lay prone on the rise to the west of the al-Shabaab training camp, eyes locked on the target below them. Derek had left to do a perimeter check, to see if there might be another spot that would give them a better view.

The morning call to prayer marked the first sign of activity. Dozens of men clad either in black or jungle print fatigues faced east and bowed to Mecca, their prayer rugs and AKs laid out in a straight grid. The familiar sound brought up memories of the places Leine had been when she'd heard the characteristic call. It was funny how sound could raise old ghosts.

Leine scanned the men, searching for anyone resembling the photos she'd seen of Samir. "Anything?" she asked Dani.

"I don't see him."

"Keep looking. He might still be inside one of the tents."

By the time of the second call to prayer, Leine had grown discouraged. The group had gone through several training exercises, but she'd seen no one resembling Samir. Derek returned from his reconnaissance and dropped to his stomach beside Leine.

"What'd you find?" Leine asked.

"This is the best viewpoint, by far. The rest of the terrain is too exposed. Al-Shabaab chose the location of their camp well."

"Lucky for us," Amira deadpanned.

"Yeh." Derek snorted. "How about you? Have you found our terrorist yet?"

"Unfortunately, no," Leine answered. "I'm beginning to think he might not be here after all."

"Bad intel?"

Leine shook her head. "The only intel. Samir appears to be a lone wolf. I expected him to be here by now."

"Perhaps he stopped at another camp, one your overlords don't know about?"

"Possibly. They weren't aware of any others except in Somalia, which is currently off line, and near where he ditched the plane near Khartoum." Leine sighed. "If that's the case, we need to check with every contact you and I have."

Derek gave her a look. "He could be anywhere. Africa's a big place."

"I know. I just hope we get a break."

"Speaking of breaks." Derek pulled out his mobile. "When I was doing recon I checked for service. The jihadis have their own cell tower." He glanced at the camp below them. "The pole near the center of the compound with the speakers."

Leine followed his gaze. "I figured it was doing double duty as some kind of comms. Makes sense it's a cell tower."

Derek made a call and waited for it to connect. "Hey. Just checking in. Got anything?" He listened, then said, "All right. Keep up the good work. We're headed your way." He ended the call.

Leine asked, "Good work?"

"Eunice and her crew have been checking villages close to Nairobi. They haven't gotten any hits yet, but she mentioned one of the villagers had heard rumors from relatives of a mysterious illness in Kibera."

"Kibera?" A suburb of Nairobi and considered one of the largest urban slums in Africa, Kibera had an unofficial population of over one million, with residents living in close proximity to each other. Most of the population lacked access to even basic services like electricity, running water, or medical care.

If the virus took hold there, it would be incredibly difficult to stop.

"Eunice says she'll wait for us to get back and then we can pay a visit to the area."

Foreboding settled over Leine. "Let's hope Samir hasn't deployed the virus." If true, it would help them track the terrorist, but it would also show that he was unafraid to use it on an unsuspecting populace.

"Agreed."

Leine did another scan of the terrorist camp, then turned to Dani and Amira. "We're going to cut our losses." She nodded toward the terrorists in the compound. "They're not reacting in any way consistent with a looming attack. If Samir had shown up with the virus there'd be more activity. More training, more meetings. More something."

Dani set down her binoculars. "What do you want to do?"

"We're going back to Nairobi. There are rumors of an illness in one of the slums there."

"Do you think it has something to do with Samir?" Dani asked.

"I hope not."

"What if Samir isn't in Kenya?" Amira asked. "What do we do then?"

Leine sighed, her anxiety growing. *What if he is and he's already used it?*

"We hope he makes a mistake."

TWO HOURS LATER, THEY ARRIVED BACK AT THE LEOPARDS' BASE camp. Eunice and her team were resting in the barracks. Leine found Eunice in one of the rooms she shared with three other women, listening to music on her phone and scrolling through her text messages. She pulled out her earphones and moved over to give Leine room to sit on the cot.

"By the look on your face, Samir was not at the camp." Eunice sighed. "We haven't heard anything more about the outbreak in Nairobi. We are taking shifts with another team. They will continue checking villages in case the rumors are just that—rumors. Your team and I will leave within the hour for Kibera."

"Thank you for your help." Leine leaned against the wall. Eunice gave her a pillow, which she gratefully slid behind her back.

"Don't despair," Eunice said, her expression brightening. "God has always been good to us in the fight for our wildlife. He will be good to you, too. This is too important for him not to take an interest."

Leine sighed. "I envy your faith. But I've seen plenty of things God should have taken an interest in and didn't."

"So, you do not believe?" When Leine didn't answer, Eunice nodded. "I was once as you are. Nothing anyone could say would change my mind."

"And? What finally did?"

Eunice smiled. "It was not a large thing, but a series of small events leading to my life changing when I joined the Leopards.

I believe that when you find your true calling, God rewards you."

"If that's true, then I haven't yet found my calling."

Eunice cocked her head to the side. "Are you sure? Has God not spoken to you?"

Leine thought about the course of her life—how Eric had discovered her as a teenager at a shooting range in Southern California after her father had died, and trained her as an elite assassin for his secret government agency. How he'd betrayed her, and she had taken things into her own hands to get revenge. How concern for her daughter, April, who was fathered by the same man who betrayed her, led her to quit her job as an assassin, meet and fall in love with Santa, a homicide detective, and become the bodyguard for an entitled, spoiled movie star. That job led her to using her considerable skillset to help rescue trafficked women and children. And finally, how she'd come through the dark guilt that had overtaken her, and rid herself of the lure of vengeance.

"I suppose you could look at it that way," she conceded. "But I'm still not convinced. If your god is as powerful and forgiving as you obviously believe, the age-old question is how can he allow atrocities to occur? Why doesn't he protect Africa's wildlife? Or children who are used in such horrendous ways?"

Eunice studied Leine for a moment. "But he does." She gestured to the building around them. "I would argue that God's work is all around us. Look at you, for instance. You ask why God doesn't protect children? What is it that you do again?"

"All right. You've made your point. But using your line of reasoning, anything good that happens in the world could be seen as 'God's work.' Where's your proof?"

Eunice smiled at Leine. "That is where faith comes in. With faith, you don't need proof."

Leine was about to argue when the satellite phone buzzed in

her pack. She pulled out the device and glanced at the screen. It was Miller.

"Hey, Paul."

"Where are you right now?"

Leine sat up straighter at the urgency in Paul's voice. "What's going on? Have you found Samir?"

"No, but we might have a lead. A contact at the WHO reached out to let us know there's an outbreak of a virus they've never seen before in a suburb of Nairobi."

She glanced at Eunice. "Kibera?"

"How did you know?"

"The group I'm working with heard a rumor about a mysterious illness in that same area."

"Think it's our guy?"

"Gotta be."

"WHO sent in a team of scientists and doctors to work with the Kenyan government. I want you to be my eyes and ears on the ground. I'll send a heads-up to the lead investigator. They'll have extra bunny suits for you and your team."

"Got it. I'm bringing a local to help with statements."

"Great idea. I'll make sure they know to make extra PPE available. And Leine?"

"What?"

"Be careful. From the initial reports, the virus is on steroids."

"Will do." Leine ended the call and slipped the phone back into her pack and nodded at Eunice. "Looks like your lead panned out."

35

———

Somewhere in Somalia

Felix Andreyev unscrewed the top of his water bottle and took a deep drink. What he wouldn't give to be back in Moscow enjoying a thick, juicy steak and a bottle of decent red wine. And cooler weather. He really missed that. Not this Godforsaken heat. He'd been relieved when they reached Kenya, leaving the choking dust storms of the Sahara in their rearview mirror.

Well, asshole, you signed up for this. Now make the best of it.

Felix glanced at Azim as he finished his bean-filled chapatti. How he'd gotten stuck with the feckless mercenary he'd never know. Out of all the losers that were on his team, why did Azim survive? At least give him someone who didn't continually brag about his conquests of the opposite sex. Felix was getting sick and tired of hearing the man's salacious stories, most of which he assumed were just that—stories.

They'd been in Somalia for two days now, had surveilled the so-called terrorist training camp his government sent him to watch. Samir hadn't been there of course, making a mockery of their attempts to find one lone terrorist in the vast continent that was Africa. When the camp was obliterated by an air strike rumored to have been ordered by US Africa Command, Felix and Azim had shifted their focus to locating the surviving al-Shabaab members. That proved to be a dead end when they scattered to the four winds. Now Felix and Azim were awaiting orders.

And more recruits.

Felix's mobile vibrated in his pocket, signaling a text. *"Limited outbreak reported in Nairobi. Suggest you find out more details."* The message was followed by the GPS coordinates of the area where the outbreak had occurred.

When his bosses "suggested" anything, it always meant a direct order. Felix never understood why his handler insisted on couching his instructions in such vague language. Give him an order or don't. Not this pussy bullshit of "suggesting" anything.

With a scowl, Felix returned his phone to his pocket.

Azim glanced at him. "Where are we going now?"

Felix smiled, and Azim smiled back uncertainly. "Don't worry. I have a big job for you."

Leine and Eunice took the hazmat suits from the WHO representative and pulled them on. Several vehicles were parked near the walkway leading into the slum, some official, some not. Derek, Amira, and Dani were tasked with interviewing anyone who wanted to talk. Curious onlookers milled near the entrance, talking among themselves and filming the activity with their mobile phones.

The WHO rep checked her watch and nodded at a tall, younger woman already dressed in a hazmat suit. "My colleague, Hani, will lead you to the containment zone. You will be allowed twenty minutes." She double-checked their suits and gasmasks to make sure they were sealed before she motioned for them to follow their guide.

"Is there a water source?" Leine asked Hani as they walked.

She nodded. "Yes. There are several. Unofficially, of course."

"I assume they've been checked?"

"Oh, yes. That was one of the first things we did."

"And?"

"We haven't received comprehensive results yet. Preliminary reports tell us there are a variety of toxins in the water, including what appears to be a particularly virulent strain of smallpox. But there's something else in the samples no one has been able to identify. They're running them through more tests in our mobile lab now."

Leine and Eunice exchanged looks. "What are the symptoms?"

"Extreme fatigue and high fever, bleeding from the ears, nose, and eyes. Abscesses. Vomiting. And death."

Leine murmured to Eunice. "I think we have Samir's test site." She asked Hani, "Can you direct us to the woman who first reported the illness?"

Hani shook her head. "I'm afraid she's too ill. All of the residents inside the containment zone are. But you can speak with one of the families in the buffer zone, if you like. I will take you."

Hani led them through a maze of narrow alleys filled with dirt and trash. A river of sewage flowed down the middle of the walkway. Thankful for the gasmask, Leine followed. Hani brought them to a rusted corrugated metal shack. She stepped aside and nodded at them to enter.

The only light came from an electric lantern that stood on a makeshift counter. An older woman with streaks of gray through her hair sat on a plastic crate in the dimly lit room. A smaller, wiry man close in age to the woman lay on a stained mattress on the floor. At first he appeared to be sleeping, but once her eyes adjusted to the low light, Leine realized he was watching them through a narrowed gaze.

Leine introduced herself to them both. Eunice did the same.

"Does she speak Swahili?" Leine asked Eunice.

Addressing the woman, Eunice translated Leine's question. The older man answered for her, using a dialect Leine didn't recognize.

"He speaks Kikamba. No Swahili."

"Ask him if he has lived here long."

The man replied that he and his wife had moved to Kibera after he lost his position as a day laborer for an agricultural company.

"What does he know about the virus?"

Eunice translated her question. "He says his brother and his family live near here. He was on his way to visit them when he was informed that they were sick and he couldn't enter the containment zone."

"When did he first find out about the infection?"

Eunice listened to his explanation and then translated for Leine.

"He says his brother's wife had come to ask for assistance early this morning, had described the horrible pustules on the brother's face. They came to help, but were turned away by the doctors."

"Ask him if he knows of any others who have fallen ill."

Eunice asked the older man, who nodded. "He says many are sick. Some he knows have it worse than others. There have been three deaths."

They thanked the couple and followed Hani to the edge of the containment zone.

"This is as far as I can take you. Someone will be here to take you back when you're finished. Remember," she said, pointing to her wristwatch. "No more than twenty minutes."

Leine and Eunice made their way along the edge of the containment zone, searching for evidence that might lead them to Samir. They split off, each taking an area to search. A short time later, Eunice returned and urged to her to follow.

"I think I have found someone with information."

Leine entered one of the tiny homes, a patched-together affair with a corrugated roof and cardboard covering open sections used for windows. Inside, a pot of something delicious-smelling bubbled on the propane cook stove. The space had recently been swept. A middle-aged woman wearing a long, colorful skirt and loose-fitting blouse watched them from nearby. Her resigned expression spoke to her lack of resources to fight whatever new scourge had infiltrated her world. Lying on a mattress on the floor in the corner was a girl of about three. Obviously too exhausted to cry, the toddler's smooth skin revealed dark abscesses forming along her arms and legs.

Leine watched the girl as Eunice introduced herself and Leine. The woman spoke Swahili, allowing them both to speak with her. Leine asked the woman if she'd noticed any strangers in her neighborhood over the past few days. The woman replied that she had.

"Can you describe them?"

"My neighbor's daughter entertained a strange man two nights ago."

"Is that unusual?" Eunice asked.

The woman shook her head. "This is how she makes a living. But it's unusual for her to bring them here."

"How did you see them?" Leine glanced out the doorway. "There are no streetlights."

"I couldn't sleep, and spent the time mending clothes. There was plenty of light. The moon was full."

"Do you think he saw you?"

The woman shook her head. "I am careful to remain hidden, especially at night." She narrowed her eyes. "There are men who prey on women here."

Eunice added, "Sexual assault is a huge problem in Kibera. The police are known to avoid the area."

"This man with your neighbor's daughter, did he ever return?" Leine asked.

The woman shook her head. "I never saw him again."

"Can you tell me what he looked like, and where we can find her?"

The woman described a man fitting Samir's description. "The daughter works at a tavern near the city center called the Acme Bar."

"Thank you for your time," Leine said. "I hope your daughter recovers quickly."

"We'll pray for her," Eunice added.

Leine and Eunice exited the house and made their way past the WHO workers and scientists to wait as someone was located to guide them out of the containment zone. Leine mentioned the plight of the little girl to one of the doctors they passed. He nodded and said he would look in on the girl and her mother.

Finally, they had a lead.

They removed their hazmat suits and gasmasks and tossed them in a burn pile outside the buffer zone before returning to the Land Cruiser, where Derek, Amira, and Dani waited. Earlier that morning, after arguing with Darwin, Leine had permanently but gently relieved Henry of his chauffeur duties. He'd been reporting their movements to the embassy. It wasn't that Leine didn't think the CIA had a right to know where she was or what she was doing, but she really hated having a minder. Even one as predictable as Henry.

Not to mention the possibility of a mole.

"Well?" Derek's expression was hopeful. "Find out anything?"

"We did. Two nights ago a waitress who works at a tavern in Nairobi brought a strange man home fitting Samir's description."

Derek smiled. "We have our break."

36

From the shade of an entryway across the busy street, Verdun King watched as the WHO rep stopped everyone on their way into the slum. Leine Basso and her team had been notified about the outbreak, were tasked with finding the terrorist before he released more of the virus. Matt Price had called in Verdun's team as backup.

He'd let Basso keep looking for Samir, since the terrorist hadn't returned his call. That told Verdun Samir might be having second thoughts about accepting the CIA's help leaving Africa. Once Basso and her team found him, Verdun and his men would save the day by swooping in to acquire the virus and eliminate Samir. The best part about this op was the potential windfall from both the virus and the vaccine, the existence of which Verdun just had confirmed.

He never dreamed that a lone scientist from a Russian lab in the middle of nowhere would change his fortunes and the fortunes of his partners so precipitously. The CIA had known that the Russians were working on a super virus—had been for over a decade. But no one understood just how close they were to weaponizing it. The scientist in question had developed a conscience and was now ready to steal the vaccine developed at the same lab, which Verdun planned to acquire. When he broached the subject with his partner at ZeniGen Pharmaceuticals, dangling the chance to be the first with a vax, the partner had quickly agreed to terms.

The idea came to him as soon as Matt told him about the outbreak in Kibera. Samir was following a known pattern, one that the owners of ZeniGen and their powerful partners could exploit. Once Verdun had the vaccine, ZeniGen would be poised to make billions, perhaps trillions with the cure.

All thanks to Verdun King.

Of course, they would all reap the benefits.

Many, many benefits.

Verdun smiled to himself as he returned to his vehicle to head back to his hotel. He'd have a drink first and check in with Matt before he spoke with ZeniGen to discuss next steps. Verdun would suggest to Matt that he be allowed to continue to direct Samir, to offer him free passage off the African continent. If the CIA balked, then Verdun would go to ZeniGen.

It wouldn't matter to Samir who offered to help him escape. He'd end up dead, either way.

But it would to Verdun.

GENERAL AL SHAMI SHOOK HIS HEAD AND LET OUT A DEEP SIGH. His son, Yusuf, sat across from him, his expression a study in defiance and shame. Ever since the general's men had brought his son back from Libya, he'd been wrestling with himself as to how he would punish Yusuf for his stupidity. The body count at the CIA safe house was another matter. His contact in Libyan intelligence had expressed dismay at the slaughter, not to mention the damage done to the structure itself. The heat was on in his department, and the contact feared his duplicity would be discovered.

The general blew out another sigh. There was no other way to achieve the end required. He drummed his fingers on the arm of his chair, considering what he was about to do. Yusuf's mother would be most unhappy, but Al Shami didn't care. He couldn't be shown to be weak, especially when it came to his own family. Especially when that family member had unleashed something so dire that he put the Assad regime in danger.

Al Shami caught his son's gaze and held it. *So young.* And yet, Al Shami himself had been close to Yusuf's age when he'd been tasked with sensitive operations. Had he been too lax with him? He'd tried to instill in Yusuf a sense of duty and loyalty to country, no matter who was in power, or what they asked of him. And the younger Al Shami had shown a marked ability toward those ends.

But.

His son's sexual proclivities, although not unheard of in Syrian society, had become an impediment to Yusuf's gaining power in Assad's administration.

Those proclivities made him weak, subject to what his Russian counterparts referred to as kompromat. And the general couldn't risk a weak link in his organization, including his own son.

"You know why you are here?" The general gave Yusuf a stern look.

Yusuf shook his head. "Has there been news?"

Al Shami noted that he avoided using Samir's name, preferring to keep his father from berating him again regarding his ill-advised relationship with a known terrorist.

"If you're asking whether we've found your friend Samir, we have not."

Yusuf winced at the mention of his friendship with the target of his father's ire. "He isn't my friend."

"Indeed." Al Shami steepled his fingers and gazed calmly at his progeny. "Would it be better if I called him your business partner?"

"Our deal was for only one vial," Yusuf argued. "Is it my fault that the Americans found out about the handoff?"

Al Shami's anger spiked, but he tamped it down. "Yes, actually, it is."

Yusuf frowned and shook his head. "How? They obviously knew about the meeting. I did nothing to help that."

"You do remember going out the evening before?" The general's ire crested. How could his son be so delusional?

"Like it was yesterday. But nothing I did could have tipped off the Americans."

"If you hadn't gone to that blasphemous club in Tripoli, there's no way the CIA would have been able to track you. And what of the woman?" Yusuf's own bodyguard, Jamal, had mentioned a woman whose services his son requested, had accompanied him to the sex club, and later, to the handoff. There had been something about her, Jamal said, that set his radar humming.

"She had nothing to do with anything. What I do on my own time is not up for discussion. Jamal was mistaken."

Al Shami picked up a piece of paper lying on his desk. "It says here that the woman whose time you purchased was forcibly detained by two unknown men waiting outside the hotel. The real Aya never made it to your appointment."

Yusuf's gaze faltered, and he shifted in his chair.

"Which begs the question, who did your imposter work for?" The general shook his head in frustration. "Have I not trained you to be wary of everything? Especially in a country like Libya?"

"She was...she was exactly what I expected." Yusuf's voice trailed off.

"Of course she was." Al Shami snorted. "Didn't I tell you your sexual aberrations would be your downfall? Don't give the enemy even the smallest opportunity to exploit you. Especially not something for which you can be blackmailed."

"The room was under surveillance the entire time. I reviewed the recordings. Aya did nothing wrong."

"Except she was an imposter." Al Shami stood and paced the room, unable to contain his fury. "Explain to me why you didn't listen to Jamal? He said he thought the woman was not who she seemed. Especially when Samir discovered the gun."

"He would have stopped Samir from going to the meeting."

"Which would have put an end to the sale of the vial to a terrorist. Which, in turn, would have stopped him from obtaining all eighteen vials of the deadliest virus ever conceived. It's only a matter of time before Samir—a member of Izz al-Din, remember—brings that death back to his own country to use against Assad's forces. Against us."

Yusuf had the decency to appear chagrined.

Al Shami stopped pacing and crossed his arms. He stared at his son. "Do you see how your actions led to this outcome?"

"Yes, father." Yusuf looked away, petulance plain on his face.

"What? You want to say something? Say it."

"You trained terrorists—with our friends from Iran. Or have you forgotten? All I did was attempt to work with one, as you did."

"That is not the same." The words ricocheted from his mouth like rifle rounds. They were wrong to train ISIS and Izz al-Din—he understood that now. Al Shami hadn't heeded the warnings from others who told him they would turn on the regime as soon as it suited their purpose. They did as predicted, and now he and Assad were paying the price. But that didn't mean his son should try to follow in his footsteps.

"You can't blame me for trying. You showed me how."

Assad would execute Yusuf for less, and be completely justified in doing the same to Al Shami. The general brushed sweat from his upper lip as he leaned forward and pressed the intercom button on his desk.

"Yes, General?" his assistant's voice asked.

"Send for security."

"Right away, sir."

Yusuf's eyes widened. "What are you doing?"

Al Shami raked his hand through his hair in frustration. "What I should have done as soon as you arrived home."

"No. You can't." Yusuf rose from his chair and backed toward the door, his eyes imploring him to reconsider. "I'm your son."

"It is precisely because you are my son that I must do this."

Yusuf spun in place and grasped the door handle. It was locked. The only way out was via a hidden button under Al Shami's desk.

"You must take your punishment like a man, Yusuf. It's the only way to restore our family's honor."

"No. You've got to believe me. It wasn't anything I did."

Al Shami sighed. Defiant to the end.

The general's mobile buzzed, signifying a phone call. He glanced at the screen. His Russian contact. Surprised, he picked up the phone at the same time a sharp rap sounded at his office door. He depressed the locking mechanism, and the door swung open to reveal three of his security contingent.

"Take him." Al Shami waved them toward Yusuf, ignoring his son's incredulous look. A small voice whispered in the back of his mind, *your wife will never forgive you.*

The guards took Yusuf into custody and, though he resisted,

frog-marched him from the room. The general waited until the door closed behind them before answering the call.

The small voice did not speak again.

"General. I have a favor to ask of you. It has to do with our... little problem."

"Certainly. What can I do?"

"I have an operative in Kenya who is in need of new recruits. *Experienced* recruits."

"Of course. Where shall I send them?"

37

Kibera slum, Nairobi

"Aren't you coming?" Through the windshield, Azim eyed the people going in and out of the entrance to the slum and gave Felix an uncertain look. "Do I need to wear one of those?" he asked, referring to the hazmat suits worn by several within visual range.

"No. They're made to wear them out of an abundance of caution. You know how those government types are. They have to protect themselves from lawsuits."

Azim grimaced. "It looks dangerous." He removed his semi-auto and placed it in the center console. "Are you sure there's nothing else I can do?"

Felix shook his head, feigning concern. "I'm afraid not. Direct orders." He pointed to the sky, indicating those orders came from the top. Azim's expression still conveyed anxiety. "Look. Would my government ask you to do something they wouldn't do themselves?" He waited a beat, then said, "Of course not." *What was it the Americans said? And if you believe that, I've got a bridge in Brooklyn to sell you.* Felix motioned to a woman standing near the entrance with a clipboard. "Go on. Just tell them you live there and need to get your things."

Azim grimaced as he climbed from the vehicle. "You'd better wait for me."

"What do you think I'm going to do? Leave? You're going in there to get information. Information my superiors need." Using the word superiors was a stretch. Felix had learned long ago that just because they paid his salary didn't mean his bosses were "superior." But he had to play it right or Azim might bolt. The loser mercenary would have no problem finding work in Nairobi. Just head into certain neighborhoods and he'd be practically assured a job with some kind of shady outfit. Organized crime always needed new recruits—for cannon fodder.

Felix adjusted his seatback in the rental as Azim spoke to the woman at the entrance. She checked her clipboard, then pointed to a group of hazmat-suited people passing them. She handed him a badge, and Azim walked into Kibera.

Felix checked his phone for updates on replacements for his team, but his handler was being cagey, which pissed him off. Did they or did they not want him to have eyes on Samir? Give me more people, Felix had told them. His handler had assured him more were on the way, but it had been some time since his request. Normally, the organization had several battle-hardened groups ready to deploy at a moment's notice. This ability to be anywhere in the world within twenty-four hours had distinguished the unofficial mercenary group from other government-sanctioned militia. Well, that, and the idea of an elite fighting force that could be disavowed by the Kremlin if necessary. Now, many of his comrades were in Central Africa, "training" troops.

A deep sigh escaped Felix as he thought how much the Group had moved away from its original mission. Now, they were lucky if their fighters had even seen military service.

Maybe it was time to retire. He tamped down the laughter threatening to burst forth from deep inside him.

Like he had a retirement.

No, he had to continue on with the farce that had become the merc group of which he'd once been so proud. Fighters who had seen war caught on early to the fact that none of them would ever earn the public honor of having fought for their country, much less earn a retirement for their service, so they'd left in droves. That, coupled with having to serve in every shithole in the world tended to have a deleterious effect on recruitment.

They were the smart ones. What the hell was he doing? He was a decorated veteran of Russian military operations around the world, including Ukraine and Kosovo, as well as several secret ops not covered in the news. Now, here he was, wasting away in East Africa, waiting to become infected by some unknown virus his government had created, and wouldn't earn a ruble for his trouble if—when he died.

"Bah." Felix shoved the thoughts deep and leaned his head back. All he could do now was wait for Azim to return with news. If he found nothing, Felix was tempted to make up a story to give his superiors something to gnaw on.

Like throwing bones to the wolves.

Fifteen minutes later, Azim returned to the car. When he tried to open the door, he found it locked. Felix inched the window down.

"Open the door." Azim knocked on the window to emphasize his point.

"Did you find out anything?"

"They think they have the illness contained, although they didn't seem certain of that."

"Did you talk to anyone? Do they know where the virus originated?"

Azim shook his head. "They're checking water samples. But people are scared. No one knows how it spreads."

"Anything else?"

"At first they would not allow me to enter the containment area. But I found another way inside."

"So you were in the containment zone?" *Stupid bastard.* Good thing he locked the doors. He pushed the button on his armrest to raise the window, leaving it barely cracked.

"Wasn't that what you wanted?" Azim looked nonplussed.

Felix waved his question away. "Of course. You did well."

Azim leaned closer to the window and said in a low voice. "It's bad, Felix. People are really sick. I've never seen anything like it." He shivered. "It's like they're possessed by demons."

Fucking superstitious twaddle. "Good to know."

"Then we're finished here? Can you open the door?" Azim jiggled the handle.

Felix shook his head. "The boss called while you were inside. They want you to stay here, in case there are any late-breaking developments. You are to call me if anything comes up." He reached into the center console for one of the burner phones he stashed there and handed it out through the passenger side window, careful not to touch Azim.

Azim took the phone. "I need my gun."

Felix shrugged. "Sorry. Can't have you found with a weapon. What would the World Health Organization think?" Not that he gave a rat's ass what happened to Azim. Felix would do better on his own, at least until they sent him replacements.

The look on Azim's face had Felix rethinking his idea—but only for a second. He'd figure out what to tell his boss. The replacements had to be better than this moron.

Maybe.

38

───────

*S*amir's father grins at him through the dust- and smoke-filled alley. "We have the rebels on the run, Samir. This is why we fight."

His brother feeds another rocket into the launcher, then stands back as his father fires it at the rebel stronghold not far from their position. He turns to Samir, his smile an exact replica of their father's. "This fight is ours to win, little brother." He ruffles Samir's hair and turns back to the pile of rockets nearby. They've been hammering the rebels since early that morning, had just heard the news that they were falling back.

They've won the battle.

Then it is as if Hell itself opens beneath them inside the alley. A searing white light explodes before him, accompanied by screaming and confusion and pain.

So much screaming and pain.

Samir finds himself lying prone, his cheek jammed against the rubble from the attack. Dust chokes his throat and coats his eyes, making it difficult to see. His leg burns as though being roasted on a spit in the market.

"Papa," he screams. There is no answer. "Papa—"

Samir woke, his body drenched in sweat. His eyes snapped open and he stared at the ceiling, his breathing heavy as he struggled to calm himself, to remember he was in a hotel room in Nairobi, not fighting the rebels in Aleppo with his now-dead father and older brother. Using a corner of the sheet, he wiped the perspiration from his forehead and glanced at the prostitute. She slept like a child, oblivious to his agony. His anger grew at the unfairness of life.

How long had it been since he'd been able to sleep like that? Now, he was lucky to rest an hour before the ghosts of Aleppo called to him.

He'd been told the air strike that had killed his father and brother had been carried out by coalition forces, ordered by the American president. This knowledge had been Samir's motivation for everything in his life after Aleppo. The fierce hatred that burned inside his heart would only be tempered by seeking revenge for the horrendous murders of his family.

Ironically, their deaths gave meaning to his life.

His American contact was lying. Assad didn't bomb the patriots fighting for him.

He stared at the ceiling for a long time, before eventually falling into a fitful, mercifully dreamless sleep.

Not long after, a whisper of movement woke him as Joan slipped out of bed and headed for the bathroom. He didn't rouse, preferring not to have a conversation with her. She'd been inconsolable at the bar, so he lured her away to his hotel room with the promise of doubling her fee. Unfortunately, she hadn't been able to contain her grief, weeping at the most inopportune times.

Samir was ready for her to go. She'd played her part in his plan. He'd be leaving Nairobi soon, anyway. The risk of getting caught gnawed at him and wasn't something he'd prepared for. After the initial exhilaration of successfully deploying the virus in Kibera, he was growing more and more certain of treachery, sensing a net tightening around him. If not the Russians or Syrians, then certainly Ali and Abdul were looking for him. He hadn't been able to sleep more than an hour or two at a time since he'd released the virus, jarring awake at every sound.

Joan returned from the bathroom and Samir feigned sleep. She hesitated next to the bed, then walked over to her clothes, which she'd left draped over a chair near the window. Samir opened his eyes to slits, giving him a silhouetted view of her against the curtains.

She reached into her purse and pulled out her phone. Curious as to who she might be messaging at this hour, Samir watched her closely. Probably just texting her mother for an update. He beamed inwardly at the thought that all the residents who drew their water from the tank would be dead soon, if they weren't already.

The light from her phone illuminated her face as she bent over the screen, her thumbs moving swiftly. She then glanced back toward the bed. Samir narrowed his eyes even more and worked to keep his breathing even.

Joan put her phone back, then crept over to the bed and slid inside the covers. Samir rolled away from her. He soon realized he needed to relieve himself. He sat up and stretched his neck from side to side, then climbed to his feet and padded to the bathroom.

On his way back to bed, he noticed something off. Puzzled, he leaned over and scanned the void area underneath the bedframe.

The duffel bag had been moved.

His shoulders went rigid. The bag with the thermoses

containing the virus had been moved. He was certain this was evidence that someone was watching, had sent Joan to keep track of him. He'd refused maid service, had employed various ways to tell if his door had been opened. It hadn't. Just to be sure, before he left his room, he'd lined up the zipper of the duffel bag with the center of the bedframe in case someone managed to enter without disturbing his "tells" and discover what was inside.

His focus narrowed to a laser-like clarity. Had al-Shabaab somehow put her in his path? Obviously, the woman in his bed had found the virus, then texted someone of her discovery. Why she decided to stay in the room with him when she'd found out he was responsible for her parents' deaths didn't occur to him.

All he knew was that she'd betrayed him.

Samir sat down and slid the bag out from under the bed, his mind churning over what he needed to do. Should he kill her now and then leave? He paid cash for the room, had used fake identification. Too risky. What if he didn't get out of Nairobi before her body was discovered? The hotel most likely had his license plate number. Although, he could always steal replacement plates.

No, he'd play the waiting game and lure her into the countryside where he could take her life with no witnesses. He'd leave her somewhere no one would find her. Slowly, he unzipped the bag and eased one of the thermoses free to check inside. Eight of the vials were there. The second thermos held nine. Relief washed through him.

The text she'd sent minutes before nagged at him. If she alerted her contact to what she'd discovered, he had no doubt her handlers would soon be surrounding the hotel. Of course, the contact may not get her text right away—it was early.

"What are you doing up?" Joan's soft voice floated toward

him, feeding his anxiety. She'd lost her only family to his hand, and here she was acting concerned. For him.

Traitorous bitch.

He turned to look at her. "I can't sleep."

She moved closer, placed her hand on his thigh. "I can't either."

Samir breathed deeply and let it go, working to control his anger. He couldn't stand her touching him, wanted to rip her hand free of his leg. His heart beat heavily in his ears as he pushed her away and stood.

"Are you all right?" Joan sat up, apprehension lacing her words. She tried to hold his hand, but he moved away from the bed. "Have I done something wrong?"

Samir closed his eyes and swallowed his anger. "Who did you text?"

"What?"

"Just now. Who did you text?"

She paused. Samir sensed her anxiety, like a strain of poison spreading through the air, circling inward, like a noose, or a spider's web, meant to capture her in her lies.

"I texted my mother. I wanted...I wanted to know if she was still alive."

Don't believe her. She's playing you, Samir.

She turned on the light next to the bed. Tears slid down her cheeks. "I can't believe my father is gone."

Samir moved to the bed and seized her wrist.

"You're hurting me. Let go."

He pulled her to him and put his face close to hers. "You will tell me who you texted. Now."

Her eyes widened with fear. "I told you. My mother. Please. You have to believe me."

"A sweet story from a bitter mouth." He tightened his grip and dragged her off the bed and across the room, where he rummaged through her clothes with his free hand, looking for her phone. He found it, and looked at the screen.

"Passcode."

Joan shook her head as she tried to pull from his grasp. "You're acting crazy. What do you think I've done?"

"Give me your passcode. Now." He transferred his grip to her hair, and wrenched her head back.

Crying, she mumbled the four-digit code.

He brought up her recent texts. The latest message was to an unknown number. He turned the screen so she could see it. "Tell me why doesn't this say 'Mother'? It's only a number."

Joan cowered at his anger, her confusion a sure sign of weakness. "It's a new…phone. I haven't had time to put her name into my contacts. Please, Samir. You must believe me."

Samir shook her, his rage reaching the boiling point. "That's a good story, Joan. If Joan really is your name." Scrolling through her texts he hit on one with a name, turning it toward her in triumph. "Why does this one have a name, then?"

"That's my friend, Maude. The woman you met last night at the tavern."

He scrolled down and read the latest messages, certain she was using a code in her communications. His frustration bloomed when he couldn't figure out their meaning. He slammed her phone on the table and dragged her back toward the bed. "What else do you know?"

"I don't understand."

"You know my name is Samir. What else?"

"You told me your name…remember? The first night we were together?" Her tone had grown wary, like a person trying to calm a rabid dog.

Well, he would give her rabid. He knelt beside her and shoved his face into hers. He could smell her fear, the rank odor that accompanies cowards who have been found out. He breathed in the sweet fragrance of her shampoo, the mixture of the two fueling him on. Cupping her chin with his free hand he kissed the side of her cheek. Tears streamed down her face as the reality sank in—he knew she knew she was going to die.

"Get your things. We're leaving."

39

———

Mirovia Lab, Libya

"What are you doing here so early?" Boris cocked his head to the side, reminding Sasha of a big friendly Saint Bernard. His shaggy brown hair and pudgy body belied the fact that he was a gun junkie, as well as an aficionado of B-rated action movies.

"I couldn't sleep. Thought I'd get an early start." She checked the clock on the wall behind him. Excited by the prospect of finally leaving the hell that was her life, Sasha had intentionally arrived well before her shift, making sure she would have enough time to carry out her plan.

"Well, you'll be in good company. Ilya is here, too."

Surprised, Sasha kept her expression impassive to cover her reaction. "Oh? I didn't know he was such an early bird."

"He isn't. The bosses asked him to compile and transmit the latest research on whatever Team One's been working on."

"Ah. Well, I'll have to look in on him, see how he's doing."

With a smile, Sasha walked through the metal detector and

waited while Boris checked her satchel. When he was finished, he gave it back to her with a suggestive grin.

"If you need any help, don't hesitate to call." He held his hand to his ear, pantomiming a phone call.

Sasha looked him in the eyes as she leaned in close, and said in a throaty voice, "I'll be sure to remember that."

Boris's cheeks flushed red and he half giggled. "Ha ha. I'm not kidding, you know."

She picked up her satchel and gave him her most serious look. "I know."

She went to her office, turned on her air-gapped laptop, and downloaded the vaccine research and several other files onto a flash drive. She made a copy on a second drive, and then, using a method Tony had given her, wiped all indications of her project from her laptop. She had no illusions about what her bosses would do once she'd stolen the vaccine. They'd demand her arrest, which would be followed by a sham trial, after which she'd be sent to a labor camp somewhere in Siberia.

Sasha wished the cliché wasn't true, but there it was.

She hid the second drive in an empty tube of lipstick, zipped it into a hidden compartment of her purse, and slid the first drive in her pocket. Although she trusted Tony, she didn't trust the CIA. She wanted to be certain to have access to the information in case they decided to renege on Tony's promise to distribute the vaccine.

Finished with her undercover activities, Sasha decided to visit Ilya one last time before she left. He'd been her only true friend during her tenure there, and she was going to miss him.

He was sitting in the main lab, in front of one of the lab's other air-gapped computers used for sensitive information.

"How's it going?"

Ilya swiveled in his chair as she entered the room and gave her a tired smile. "It's going." He gestured toward the computer he was working on. "You'd think our overlords would invest in more RAM. This is taking forever." He shrugged, then gave her a sidelong glance. "What are you doing here so early?"

"Couldn't sleep." Sasha took a seat next to him at the workstation and nodded at the screen. "What are they having you do?"

"Somebody high up demanded a full report on our progress. Obviously has to do with the fucking debacle with the Syrians." He glanced at the screen, which showed twenty-three percent remaining until the download was finished. A loud sigh escaped him. "Fucking government," he muttered under his breath.

Sasha wanted to tell him she was leaving, that she was going to be fine, more than fine, but realized anything she said could be misconstrued, as well as mark Ilya as a co-conspirator. Everyone assumed the facility was wired for audio, and she didn't want to implicate him in her disappearance.

The day before, she'd finally received the text she'd been waiting for from Tony. He planned to get her out of Libya today. The last thing she had to do before she left was wipe the research on her laptop and anything else that might point to her relationship with Tony or the CIA. She was sure there wasn't anything incriminating, but she checked just the same. He'd asked when she was going to the lab for the last time, and she told him she would make an excuse and go in that evening. He replied that he would send a team to pick her up the next morning at her apartment. She was to feign sickness and not go in that day.

But she'd decided to wait until morning. Her presence at the lab late at night would not go unnoticed. Better to go early in the morning, before her colleagues showed up, do what she needed to, then fake an illness and leave.

She could barely contain her excitement. She would be able to follow her dream of curing infectious diseases with the blessings and resources of the United States government. She wondered where she'd be living—perhaps some small college town in the Midwest? Sasha required little, nothing more than a laboratory where she could spend the rest of her days chasing the next discovery, and a little place to call her own.

She rose to leave. "Be well, Ilya."

He gave her a puzzled look. "Are you going somewhere?"

She grinned to cover the slip. "Only the hell that is my office. Have you noticed how much paperwork I have to wade through? You may never see me again." With a forced chuckle, she walked out the door and headed toward her office.

She hoped he wouldn't think twice about her little mistake.

THE FIVE-MAN TEAM BREACHED THE FENCE SURROUNDING THE LAB and ghosted across the pre-dawn desert landscape, avoiding the security cameras. Each man wore tactical gear with pac4 laser pointers with Aimpoint scopes mounted on the top of M4s. Two veered off, headed for the entrance, while the remaining three moved to the rear of the facility.

The early morning hour guaranteed an absence of personnel. According to the brief they'd received, a lone guard was stationed at the entrance with interior security cameras throughout the facility. As the three-man team breached the rear door, the second team would neutralize the security guard at the entrance and destroy the security footage. The guard on duty that morning wasn't much of a threat—he was thought to be untrained for an attack of this kind, his function only to ensure no prioritized information left the premises.

If things went as planned, they wouldn't need to engage.

Forming up at the back door, a member of the three-man team disabled the camera while another used a handheld thermite breaching torch to cut through the hinges. The third gunman then used a Hallagan tool to pry open the door.

With no time to spare, the group cleared the hallway, several labs, a set of bathrooms, and the breakroom before heading for their objective: an office near the center of the building.

Although each wore Peltors for comms the team didn't speak to each other—no words were necessary to carry out their mission—only hand signals and standard operating procedures. They'd worked together before, knew each other like family, moved like a singular machine.

As they neared their objective, they tightened formation. One glance through the large office window told them the target wasn't there. They split up, each moving in separate directions.

The sound of gunfire erupted near the front of the facility. Tensing, the team leader stopped and keyed his mic. "Bravo, sitrep."

There was a slight pause before Bravo replied. "Security neutralized."

"Status?"

"Spartacus received a flesh wound. Subject was armed."

"Hold."

"Roger."

The team leader resumed searching and clearing the offices and labs, inserting a flash drive into each computer he encountered, uploading spyware. As he backed out of what appeared to be a conference room, the door to one of the bathrooms down the hall swung open, revealing a dark-haired woman of indeterminate age. The sound of a flushing toilet could be heard behind her.

She matched the photographs.

She wasn't supposed to be there.

The woman froze, her eyes widening. "Did Tony send you?" she asked in a low voice.

The leader nodded. "Sasha?"

The woman visibly relaxed. "I thought we were going to meet at my apartment." She cut her eyes left and right. "They'll know," she said, nodding at a security camera positioned near the ceiling a few yards away.

"Taken care of." He moved a few steps closer, and lowered his rifle. "Do you have the drive?"

She nodded. "Of course. I—"

"Give it to me." It would be safer with him, in case the extraction went sideways.

Sasha frowned at his outstretched hand and took a step backward. "I'd rather give it to Tony."

"You're to give it to me. I'll keep it safe."

Some kind of emotion passed over her face that he couldn't read. "I need to speak to Tony first."

"Fine. But before we do that, I need to verify that you have the drive. Operational protocol," he added. He'd take it from her by force if she continued to object.

She paused for a moment, then said, "All right. I hid it in my lab." She pointed behind him. "Down the hallway, to the left."

The leader took a step back. "After you."

Sasha skirted his position, her head down. The leader followed.

40

Sasha's heart beat wildly as she led the gunman to one of the smaller labs at the far corner of the building, away from where Ilya was compiling his report. She didn't want him involved in anything dangerous, and this man appeared dangerous. He'd murmured something into the microphone he wore, leading her to believe he wasn't alone.

Who was he? Had someone gotten to Tony? That was the only explanation that made sense. Tony would have told her if he'd planned to break into the lab. What was this commando doing here? She had to try to contact Tony, but how? What if the gunman was here to kill her? Her delaying tactic would only buy her so much time.

As she reached for the door to the lab, a thought struck her. Had the CIA decided to bypass Tony's commitment to extract her, in order to steal the research? Growing up in Moscow, she'd heard horror stories about the CIA and their methods, had always assumed it was propaganda pushed by her government, but now she wasn't so sure.

Or had her own government found out about her successful

attempts to create a vaccine and sent someone to steal the information? No, the gunman had known Tony's name. Or had he? She tried to remember exactly what she'd said to him. Then she remembered: she'd been stupid and asked if Tony had sent him. All he had to do was say yes. She hadn't used the pass phrase she and Tony had come up with. She slowed, thinking through the idea.

What if she used it and he didn't respond correctly? Would that be evidence that he was from her government? Maybe not, but it would definitely tell her he wasn't on her side.

But then what?

Either way, she had to escape with the drive. Whoever the man behind her claimed to be, she didn't trust him.

They reached the small lab. She started to swipe her card to unlock the door, but hesitated. The gunman stood less than a meter from her. She had to try.

"The scale in my bathroom is broken," she said, reciting the first half of the pass phrase she and Tony had thought up.

The gunman nodded. "Then you should buy a new one. I hear they're on sale."

She studied the man. He'd answered the phrase perfectly. He wasn't from her government—they wouldn't have known the response. Why did she still not trust him? She swiped her card and unlocked the door. The lab itself was fully equipped but had been offline for maintenance. Over a series of days, staff had been sterilizing beakers and pipettes, and getting the room ready for use.

She just hoped they hadn't finished yet.

They walked in and the lights blinked on, illuminating the sterile lab. Sasha's mood plummeted—it looked like maintenance had finished their work. The surfaces gleamed. An autoclave stood next to a cooler, all shiny clean and ready for use.

Everything had been neatly put away. She scanned the room for something, anything that she could use, her gaze landing on a plastic bottle left on a counter. A large stainless sink was nearby.

"It's just over here." Sasha walked to the counter and glanced at the bottle's label. Relief washed through her. She'd been right—maintenance had used hydrofluoric acid to clean some of the items in the lab.

She checked her periphery to gauge the gunman's position. He stood behind her and to the left, about a meter away. Making sure to block his view, Sasha turned her back and opened an upper cabinet with one hand while unscrewing the top on the bottle of acid with the other. Holding her breath, she placed the top on the counter and grasped the bottle. It was nearly full.

It was now or never.

She pivoted and threw the corrosive acid into the gunman's face, squeezing the bottle to force out as much as she could. The gunman raised his hands to ward off the attack, but she'd taken him by surprise and he was too late. His screams reverberated through the room as the chemical saturated his exposed skin. His tactical gear wouldn't help him now—the acid seared his face, neck, and hands, and ate through his clothes.

Sasha looked down at her fingers. A small amount had landed on her hand and was eating through her flesh, burning her skin. She ran to the sink and flipped on the water, dousing her hand in the cold stream.

The gunman writhed on the floor, his tortured screams filling the air, hands clawing at his face. The acid had burned through his tactical strap and his gun lay on the floor next to him. She hesitated, tempted to take his gun, but decided against it. She had no idea how to operate the complicated-looking weapon, would probably end up hurting herself.

Still holding her breath, she skirted the gunman and moved

to the door, quickly programming it to remain locked. Then she exited the lab. The hall was empty.

For now.

Sasha sprinted back to her office and grabbed her satchel.

Her heart thundering in her chest, she stood next to the door, listening for movement. Were there others? There must be. If not, who was the gunman communicating with on his radio?

She cracked the door open and looked both up and down the hall. Empty. Sasha slipped from her office and hurried along the corridor, headed for Ilya's lab.

As she rounded the corner, she realized he had company. Two gunmen wearing the same gear as the man Sasha had thrown the acid on stood near Ilya. She ducked down before they could see her through the windows. He looked scared but calm as he spoke to them. He didn't appear to be hurt, giving her the impression they were most likely only interested in her.

She couldn't help him. She didn't have a weapon, wouldn't last a second against the gunmen.

Giving up on the idea of trying something stupid to rescue her friend, she stayed down and crab-walked past the lab windows. She stood once she was clear, intending to leave by the side door, near where she'd parked her car. The only problem with the plan was that she would have to pass the entrance. Hopefully Boris wouldn't ask any questions.

She glanced back through the window at Ilya and the two men. One of them raised his rifle. Ilya jerked in his chair. Blood blossomed on his shirt.

She froze, terror rocketing up her spine. *Oh my God. They killed Ilya.*

Blinking back tears, Sasha tamped down the panic rising in her chest, using it to fuel her escape.

Voices reached her as she neared the security guard's station, and she stopped near the corner, not sure who was talking. Heart still thrumming wildly, she tried taking deep breaths to calm herself. It was no use.

She eased closer, then peered around the corner and caught her breath. Boris lay sprawled on the floor next to the front desk, a pool of blood near his head. Two gunmen stood nearby watching through the door, chatting as though there wasn't a dead body at their feet. She snapped back to her original position, heart pounding as adrenaline spiked through her.

They killed Boris. How do I get out?

She had to escape or she'd be next. There was nothing she could do to help either Boris or Ilya. If she gave up now, the vaccine would be lost.

Her car would be of no use. Not with the two gunmen at the guard's station. They'd shoot out her tires or disable her car before she made it through the front gate. Her only chance was to leave through the back door. There was a section of fencing under which water had eroded the dirt, leaving a void area. She'd be able to crawl through and take off on foot. On the way, she'd send a message to Tony to let him know what happened. He'd know what to do.

The gaping hole where the back door should have been made her wonder anew who sent the gunmen. The man she'd thrown acid on wouldn't have had to breach the lab this way if he'd been one of Tony's guys. They were supposed to meet on the road back to her apartment, not break into the lab.

But who was he, if not CIA?

Sasha hesitated, torn between escaping with her life and finding some way to stop her colleagues from entering the lab. The gunmen had killed Boris and Ilya. Because of her. They wouldn't stop at two.

Her optimism waning, she stepped through the open doorway into the predawn air.

There's nothing you can do. You're not an action figure. They were after you, Sasha. Once they realize you've gone, they'll leave.

Tony would know what to do. With a determined sigh, Sasha hurried toward the perimeter fence.

41

Leine entered the Acme Bar and waited for her eyes to adjust to the dark interior. A breeze wafted in from the open doors to the patio, a welcome relief from the relentless heat outside. The place was empty, except for a bartender polishing glasses and one other man seated at a table alone. Eunice strode up to the man behind the bar.

"We need to speak to Joan Kibet. We've been told she works here. It's an urgent matter."

The man, of medium build with a sparse goatee, shook his head, eyeing them both. "I haven't seen her since last night, after she found out her father died."

"Is there some way we can contact her?" Leine joined them at the bar. "It's urgent."

"I'm sorry, but we don't give out employees' contact information."

Leine rummaged in her bag for some cash and laid it on the bar. "For your child's college fund."

The man slid the money back toward her. "I don't have children."

"Well, then use it for whatever you like." With a smile, Leine pushed it back toward him.

He eyed them both warily. After a few moments, he pocketed the cash. "Her friend Maude may know how to contact her."

"How do we find Maude?" Eunice asked.

"I'm Maude." The voice came from behind them. Leine and Eunice both turned to see a tall, slender woman carrying a plate of food. In her late thirties, she was pretty with graceful shoulders, giving her a dancer's appearance. Upon closer inspection, though, she had the look of a person who'd been through too much, for too long. She delivered the plate to the lone diner and joined them at the bar. "What can I do for you ladies?"

"We're looking for Joan Kibet," Leine said.

"I haven't heard from her since last night."

"Is that unusual?" Eunice asked.

"It most certainly is. Especially since her father just died."

Leine asked the next question. "When did you see her last?"

"Yesterday evening. Here. She left with a man she's been seeing off and on for a couple of days."

Leine and Eunice exchanged glances. "Do you know his name?" Leine asked.

"Samir. I thought he was a little sketchy, and I told her so, but apparently he tipped well."

Leine's heart rate ratcheted up. "Can you tell me where they went?"

Maude shook her head. "The first night they went to her place—God knows why. I'm sure they didn't do that the last couple of nights."

"Why?"

"Her neighborhood had an outbreak—some kind of virus. No one knows exactly what caused the infection, but it's quite deadly. It's what killed her father." Maude glanced at the bartender, then back to Leine and Eunice. "It was only a matter of time. The place is filled with trash and sewage. There are always cholera outbreaks and hepatitis. It's a wonder the place hasn't produced anything worse. Of course, the city refuses to deal with Kibera."

"You said you haven't heard from her since last night. Have you tried to call or message?" Leine asked.

"Of course. She hasn't messaged me back yet." She narrowed her eyes at Leine. "Who did you say you were, exactly?"

"My name is Leine. And this is Eunice. Like I said, we're looking for Joan. She's the only person who has had contact with Samir. We think he may have knowledge regarding the outbreak."

Maude folded her arms across her chest. "I *knew* there was something sketchy about him. He took her to a hotel not far from here the night before last. He may have done that again."

"Which one?"

"The Golden Meridian." She searched for the address on her phone and gave it to Leine.

"Can you text that to me?"

"Of course."

Leine recited her mobile number and Maude sent her the link.

"I'll text you if he comes in again."

"That would be extremely helpful," Leine said.

Maude slid her mobile into her back pocket. "Be sure to let me know if you find out anything about Joan, all right? I'm worried."

Leine nodded. "We will." She laid more cash on the bar and nodded at both Maude and the bartender. "Thank you for your time. Be careful around Samir. He's dangerous."

She and Eunice walked out of the tavern. Leine slid on a pair of sunglasses as they crossed the busy boulevard to the shady side of the street. Motorbikes and scooters whizzed by, adding to the cacophony of the busy neighborhood. A lorry belched thick smoke from its tailpipe as it raced past.

"Think she's right to be worried?" Eunice asked.

"Absolutely," Leine replied.

MAUDE PULLED UP THE TRACKING APP ON HER PHONE AND scanned for Joan's avatar. Like women the world over, she and Joan had agreed to monitor each other's whereabouts whenever they went out with someone they didn't know. According to the app's GPS, Joan was somewhere on the outskirts of Nairobi, headed southeast.

That was odd. Joan didn't own a car, and she rarely traveled outside of the city. Maude tried calling her friend for the tenth time, but there was still no answer. Maude's alarm built, having reached claxon horn levels after the two women came into the bar looking for Joan. Maybe she should have told them she could track her. She brought up the Leine woman's mobile number and hesitated. What if they meant Joan harm?

What if Samir meant her harm?

Perhaps she should follow Joan to see if she was in trouble and needed help. If she was with Samir, then Maude would call Leine.

42

Derek pulled up to the entrance to the Golden Meridian Hotel and parked. The circular drive curled around a large, non-functioning fountain, although the grounds appeared well-groomed.

Eunice opened her door. "I'll check the perimeter west to north," she said to Leine. "Text me if you see anything."

"Will do. I've got the lobby." Leine gestured to the two women in the back seat. "Dani, you and Derek stay with the car in case Samir shows up. If he does, be sure to text one of us. Amira, recon east to north and meet Eunice at the back of the property."

"Roger that."

Amira and Eunice exited the vehicle and split off in opposite directions, while Leine walked through the sliding glass doors into the air conditioned lobby. A young man wearing a tan blazer stood behind a long counter with the words "Check in" on a sign above his head.

He looked up and smiled as Leine approached. His nametag read Joseph. "Good afternoon, madam. May I help you?"

Leine returned the smile. "I hope so, Joseph. I'm looking for a man named Samir Fakhri."

Joseph's eyebrows knitted together. "I'm sorry, but we don't have anyone by that name as a guest here." He looked like he was going to say something but stopped himself.

"You answered awfully fast. What were you about to say?"

"It's just that you're the second person to ask for him today. A gentleman was in here a short time ago, asking for his room number."

"What did this gentleman look like?"

"Dark hair, tall. Dressed casually."

"Do you know where he went?"

"I'm sorry, no."

"How long ago did he leave?"

"About twenty minutes."

"Did you happen to see what kind of car he was driving?"

"I'm sorry, no."

Leine took out her phone and pulled up a photo of Samir that Miller had sent her. She showed Joseph. "Have you seen this man?"

He blinked rapidly, then squinted as he leaned closer to peer at the picture. He shook his head and straightened. "He doesn't look familiar."

Leine studied the desk clerk for a moment. He shifted on his feet, obviously uncomfortable.

"Think harder, Joseph. It's very important that you remember. This man may have important information that could save lives."

He busied himself shuffling papers on the counter in front of him. "I'm sorry. We can't give out guest information."

"So he is a guest?"

Joseph grimaced, realizing he'd been caught. He nodded.

"Can you at least give me the name he's registered under?" She pulled some cash from her pocket and set it on the counter.

His gaze flitted from the cash to his computer terminal and back to Leine. He scanned the lobby before surreptitiously sliding the money from the counter and nodding. "Mr. Cirillo."

"Thank you." Leine smiled. "Is he still checked in?"

Joseph typed something into his computer. "He has paid for two more nights."

"Did he register his vehicle, by chance?"

Joseph scanned the screen before him. "I'm sorry, there's no record of the number. Only the make and model."

"Which is?"

Joseph hesitated. Leine put more cash on the counter. He pocketed it and said, "2014 Toyota Fortuner."

"Would you mind having security check his room? I'm afraid that either he or his lady friend might be up there." Leine leaned over the counter and lowered her voice. "You see, his friend has just lost her father to that mysterious illness they've been talking about on TV and doesn't want anyone to know she might have been exposed." Leine looked side to side as she delivered the last sentence in an even lower voice. "I'm afraid she may have succumbed to the illness."

The horrified look on Joseph's face told Leine her gambit had worked. Tiny beads of sweat broke out on his upper lip as his motivation to find Joan and Samir apparently ramped up to Def Con One.

"Of course. Please excuse me." Joseph grabbed a handheld radio from a bank of radios on the back credenza and stepped away from the desk.

When he was several paces from her and muttering into the mouthpiece, Leine leaned over the counter to see the screen and Samir's room number, then moved back to her original position.

Joseph returned and placed the radio back on the charger. He wiped his brow before he turned to Leine and pasted on a smile. "I've just called maintenance to check the room." He gave her an uncertain look. "Do you think I should call the police?"

Leine shook her head. "I'd wait until your maintenance person confirms whether anyone is in the room." She didn't want city police scouring Nairobi for Samir. Not when he still had seventeen vials. There was no telling what he would do with the virus if he thought he was being hunted.

Joseph nodded as relief washed over his features. "Right. Of course. We must wait to see if she's even there."

"Make sure your maintenance people put on protective equipment before entering the room. We wouldn't want them to contract anything." The threat of becoming infected with an unknown virus should delay the maintenance staff from checking the room, at least for a while.

Joseph's eyes widened. The perspiration on his upper lip and forehead had increased.

"I'll be outside. Let me know if you find out anything."

"Of course," he said, nodding. He snatched up the radio and walked away from the desk. Leine left him to his pacing.

She met Eunice and Amira in the gardens on the north side of the property.

"Did you find out anything?" Eunice asked.

"Samir is staying in room 506. An unknown male came in earlier looking for him."

"That's odd. Who do you think that might be?" Eunice asked.

"Not sure. Possibly a buyer. Or a contact for something else."

It wasn't al-Shabaab. Not with Joseph's description. Miller would have alerted her if Darwin or his team had a lead. Probably. Then again, the CIA might be working another angle. They didn't have to coordinate with Leine. The op would work a whole lot better if she didn't duplicate their efforts, but Miller had been adamant about operational security, especially once the possibility of a leak reared its head. He was a fan of not letting one hand know what the other was doing but still coordinating everything to keep everyone safe. Which was why he insisted on Leine checking in with Darwin, as well as Matt Price, on a regular basis.

She hated working for someone, especially her old employer. Hated not calling the shots. Like she always said, the people on the ground knew the score better than anyone else. Those who distanced themselves from the action and directed the troops didn't get the nuances of the enemy, of the operation itself. In her opinion, the only thing upper management was good for was a bird's-eye view and financing. And even that could be achieved if someone on the ground had the right equipment and contacts.

Get over it, Leine. You signed up for this, remember?

Leine eyed the staggered balconies marching up the side of the building, estimating how long it would take her to climb to the fifth floor. "What kind of security are we dealing with here?"

Eunice shook her head. "There isn't any." She nodded at a glass door with a digital card reader next to it on the wall. "The readers are for looks, apparently. I was able to easily open the door."

"What about the cameras? Same thing?" Leine glanced at the security camera mounted over the side entrance.

Amira shrugged. "There is no indicator light, so I don't think that one's active."

"Then follow me."

The three of them slipped in the door to the hotel and hiked up the stairs to the fifth floor. Maintenance was nowhere to be seen—the hallway was empty.

"I'll check the room. No sense in all three of us getting infected if he was careless with a vial."

Eunice narrowed her eyes. "Why does that mean you, then?"

"Because this is my op and I'm responsible for the team. Your objection is overruled." Leine gave Amira a look that told her not to argue. "May I use your scarf?"

Amira unwound the colorful fabric and handed it to her.

"Thanks."

Leine gestured toward the stairwell as she pulled on a pair of nitrile gloves and covered her nose and mouth with the scarf. "Text me if maintenance or the desk manager shows up. I'll be in and out as quickly as I can." She pulled out her lock picks as she crossed the hall to room 506. Even though programmed to open with a key card, she worked the emergency keyhole and had the door open in under a minute. With one last glance up and down the hallway, she slipped inside, closing the door behind her.

The drawn shades blocked the sun, giving the space a gloomy look. Leine switched on the light next to the bed and scanned the room. Leine sincerely hoped Samir hadn't mistakenly released the toxin—she was betting her life he wouldn't waste a drop.

The bed looked as though it had recently been slept in. She bent down and plucked a strand of dark hair from the pillowcase. It was longer and curlier than what the picture of Samir showed, leading Leine to believe it was most likely Joan's. She went through the dresser, checking for clues to where Samir might have gone, but the drawers were empty. After thoroughly searching the room, she went to the closet and opened the double doors.

Nothing. No clothes, no suitcase, no shoes.

She returned to the hall door and cracked it open. The corridor was empty. She exited the room and met Eunice at the entrance to the stairs just as the elevator at the end of the hall pinged. A pair of male voices arguing in Swahili floated toward them as Eunice followed Leine into the stairwell to join Amira. Leine untied the scarf, and, finger to her lips, led the way to the first level.

"What did you find?" Eunice asked when they reached the door leading outside.

"There's nothing in the room. No clothes, no bags."

Amira followed the other two out the door into the garden. "Think he might have left town?"

"Not sure. He paid for two more nights, so it's possible he'll be back. I'm pretty sure Joan has been in the room. I found a long strand of dark hair on the pillowcase."

"So what do we do now?" Amira asked.

"I'm going to give Miller a call, see if he has any leads." She was betting she'd be able to hear in his voice if he was lying. She didn't know Matt Price or Darwin well enough. They returned to the Land Cruiser and briefed Dani and Derek on what they'd found. Then Leine called Miller. Matt Price answered.

"Where's Paul?"

"He's not available. What can I do for you?"

"We found Samir's hotel."

"Good work. I take it from your tone you didn't find him." He sounded genuinely interested in her report. Then again, she didn't know him all that well.

"Looks like he's gone—there's nothing left in his room."

"You went into his room? Did you protect yourself in case some of the virus leaked?"

"I sincerely doubt he would have mishandled it. Too much to lose if he winds up dead."

"Yeah, well, get yourself tested if you start experiencing symptoms."

"Where did you send Verdun and his guys after Khartoum? I

can give them a heads-up if we're covering the same area." She assumed it wasn't only her team searching for Samir. The high priority threat and the presence of the dark-haired man asking about Samir told her otherwise.

"They're in Nairobi, but that's all I can say."

"Do they know which hotel Samir's been staying at?"

"Don't you think I would tell you if I had that information?"

"Sure, Matt. Of course."

There was a pause before he spoke again. "Is there a problem?"

"No, no problem. Someone else was looking for Samir right before we got there."

"Did you get a description?"

"Pretty standard. Could be anybody." She gave him Joseph's description.

"That's not good."

Just then, Leine's burner phone buzzed, indicating a call. "Gotta go. I'll call you if I find out anything else."

Leine checked the screen. It was Joan's friend, Maude.

There was an edge to her voice. "I found Joan."

43

"Where are we going?" Joan eyed the duffel bag in the backseat. She was scared, that much was obvious. Samir had bound her wrists and ankles and belted her into the passenger seat, like he'd done with Yusuf's slut, Aya.

"Be quiet." Stress spiraled through Samir, making it hard to think. Her blathering didn't help. He glanced in the rearview mirror, certain someone was following him. Were they CIA? Or al-Shabaab? Perhaps Syrian Intelligence? The Russians could be tracking him, too. The beat-up white sedan had been behind them for several kilometers. He'd taken random turns, but each time the vehicle had kept pace. He cursed the sun's glare on the other's windshield. He couldn't make out who was driving or how many passengers there were.

"Who do you work for?"

Joan shook her head. Tears sprang to her eyes and she blinked reflexively, trying to hold them back. "I've told you before. I don't know what you're talking about. I work at the Acme Bar. That is my only job. I have no other employer."

He slammed his fist on the steering wheel. "You're lying," he yelled, his voice shaking. "I know you were sent to follow me."

Joan stared at him, a wary look in her eyes. "You're crazy."

"How else could you have known I needed to test the virus on a smaller populace first?" Joan's eyes widened at his words. "Oh, don't look so surprised." He shook his finger at her, convinced she was some sort of double agent. "You knew who I was when I walked into that bar. You were the perfect plant. How does it feel to be responsible for the deaths of so many?"

A look of horror washed over her face. Tears streamed down her cheeks as she began to sob.

"Silence!" He swerved, narrowly missing a motorcyclist.

She squeezed her eyes closed, obviously struggling to contain herself. Her sobs grew quieter.

Good. His anger had subdued her. Samir drummed his fingers on the steering wheel, trying to figure out what to do. He checked the time on the dash—he needed to leave the city, now, before anyone found him. Obviously, he couldn't stop to kill her and dump the body somewhere—not when he was being followed. He surely couldn't take her with him. If he let her off somewhere, would the people tailing him stop to pick her up? He had to buy some time. Once he was free of Nairobi, he'd call his contact in the CIA. The man at the café had assured him they could get him out of the country with the vials.

The vials. The temptation to stop somewhere and hide them was overwhelming. That way he'd ensure that anyone sent to track him down wouldn't get the virus.

Don't be stupid. Whoever caught him would interrogate him. He knew what the Russians and the Syrians were capable of— had heard stories from Izz al-Din members who'd been captured during the Syrian war and survived. He assumed the CIA would be the same. His heart raced as thoughts of what al-

Shabaab could do to obtain the virus filled his mind. No, he had to stay ahead of all of them. He couldn't be captured.

Not alive.

As long as he survived, then he could be certain he had a place in paradise alongside his brother and father. A wave of grief flashed through him, but he tamped it down. He would avenge his family's deaths. He alone would right the wrongs of the powerful West. When his father and brother were cut down by the air strike, Samir had been inconsolable. If only he'd done something. He might have been able to stop their deaths.

Or at least have his vengeance against those responsible.

It was obvious that Allah had another path for him. Samir prayed that he would be up to the task to which he was driven. How else could a man like him possess such righteous destruction? He alone would change the course of the world. He held the keys to triumph over his adversaries.

Assad's march to destroy the Islamic State had ignited Samir's own personal jihad. But America's actions in his own country had set him on his righteous path.

Adversary was too gentle a word to describe the evil propaganda belched from the belly of the Great Satan. He'd been blind to the lure of luxury and decadence played over and over by the West's media. He and his brother and father had rejoiced when the people of America rose up against the false witness of their nation's leaders, only to be crushed by the same pablum their government offered to control the masses.

Americans were weak. No one had the courage of purpose. Even America's minorities had succumbed to the yoke of money and opulence, rising up for a short period, but then backing away from the fight when their government offered them some minor redress to make them think they'd won.

But it would happen again and again. How many times would the people of America allow their government's repressive actions to upend their lives? He'd been heartened when the highest court in the land, the Supreme Court, had ruled in favor of Christianity, paving the way for the Great War. The Chosen against the Christians. Not this talk of all religions and faiths being equal in the eyes of the law. Or God.

That wasn't true, just as Samir believed his faith was the one true way. The Great War between good and evil would soon be fought. And Samir's side would win.

He'd make sure of it.

———

THE SUN WAS WARM AGAINST SASHA'S BACK AS SHE TRUDGED THE rest of the distance to her apartment. She'd hidden each time a car passed by, which thankfully wasn't often.

Throughout the harrowing morning, she'd tried to forget Boris's body lying on the floor by the guard shack, or Ilya being cut down by the gunmen in his lab. Who were they, and why had they killed her friends?

She'd never forgive herself for going into the lab that morning. *This isn't a game, Sasha,* Tony had said on one of their infrequent calls. Well, she certainly knew it now.

Sasha brought out the burner phone Tony had sent her and checked the service. Three bars.

Maybe now she would get some answers.

She stopped near an abandoned storefront not far from her apartment, one of many bombarded by Izz al-Din in one of the dozens of battles between the terrorist group and the Libyan army that had taken place years before. There, she took shelter from the insufferable sun to text Tony.

She had a new message.

Her hope building, she accessed the encrypted app and opened the message. It was from Tony.

Tony: *Are you all right?*

Sasha replied: *I'm here. What the hell happened?*

It didn't take long for him to answer. He must have been monitoring the app.

Tony: *You weren't supposed to be at the lab.*

Sasha: *I was doing what you asked.*

Tony: *But you said you were going in last night, not this morning.*

Sasha: *Were they your men?*

Tony: *??*

She stifled a sob as she typed.

Sasha: *They killed my friends.*

Tony: *You were supposed to wait for the extraction team at home.*

Sasha: *THEY KILLED MY FRIENDS.*

There was a pause before he responded.

Tony: *Sometimes terrible things happen. It shouldn't have. I'm sorry.*

A thought that had played at the edge of her mind during the walk home finally made itself known.

Sasha: *Did you order them to kill me?*

There, she'd said it. Heart beating wildly in her chest, she waited for his reply.

Tony: *Of course not. We lost a good soldier at the lab. He didn't need to die.*

Sasha: *Neither did my friends.*

Tony: *In this business, there's a thing called acceptable losses. It's terrible, I know.*

Acceptable losses? Sasha couldn't wrap her mind around the words. Tears filled her eyes as she texted him back.

Sasha: *I want no part of an organization that believes that.* She hesitated, then added, *I want no part of you.*

She powered down the phone and opened the back to remove the battery and the SIM card. Tony would likely be able to track her otherwise. She tossed the components in opposite directions, making sure no one would find them.

Despair clouded her mind, threatening to swallow her whole. She sucked in deep breaths, willing the horrific sense of betrayal away.

Tony never loved her. He was only using her for his own ends.

A little voice inside insisted, *Isn't that what you were doing, too?*

"It's not the same." She'd said the words out loud, startling herself. But it wasn't the same. Tony used her. Yes, she was using him to get out of a bad situation, but she *loved* him, would have done anything for him.

What was she going to do now? She didn't have a passport. She wouldn't be able to get one and leave Libya unless she contacted her embassy. But she didn't want to be associated with her country ever again. Not when they'd created such a powerful virus and were willing to sell it to their allies to use.

But where could she go? Maybe if she went to the American embassy in Tunisia and told them what she'd done, that she had a vaccine for a lab-created super virus and wanted to defect —maybe then she'd still be able to follow her dream of finding cures in an American lab.

She started for her apartment, but stopped when she spotted a large white SUV in front of her complex. Two men in camouflage and mirrored sunglasses stood outside in the sunlight, obviously waiting.

A surge of adrenaline flowed through her and she ducked behind a nearby parked car.

She couldn't go back to her apartment to get her things. She'd have to find another way.

Warehouse in Nairobi, Kenya

"The Basso group is headed southeast, out of the city."

Felix pulled up a map of the vicinity on his phone and mentally charted a course. "Do we know their objective?"

"Negative. They abruptly changed direction, so we're operating on the assumption they received intel regarding the target's whereabouts."

"On our way."

Felix turned to the group of men assembled inside the warehouse his government used to store weapons in Nairobi. He'd been heartened to see that the quality of recruits had gone up from his previous contingent. Many of the men were hardened fighters flown in from Syria. Some were Russian, some Syrian, but all had experience.

Score one for General Al Shami.

Felix made sure everyone was well-armed and then briefed them on the mission. "The man we are after is called Samir

Fakhri. He's rumored to be a member of Izz al-Din and has in his possession something concerning that we must recover."

"And this concerning thing is..." Karam, a tall, muscular Syrian, crossed his arms and speared him with a look.

"Just know that it's vital we recover it."

"How can we recover something if we don't know what it is we're looking for?" Fayed asked. Another of the Syrian fighters, Fayed was shorter than Karam, but just as powerfully built.

"I'll be sure to tell you." Felix texted the grainy photograph of the lone terrorist obtained by his handler to the recruit's mobiles. "The picture I just sent to your phones is a photograph of the man we're after. Be warned. We need him alive."

"And if that isn't possible?" Karam asked.

"You need to make it possible," Felix growled, reminding himself they were mercenaries and would do what they liked. He needed to sweeten the pot. "There's a juicy reward to anyone who recovers him alive."

The group murmured among themselves. Always a motivating factor, the promise of more money raised the recruit's spirits considerably. When and if the time came to pay the reward, Felix would figure something out. Until then, he wasn't above bribery to maintain operational control.

"The CIA wants Fakhri too, so be aware that we are not the only ones looking for him. Currently, they are running two teams. A woman leads one, and Ground Branch leads the other."

"What is this woman like?" Fayed asked, wiggling his eyebrows.

Felix shook his head. "This is one you will want to pass by."

"Is she ugly?"

"Far from it. But she is deadly."

"Are there other women? I mean, it has been a while..."

Qasim said with his hand on his crotch, eliciting laughter from the others.

"There are two Kurds that we know of."

That got the Syrians' attention. Karam flashed a smile at his two compatriots. "You've just made this job even sweeter. There's nothing better than getting paid to exterminate Kurds." Chuckling, Qasim and Fayed both nodded.

"Then we'll be sure to leave them for you." Felix checked his watch before he directed the men to two armored Land Cruisers. An international arms dealer had been more than happy to extend a favor to the Russian oligarch who funded the mercenaries—so long as he received adequate compensation in return. Extra munitions had been placed in the cargo areas of both vehicles, even though Felix didn't anticipate a protracted fight.

It was good to be prepared.

Felix slid behind the wheel of one of the Land Cruisers, while another Russian, Ivar, climbed into the other. Not that he didn't trust the Syrians to drive. But he'd rather the Russians remained in control.

Samir continued to try to shake the vehicle behind him loose but was unsuccessful. As soon as he thought he'd managed, the sedan appeared behind him yet again. He would have to stop somewhere no one would see them and confront whoever was inside. Perspiration dripped down his forehead and he angrily wiped at his eyes. How could they have found him so quickly? He thought he'd covered his tracks well enough. Thought he'd be on his way to Europe by now.

He glanced at Joan. Eyes closed, she leaned her head against the window, her tear-streaked face the only evidence of her fear.

He had to get rid of her, but how? All he had to fend off his trackers was the semiauto that had belonged to Yusuf's whore. He didn't think he'd have to defend himself from anyone. Thought he'd be well away from Nairobi by now.

He scanned the terrain, looking for a place to go off-road, hoping that whoever was following him would balk at navigating the wilderness. Traffic was beginning to thin somewhat, although he'd been told by a local that he would encounter much more if he meant to take the main highway to Mombasa. A train or flight was the only realistic mode of transportation to the coast.

The people following him weren't CIA, of that he was certain. The Agency would employ a drone to track him. They wouldn't risk personnel—not until they had positively identified their target. Nothing but clear blue sky met his gaze.

If it was the Syrians, he doubted he'd still be alive. They wouldn't follow him for so long without disabling his vehicle. Same for the Russians and al-Shabaab. Who did that leave?

While Samir's mind whirled with the possibilities, the perfect place to leave the main road presented itself. A red dirt road branched off the highway up ahead. A maintenance road for the power lines along the highway, it disappeared over a rise. If he could manage to make it over the rise, stop, and exit the vehicle, he'd have a chance to ambush his pursuers. Maybe he could disable their car, or at least hold them off.

He'd deal with Joan then.

Without slowing, Samir veered off the highway and onto the dirt road, kicking up a rooster tail of reddish-brown dust behind him. He couldn't tell if the other vehicle followed. He punched the accelerator to the floor and rocketed up the rise, catching air as they crested, and came down hard on the other side. Joan gripped the armrest with her bound hands, her expression grim.

The red ribbon of dirt road stretched into the distance, leading up yet another hill. He stomped on the gas, barreling up the rise, coming down on the other side of the second hill. He needed to put distance between himself and the busy highway, in case he had to exchange gunfire with his pursuers.

Sliding to a stop next to an acacia tree surrounded by thick bushes, he hurtled out the door and took a position near the engine block, steadying his aim on the hood. He was a third of the way up the rise, giving him a tactical advantage of being on higher ground with the hill at his back.

The other vehicle didn't appear. Adrenaline coursing through his body, Samir remained in place, expecting the sedan to come over the rise, but it never did. He searched the sky for the telltale glint of a drone, but didn't see anything.

Had he been imagining things? He wiped his face with his sleeve and took a deep breath. Perhaps his pursuers were afraid the car didn't have high enough clearance for the terrain.

A series of thuds came from inside the vehicle. Samir peered over the hood through the windshield. Joan threw herself against her restraints, trying to get free. His nerves already frayed, a potent mixture of anger and fear lit the fuse of his wrath. He stormed to her side of the SUV and yanked the door open. Then he unbuckled her belt and hauled her onto the ground.

Samir towered over the woman, his shadow darkening her features. With a wince, she held up her hands to absorb the expected blow.

"You will *never* try to escape, or I will kill you on the spot. Is that clear?" Samir clenched and unclenched his fists, working to control the potent rage simmering inside. He'd have liked nothing better than to snap her neck right there, but stopped himself. He needed to think before doing something he'd regret. What if the people following him called for reinforcements? If caught, not only would he lose the vials, but he'd be brought up on murder charges.

Or be murdered himself.

He needed time to think. A glance at the empty crest of the hill told Samir they were wary of him. As much as he was of them.

That would give him time.

45

Leine floored the accelerator as she skirted traffic. Determined to reach Maude and Joan in time, she raced past slow-moving vehicles trundling along the highway, a chorus of honks left in the Land Cruiser's wake. If their luck held, they'd be able to save both Joan and the vials.

"How far?" she asked Eunice, who was navigating.

"Three kilometers to the turn-off."

Leine scanned the road ahead but didn't see anything. Derek, Dani, and Amira were in the back, loading weapons.

Leine glanced in the rearview mirror. "How's it going back there?"

"Good," Derek answered. "We've got three full magazines for each of the AKs, five grenades, and plenty of ammo for the semiautos."

She nodded. "Good." She passed a line of vehicles and crested a rise. "There's the turn-off."

Up ahead, a dirt service road T-boned the highway, leading west, paralleling a power line.

Leine turned off the highway and rocketed up a short rise, then down into a valley surrounded by shrubs and acacia trees.

Maude's car was parked at the base of an even steeper rise. Leine had warned Maude under no circumstances was she to follow Samir. Obviously, he realized Maude was following him, panicked, and veered off-road. When Leine asked Maude how she found them, she confessed to their tracking each other for safety.

"Why didn't you tell me at the bar?"

"I didn't know who you were," Maude had replied. "What if you wanted to hurt Joan?"

"Why trust me now?"

"You're the only person who knew Samir was dangerous. Call it a feeling."

Leine stopped next to Maude's car and everyone got out. Maude stood next to her sedan, a mixture of relief and anxiety on her face.

"Thank you for coming so quickly." Maude pointed to where the dirt road disappeared over the steep rise. "He raced over that hill, but I don't think he kept going. I didn't see any dust rising."

Leine glanced at the dry ground. "Hasn't rained lately. He might have stopped." She nodded at Maude. "You're lucky you didn't follow him. You'd most likely be dead."

Maude's face blanched at Leine's blunt assessment.

Leine turned to her team, who were donning their tactical vests. "Samir's most likely on the other side of that rise. We don't know if he's armed, so proceed with caution."

"What should I do?" Maude asked.

"Thank you for your help in tracking Samir and Joan. We would never have found her if it wasn't for the tracking app," Leine said. "But it would be best if you got in your car now and drove away. This could get ugly."

"But—"

She gestured at Amira's AK-74. "Can you shoot one of

those?" Maude shook her head. "Then you're better off far away from here."

"All right."

Maude climbed into her car. Leine and Derek advanced along the dirt road and climbed to the ridge, moving into opposite positions at the crest to get a visual on Samir. Peering through binoculars, she caught a glint of metal behind a stand of shrubs partway up the rise. Upon further investigation, lettering that read Fortuner could be seen on the tailgate. She gestured to Derek, and he confirmed the same. Leine called in their location to Matt Price, who said he'd relay the message to Verdun and his team, as well as redirect one of the CIA's surveillance drones. Derek and Leine returned to the SUV, discussing their next move. Maude was still there.

"Why aren't you gone?" Leine asked her, nodding at her car.

"I'm wondering if I might still be of some help?"

"The best thing you can do for both yourself and Joan is get to safety. She may need you, and I can't guarantee you'll be safe here."

"Okay. If you're certain?"

"I couldn't be more certain." Leine walked her back to the sedan and opened the door. Reluctantly, Maude climbed behind the wheel.

"You'll be sure to text or call me when you know something about Joan?"

"You have my word." Leine shut the door and watched her drive away before she joined the others.

Derek was sketching out the operation in the dirt with a stick. "—and Dani and Amira will come up behind from the south." He glanced at Leine. "All settled, then?"

Leine nodded. She looked at Eunice, Dani, and Amira. "Derek told you Samir's vehicle is parked facing west?" When the three confirmed, she continued. "That means he's primed for escape. I'm sure I don't have to say this, but if he's there, don't let him leave. We didn't see anyone, meaning he and Joan could either be inside the vehicle, or he's abandoned it." She didn't voice her concern for Joan's life. If he abandoned his vehicle, he'd have killed her, then run.

"What should we do if we see him?" Amira asked.

"Try to keep him alive for questioning. It's a safe bet he's still got the vials with him, so if you have to eliminate him to protect either Joan or yourselves, do it." She glanced at the sky. The sun was inching toward the horizon, casting long shadows across the landscape. The afternoon shade worked to their advantage, allowing for more cover. "Everyone ready?" The group answered in the affirmative. "Let's go."

SAMIR PEERED THROUGH THE THICK LEAVES AT THE DIRT ROAD, wondering when or if someone was going to come after him. The long shadows cast by the afternoon sun played tricks with his eyes. He thought he'd seen movement near the crest of the hill, but he didn't have binoculars, so wasn't sure. The remaining light would illuminate anyone who came over the ridge, giving him time to get into position.

Maybe he should have kept going instead of stopping to confront his trackers. But running in fear wasn't in him. He'd never been afraid of confrontation—a quality his father and brother had admired.

Even so, something whispered in the back of his mind that he should go, now, and leave the woman.

He'd dragged Joan away from the Fortuner, had left her at the base of the tree, while he decided her fate. Could he use her as leverage? Doubtful. No one would care about a woman from Kibera. Her death would be just one more in a long line of missing prostitutes. He doubted the CIA would endanger their mission just to save her life. Not when the stakes were so high.

He decided to kill her, then leave. His pursuers might stop to see what he'd left in his wake, perhaps even try to save her, allowing a slim margin of time to escape.

He glanced through the window of the SUV at the duffel bag in the backseat. He'd have to find a different way to transport the vials—the duffel was too unwieldy, especially if he had to abandon the SUV and travel on foot. His gaze drifted to the floor of the passenger seat. Joan's backpack was much easier to handle and would leave his hands free.

He climbed into the vehicle and moved the duffel bag to the front. After dumping the contents of her pack onto the floor, he transferred the vials, his gasmask, and what was left of the money from Beni Haddad into the main compartment of the backpack, all the while keeping an eye on Joan. Then he loosened the shoulder straps and tried it on, testing the fit.

Perfect.

Leaving the backpack on the passenger seat, he grabbed his sweatshirt and returned to where he'd left his captive. She appeared to be asleep. He pulled the gun from his waistband and wrapped the sweatshirt around the muzzle. Although not perfect, the material would deaden some of the sound.

He stepped closer to make certain he killed her with one shot, and raised the gun, his finger curling around the trigger. Joan's eyes snapped open. At the same time, she swung her bound legs in an arc, sweeping Samir off his feet.

He landed on his back with a grunt and dropped the gun, a sudden, sharp pain jabbing his spine. Hot fury erupted at her insolence and he struggled to his hands and knees, scrambling for the gun. Growling like a wild animal, Joan launched herself onto his back, tearing at his hair and clothes, scratching his face, his neck, his exposed skin.

Her hands were unbound. How had she broken free? Samir reared up and threw her off. She landed hard behind him. He scrambled for the semiauto and climbed to his feet, weapon raised. Joan hurled a stone at him, knocking his firing arm to the side. The gun went off, the shot reverberating through the still air. A nearby flock of egrets took flight, squawking their alarm.

"Devil," Samir cried. The people that followed him would surely attack after hearing gunfire. If he didn't leave now, he'd be killed and the virus would fall into the wrong hands. Samir slammed the gun against Joan's head. The loud *crack* and resultant blood suggested a mortal blow. Like a cloth doll, she slumped to the ground. If she wasn't dead yet, it wouldn't be long before she bled out.

Samir jammed his hands into his pockets for his car keys as he sprinted to the SUV. The crack of a gunshot echoed in the air. A millisecond later the metallic *ping* of a round slammed into the door next to him. He dove behind the engine block.

They were here.

46
______

Amira and Dani went wide to approach Samir from the south, remaining out of view until signaled. Derek, Eunice, and Leine came in from the north, tightening the noose around the terrorist in a modified pincer movement.

A gunshot cracked through the air.

"Dammit." Leine scanned the terrain but didn't see any sign of Joan. "Who's got a visual?" She checked to make sure her gun was switched to full auto.

"He's behind the engine block," Amira answered. "I don't have a shot. Moving to a better location."

Dani's voice came over Leine's earpiece. "Someone's on the ground in front of the vehicle. I can't tell if they're alive."

Leine and Derek moved to close the pincer, pinning Samir. The terrorist fired at them, but missed. Chips exploded from the rock outcropping Leine had chosen for cover.

"Well, now we know he can aim." It was clear to Leine he didn't have an automatic weapon, or he'd be using it.

"I'll try to draw him out." Derek broke cover and sprinted to a stand of trees closer to the terrorist's position. Leine watched, finger on the trigger, waiting for Samir to show himself.

He popped up and fired over the hood. Leine fired back and Eunice joined her. The rounds pinged off the SUV, and he disappeared behind the vehicle.

"Did they get him?" Dani asked.

Amira replied, "I can't tell. Give me a second."

Leine checked to see where Derek had landed. He was closing in on Samir's position. "Eunice and I will draw him out —" she started to say.

Gunfire erupted behind her, and she dove behind the outcropping as bullets bit the dirt nearby.

"We've got company." She scanned the area above them to get a bead on how many new shooters there were. Lit by the sun, two gunmen wearing tactical gear and carrying rifles moved in a crouch along the ridge. Leine fired. Both ducked behind the crest.

"Who the hell are they?" Derek barked.

Three more gunmen moved along the ridgeline, staying low.

"Don't know, but I count at least five." Leine followed their movements. A classic flanking maneuver. They had the advantage of the higher position. "Looks like they're trained."

"Shit."

Leine sprayed the ridge with her AK, dozens of rounds punching holes in the dirt. She hit one of the gunmen, while the other two dove for cover. "One down." She reloaded. "Keep your eyes on Samir. Don't let him leave."

Dani and Amira keyed their mics, acknowledging transmission.

"I'm headed your way," Derek said.

"I'll cover you, Derek," Eunice added.

"This would be a great time for backup, Miller," Leine muttered. She wasn't going to hold her breath.

Two of the gunmen popped up and fired. Rounds slammed into the rock in front of Leine. Eunice fired at them from her position as Leine fired back, and Derek joined in. One of the figures dropped out of sight, while the second fell forward, obviously hit. Several shots fired behind Leine, from Dani's and Amira's positions.

"Dani—Amira. Report."

No answer.

"Dani, report." Leine caught movement out of the corner of her eye. Derek was in position.

At that moment, a barrage of gunfire erupted near the crest of the hill.

"Engage," Leine yelled into her mic.

Eunice, Derek, and Leine attacked the gunmen on the ridge with a fusillade of gunfire.

"Cover me." Leine pulled the pin on a grenade, broke cover, and heaved it at their attackers. The explosion fell short of the enemy's position, but took out a section of the berm they were using for cover. Derek, Eunice, and the gunmen exchanged fire.

Reloading, Leine yelled, "Who are you, and what do you want?"

"We have the woman." The man's voice echoed across the expanse separating them.

"What woman?" Leine narrowed her eyes. She knew that voice.

"She says her name is Maude."

A muscle near Leine's eye twitched. "Let her go, Felix. She's got nothing to do with this." Joan's friend had come back against direct orders, and now the Russians had her.

Of course.

There was a pause, then, "Is that you, Leine Basso?"

"I said, let her go."

"Shall we make a trade? Samir for Maude."

"Wait." Dani's breathless voice came over the radio. "It won't work. Samir's gone."

Leine froze. "Gone?"

Amira answered. "He escaped in the SUV. I managed to shoot out his windshield and one of his tires. Dani got his back window. But he's still gone."

"What about Joan?"

"We're already on it. She took a blow to the head." Dani paused. "She's unresponsive, but still has a pulse. She needs help. Now."

Leine turned toward Felix and his men. Anger at losing her target boiled over, seeping into her voice. "Because of the little gunfight you and your team just initiated, Samir escaped. Let Maude go," she said, the words exiting her mouth like railgun fire. "We've got an injured party that needs medical attention. Maude can drive her to the nearest hospital."

"And what do I get in return?" Felix asked.

You get to fucking live, Leine thought. "You get a head start after Samir."

Felix and his contingent were silent. Impatient, Leine called out, "Well? What's it gonna be?"

The sound of a gunning engine shattered the stillness of the temporary ceasefire. Leine scanned the ridgetop through her field glasses. A white SUV launched over the ridge, landed hard on its front wheels, then bounced onto all four as it raced past. The closed tinted windows made it impossible to see inside. Leine got a glimpse of the vehicle's suspension as it screamed past.

"Hold your fire," she growled into her mic. "It's up-armored." The white behemoth disappeared in a cloud of red dust, headed after Samir.

"Hold your positions," Leine said. "I'm not convinced everyone's gone."

"And we don't have Maude," Eunice added.

"Exactly." Leine checked the ridge. She didn't see any gunmen, but that meant little.

A moment later, the sound of a second engine shattered the air as another white SUV flew over the ridge, headed straight for Leine. She dove behind the rock, emerging on the opposite side. The vehicle slid to a stop several yards from her, enveloped in a cloud of red dust.

"Hold," Leine breathed into her mic.

The engine idled as the dust settled. Somewhere, a hyena yipped. Leine waited for the occupants to make their move.

It didn't take long.

The side doors exploded open. Four gunmen let loose with a hail of bullets from behind the armored panels. Leine, Derek, and Eunice returned fire. One of the gunmen popped out, firing at Derek's position. Leine acquired the target and fired. Rounds slammed into the reinforced steel, gouging a path to her adversary. His head snapped back with the impact and he slid to the ground.

A second gunman fired, forcing her behind the rock. The heavy staccato beat of automatic fire from Derek's and Eunice's positions echoed around her. Two of the gunmen returned fire, while a third pinned Leine down.

"Behind you, Leine." Amira's breath came fast, like she was running.

Dani added, "I'm headed for Eunice's position."

Leine glanced behind her to see the two women closing the distance.

The driver shouted something and fired into the air. Three more gunmen popped up near the ridge and fired on Leine, Derek, and Eunice, while the driver disappeared inside the SUV and slammed his door closed. The two gunmen using the doors for cover did the same, and the vehicle catapulted downhill toward Dani and Amira.

"Dammit," Leine said. "Three of 'em coming at you, Dani and Amira."

"Got it." Dani's assured tone was just what Leine needed to hear.

"Piece of cake," Amira added.

Leine's mouth twitched up in a grim smile. Two of the gunmen on the ridge showed themselves.

She opened fire.

47

The second armored SUV hurtled down the rise, headed straight for Dani. She scrambled for cover behind a dense thicket of shrubs and hugged the ground, tensing for the attack. Amira took cover behind an outcropping.

The white Toyota skidded to a stop and the doors opened. Two gunmen moved into position behind the passenger doors, aimed at Dani, and opened fire, shredding foliage and halving the size of the shrubbery. Amira popped up and sprayed them with bullets. The driver materialized and returned fire.

"Amira, fall back," Dani yelled in Arabic, forgetting the mic. "You're playing into their hands."

The driver stopped shooting and shouted in the same language. "How lucky are we? These must be the Kurdish whores we've heard about."

Dani froze. How did they know they were Kurds?

"And you must be a son of a goat to have to stoop to work with Russian scum," Amira spat back. "What's the problem? Did the SDF not want you?"

Dani stifled a smile at her friend's bravado. Dani joined in.

"Why are you here and not in Syria? Obviously, you don't know how to fight if you take your orders from a Russian."

The driver scoffed. "This shows how stupid Kurds are. We are part of an elite force of fighters, called up by General Al Shami himself."

"And did the esteemed general explain what you were fighting for?" Dani asked, her voice dripping sugar.

Silence.

"Your mission is to recover a weapon of mass destruction Assad is prepared to use against his own people. Your people."

"How do you know when a Kurd is lying?" one of the other gunmen quipped. "When she opens her mouth." The others erupted in laughter.

"She isn't lying," Amira replied. "But I know how hard it is to reason with one of Assad's thugs. Especially one who is so obviously ignorant."

"But aren't *all* of Assad's men ignorant?" Dani and Amira's laughter replaced the gunmen's.

"Enough," the gunman on the front passenger side shouted, and opened fire, stitching a path of bullets across the ground from Dani's position to Amira's.

"Apparently we struck a chord." Amira's derisive laughter left no doubt how she felt.

"I say we help them waste more ammo," Dani said into her mic.

Amira's deep-throated chuckle made her smile. "Good thinking."

"The gunman in the back hasn't said or done anything," Dani warned.

"Think he's up to something?"

As if to answer Amira's question, a round cylinder appeared over the top of the rear passenger window. The gunman in front of him ducked.

"RPG," Amira roared. "Get out of there, now!"

The familiar hiss of the grenade set Dani in motion. She leapt from the thicket and rolled as the RPG detonated.

Clods of dirt and stones and plants showered down around her. Disoriented, Dani clambered to her hands and knees, shaking her head to clear the ringing in her ears. She reached for her radio, but it was gone. Her AK lay several feet away. For a moment, she thought she was in the middle of the battle for Raqqa, and she scrambled for the gun, then to the nearest cover she could find—a slight rise in the earth. Dirt hit her in the face. They were shooting at her.

Keep going—a moving target is harder to hit.

The distant sound of gunfire fought its way through, bringing her back to the present, but she couldn't tell where it was coming from. She crawled in the opposite direction of the gunmen and threw herself behind a copse of trees. Her hand touched something soft, and she turned.

Joan.

Dani had forgotten her in the melee. She felt her pulse. Still weak, but steady. Blood matted her hair. The woman needed medical attention. Now.

Anger surged through her and she climbed to her feet. Those assholes needed to go. She ejected the magazine and slapped in a fresh one, then came around the side of the tree, careful to keep foliage between her and the gunmen.

Amira was doing a good job keeping them engaged, but Dani could tell she was flagging. She peered through the leaves. The gunman nearest her was exposed. She squeezed the trigger.

Her target shuddered from the impact as the bullets ripped through him. He dropped his weapon and slid down the side of the SUV, crumpling to the ground.

One down, two to go.

Obviously surprised, the remaining gunmen turned toward

her and fired. Amira broke cover and moved into the open, where she let loose with a volley of rounds, hitting the driver.

The last surviving gunman from the SUV pivoted and fired, leaving himself open for an instant. Dani fired.

The gunman fell.

Amira ran to check the gunmen to make sure they were dead, as Dani raced back to Joan. A moment later, Amira joined her. The two women hoisted Joan to her feet and carried her to the SUV. Amira popped the cargo door open.

Dani whistled as she pushed aside the stash of weapons and ammunition to make room for Joan. "They were ready for a war."

"Well, they got one, didn't they?"

After securing Joan in the back, Amira hauled the now-dead driver off the running board and climbed behind the wheel. Dani kicked the rear door closed and joined her. Amira threw the SUV in gear and stood on the accelerator, kicking dirt and rocks behind them as they backed down the rise.

48

Derek, Leine, and Eunice continued to exchange fire with the gunmen on the ridge, but they were running low on ammunition. Derek had managed to kill one of them, leaving at least three, although there could have been more.

"On your right, Leine," Amira shouted.

Leine swiveled as the white SUV came barreling up the steep rise. "You're in the truck?"

"We are. I'll pull up broadside to give you cover."

"Where's Dani?" Leine asked.

"She's here. She lost her radio when that asshole fired the RPG at her."

Relieved, Leine asked, "I take it the asshole and his friends are dead?"

"Yeah. If only we could kill them twice."

"And Joan?"

"In the back. Dani says she's still alive, but just barely."

Leine waited until Amira was in position, then sprinted for the SUV. Derek and Eunice did the same.

"Get us closer," Derek said. "Go slow and angle up toward the ridge."

Leine and Eunice hopped on the running board, while Derek walked alongside, using the reinforced vehicle for cover.

"How many are left?" Amira asked.

"At least three. There could be more."

"Get in."

"What?" Leine asked.

"Get in," Amira repeated. "I have an idea."

"I don't think—" Derek began.

"This is an armored SUV, right?"

"Yes."

"Run-flat tires?"

"Probably."

"I'm going to use the SUV as a missile. When they scatter, pick them off from the windows. We have enough guns."

Leine glanced at Eunice, who shrugged.

"It could work."

Derek nodded. "What the hell."

Leine opened the door and slid across the seat to the opposite window. Eunice and Derek piled in after her.

Dani nodded toward the cargo area. "Joan's back there, but so is a whole lot of ammo." She held up an extra magazine. "If you need to reload, that is."

Amira glanced at Leine in the rearview mirror. "They don't stand a chance."

Aimed at the ridge and the remaining gunmen, the SUV took heavy fire, but the reinforced steel and polycarbonate windows held. When it was obvious Amira wasn't going to stop, the gunmen scattered. Everyone except Amira laid down fire, cutting the last three to the ground. Leine and Eunice jumped out to make sure they were dead, and Amira raced to Maude's car, which was parked next to the Land Cruiser. The driver's door had been left wide open.

Leine and Eunice sprinted down the hill to join them. As they neared Maude's sedan, Leine's heart dropped into her stomach. The rest of the team had gathered near the open front door and were looking down.

"We're too late," Leine muttered to Eunice. Eunice didn't reply.

They cleared the front of the car and glanced at the ground. Dani crouched beside Maude. Leine's mood rose as she drew closer.

"Is she—?"

Maude tilted her head back and gave Leine a wan smile. "I'm alive."

"It's a goddam miracle," Derek muttered. "You could've been killed."

Maude had the good sense to look chagrined. "I realize that now." Dani and Amira helped her to her feet. "They were going to kill me. Whatever you told them to make them drive off, it was enough to save my skin. I'm grateful." She nodded at the armored SUV. "We need to get Joan to hospital."

"You'd better have a doctor look at you, too," Leine added.

Maude handed Leine her phone. "I think he still has Joan's mobile with him. The tracker is moving."

"I shot out his rear tire, so Samir can't have gone far," Amira said.

"Unless he stopped to put on the spare," Derek replied.

"With a truckload of Russians after him?" Leine glanced at the screen. Sure enough, Joan's blinking avatar showed it had traveled several miles west of their position. "Either way, we need to leave. The Russians have a good head start."

Amira and Derek loaded Joan into Maude's car, and Maude got behind the wheel of her sedan.

"You all right to drive?" Leine asked.

"I'm fine." Maude gave her a determined look.

"We'll pray for Joan," Dani said to Maude.

Amira headed for the Russian's SUV, but Leine stopped her. "What?" Amira asked. "It's an armored SUV. It will come in handy when we find Samir."

Leine shook her head. "That's an expensive ride. Guaranteed there's a tracker baked into the thing."

Amira gave it a longing look before she shrugged and joined the rest of the team in Derek's Land Cruiser. Derek started the engine and pulled onto the dirt road as Leine brought up the tracker on Maude's phone to guide them to Samir.

49

Samir drove as far as he dared and parked. He'd gone off the dirt road and ridden on the rim of the back tire for several kilometers. He climbed out of the Toyota and inspected the tire by the light of his mobile. The rubber was shredded, leaving only a slim band intact. The rim itself was badly warped.

And it was slowing him down. He couldn't use the spare, had found none in the cargo compartment after he'd stolen the vehicle. Besides, even if he'd had one, his paranoia wouldn't allow him to take the time. What if he pulled over to change the tire and his enemy found him? All he had left was the whore's semiauto, a few rounds, some detonators, and a block of C-4. He had no way of fending off automatic weapons—and his enemies had several. At least now it was dark.

The fierce response of his attackers had surprised him. How many were after the virus? His hope of making his way to Europe without help had evaporated. Much as he hated the idea, he would have to accept the efforts of the dark-haired man from the restaurant to leave the continent with the vials intact.

As Samir searched the backpack for the phone, his hand

brushed something hard. He inspected the bag and realized there was a zippered compartment he'd missed. He unzipped it and looked inside.

A mobile.

Joan's mobile.

He pulled it free and used the passcode he'd gotten from her at the hotel. An icon at the top of the screen appeared to be active. Curious, he swiped down to see what it was. A logo appeared, and he tapped it to open the app.

He froze. A geo-tracker. That must have been how they'd found him. Rage against the prostitute bloomed in his chest. Breathing heavily, he raised his fist, intending to hurl the phone as far as he could.

But then he stopped.

If they were tracking him, they'd find the Toyota.

He'd have to leave a surprise.

Twenty minutes later, he checked his work. Satisfied the makeshift device would do what he intended, Samir grabbed his burner phone and shrugged on the pack. Then he pressed speed dial and waited.

"Yes?" The voice was that of the man he'd met at the café.

The annoyance of being handed off to an underling came back, angering Samir. Apparently having seventeen vials of the virus deemed him worthy only of the second in command.

"Have you made arrangements?" Samir asked.

"I have. Where are you?"

"Southeast of Nairobi."

"On a main road?"

"No."

There was a pause before the other man replied. "Do you have access to GPS?"

"Yes."

"Write down these coordinates. They will lead you to a

private airfield near there. A plane will be waiting to fly you to Mombasa. From there, a container ship will take you to Yemen, then continue on to Syria to complete the original plan."

Which, of course, Samir would not do. Once the ship landed in Yemen, he'd escape and find another way to Europe. He just had to leave Africa safely. "How will I board this container ship?"

"Don't worry. I've got that handled. Just get to the airfield."

"I want to speak with my original contact."

"He's unavailable."

"Then I'll wait until he's available."

The contact sighed. "All right. I'll have him call once you've reached the airfield."

The man ended the call and Samir powered down the phone. He removed the SIM card and slid it inside his pocket. He didn't trust this new contact, but what else could he do? He'd make his way to the airfield and go from there.

It could be a trap.

The voice of fear had grown inside him, had taken over his mind. It was just as well. His thought processes sharpened when fear dominated. Situational awareness remained high as a result, as did his ability to outwit his adversaries.

He wouldn't just blunder onto the airfield. He'd watch the area, make certain it wasn't an ambush, before showing himself.

Then he would kill the pilot and steal the plane.

Just like he did in Algeria.

50

Felix stared at the ground. The SUV's high beams illuminated a wide expanse of red dirt. There was a decided dearth of tracks.

"Fuck."

They'd lost Samir. The wind had whipped up in the past hour, apparently enough to obliterate the terrorist's tire tracks—even though he'd kept driving on the rim of his rear tire. Why Samir hadn't stopped and changed to the spare, he'd never know.

Fucking ignorant terrorist.

He frowned and gestured at his comrades. "Why are you standing there? Find the fucking tracks."

The four gunmen immediately fanned out, NVGs directed at the terrain in front of them, reminding Felix of a group of bloodhounds.

How did an A-Number-One asshole like Samir slip through his grasp? He'd never live this down. Not only that, but the kill squad Felix had left to take out Basso and her team weren't responding to his calls. Now he was second-guessing himself, wondering if leaving before that phase of the op was completed had been such a good idea. The Syrians might have allowed their animosity for the Kurds to dictate their response.

Using emotion to drive actions was never a good idea. Although that wouldn't explain the other gunmen who were there. The rest of the team couldn't have cared less if the women were Kurds or little green men—they had a job to do, and would do it with ruthless efficiency. That's what these men had been paid for.

Apparently, he'd underestimated Basso and her team.

With a deep sigh, Felix returned to the SUV.

He was cursed.

The general had sent his worst men—that was the only explanation. Sure, Karam had seemed like his kind of mercenary, but looks could be deceiving. Felix didn't blame the general, though. He had a lot on his plate, what with an asshole for a son and the resurgence of the Islamic State.

Maybe he'd ask for a transfer, head to Central Africa and the mines. Becoming a killing machine wasn't necessarily something he could list on his resume, but the experience might help him remember there was more to life than pride in a job well done.

***

"UP AHEAD." EUNICE POINTED TO THE REMNANTS OF SAMIR'S vehicle. The sad looking shell of the SUV showed plainly through the NVGs. A jagged ridge of broken glass from the impact of Amira's and Dani's rounds was visible in the rear window, as was the flattened rear tire.

Leine slowed to a stop and checked Maude's phone. Joan's avatar blinked steadily, indicating her cell phone nearby. "He's close."

"He didn't use an automatic weapon back there," Dani said. "He used a pistol."

"Doesn't mean he hasn't got something up his sleeve," Derek warned.

Leine added, "Watch for tripwires and explosives. Never, ever underestimate your enemy."

The four of them quietly exited the vehicle and moved toward the wreck. As they neared the vehicle, Leine signaled them to fan out and surround the Toyota.

There was no sound or movement from inside. Leine gestured to Amira and Eunice to hold before investigating the SUV. Then she and Derek split off to follow the beacon on Maude's phone.

Where was Samir hiding? Had he seen their approach? How would he defend his position? He might have rigged explosives inside the Toyota or somewhere in the terrain, might be watching them, waiting to detonate via his mobile. Endless possibilities raced through Leine's mind as she and Derek neared the tracker. Leine's NVGs picked up a rectangular object lying on the ground a few yards away.

"Over there." Cautious, she edged closer, scanning for wires or disturbed ground, signifying a buried IED.

Derek approached from the opposite direction. "What'd'ya think?"

The object appeared harmless enough. "Looks like a discarded cell phone." Leine searched for something she could use as a probe. She settled on a slender branch that had fallen at the base of a tree.

"Found something interesting," she said into her mic. "You guys see anything?"

"Negative," came Dani's voice. "That doesn't mean he didn't do something to the vehicle itself. In Syria, ISIS was known for rigging abandoned cars with explosives. And bodies."

"Move away from the truck and take cover," Leine said. "This could be a detonator."

"Roger," Eunice confirmed.

A moment later, Dani reported they were clear.

Using the end of the branch, Leine nudged the device. Nothing happened. "It's definitely a mobile," she said to Derek.

"Make sure you're far enough back from the SUV, yeh?" Derek said into his mic.

"We're good," Dani confirmed.

Leine used the branch to flip the phone over. The screen lit up.

A loud explosion rocked the SUV, blowing its doors and the remaining glass from the windows. The fuel tank ignited, and a bright, orange fireball erupted in a secondary explosion, lighting the evening sky. Having consumed whatever fuel was left, the flames decreased and the sky went dark, leaving only the interior to burn.

"Well, that was exciting," Eunice deadpanned.

"You guys all right?" Leine asked.

"All good," Dani chimed in.

"At least we know he wasn't inside the Toyota," Derek quipped.

Leine picked up Joan's mobile and tucked it inside her pocket before joining the others. "Doesn't mean he hasn't rigged other stuff, though."

"Yeh, and that big, bright explosion is going to attract all kinds of riffraff." Derek glanced at the burning wreck. "We should probably move out."

Leine gave Eunice and Derek a sidelong glance. "We could sure use someone with tracking skills about now."

"Then you're in luck," Derek said with a grin.

Eunice was already searching the ground near the SUV for tracks.

Leine looked at Derek. "Well? What are you waiting for? A cookie?"

Derek snorted as he circled the SUV. "Don't be a smartass, Basso."

Leine arched an eyebrow. "No? Where's the fun in that?"

51

Verdun King checked his team's position in the rundown hangar. Satisfied that everyone was out of sight of the abandoned airfield and had their orders, he walked onto the dirt runway. He'd made sure this group was made up of his most trusted men—fighters he'd gone through hell with, who'd take orders and collect their pay, no questions asked.

Matt Price had intercepted the Basso team's sitrep before it got to Miller, detailing how they found Samir's SUV and exploded an IED the terrorist left for whoever was foolish enough to mess with it. There were no casualties. But due to exigent circumstances, what had originally been a seven-member team in Libya was now down to five—even after taking into consideration the two unknown operators they'd picked up along the way.

Five was better than seven. Fewer distractions that way. If Samir showed up before Basso's team did, she and her recruits might even survive. He'd been wary of her at the warlord's camp after his guys took out the Russian mercs, had been surprised when Basso let the leader and his ass-licker bounce. She turned out to be a shrewd operator, but nothing he couldn't handle.

Once Verdun obtained the virus, he'd be golden. All he had to do was deliver the vials to his contact at ZeniGen. Dude promised a huge payday, whether he had the vaccine or not. It sucked that the lady scientist had escaped the lab strike, but Verdun was pretty sure he'd be able to hunt her down and persuade her to part with the formula.

Either way, they'd still have the virus.

He checked the time—Samir had called thirty minutes ago to let him know he was close and should be arriving within the hour. Basso's team still had to track Samir to the airfield—hard to do in the black of night, even with NVGs.

Verdun walked over to inspect the Cessna 208 Caravan he'd had his guys fly in—first, to give Samir the impression he'd be going to Mombasa as planned so he wouldn't rabbit out of there; and second, to transport Verdun's guys back to base as soon as the operation was over.

The Chinese manufactured turboprop was perfect for short, rough takeoffs and landings, and had a hell of a payload, making it a workhorse for ferrying personnel and equipment all over Africa. The rear cargo door made for easy loading, which would reduce his team's time on the ground once their objective was met.

"Movement to the east. Over." Cass's voice had an edge. Verdun's second-in-command, Cass was his first choice in all things mission critical.

"Report." Verdun's heart sped up in anticipation. Fortune favored the bold. He'd be able to fund anyone, anywhere with the kind of scratch he'd soon be getting.

"Single military-aged male with a backpack. Looks like our guy."

"Let him get to the plane." Verdun turned as a lone figure

materialized at the edge of the airstrip. Sure enough, it was Samir. Verdun waved him over, but he hesitated. He tried waving again.

Still no movement.

"Everybody's invisible, right?" Verdun hissed into his mic.

"Affirmative," Cass reported. "He can't see a thing. Not without thermal imaging."

"Then what's he waiting for?" Verdun narrowed his eyes, trying to read the terrorist's intentions.

"Maybe he wants you to come to him?"

"Fuck it." Verdun started for Samir, reassured by his tactical vest and the weight of the fully loaded Glock in his shoulder holster. Normally, he didn't allow himself to be exposed like this, but with six of his best guys' weapons trained on Samir, he was safe enough.

And the payday was too big to dick around.

"Samir," he called, plastering a smile on his face. The terrorist watched him warily from the edge of the airstrip. Verdun gestured toward the cargo plane. "See? Just like we agreed. It's all fueled up and ready to go."

"Where is Matt?"

Verdun stopped, frowned. "You thought he'd be here?" He shook his head. "That ain't how this works, cowboy. First, we get on the plane, then I call him and hand you the phone."

Samir shook his head. "I want to speak to Matt." He held his hand up and Verdun froze.

A dead man switch? What the fuck? He wired the pack?

"Uh-uh, pardner. That there dead man's switch is a no-go." Verdun shook his head, hoping his boys didn't shoot Samir where he stood—he was a little too close to the blast zone for comfort. "We had a deal. I was supposed to get you to Mombasa, where you were gonna load onto a cargo ship headed for Yemen. From there, we'd get you to Syria. We never discussed this suicide backpack shit. And frankly, I'm a little miffed."

Samir's brows drew together. "Miffed? What is 'miffed'?"

"It means pissed off. Now either you fucking dismantle that thing and start acting like a big boy, or I'm gonna take away your toys." He nodded at the Cessna.

The look on Samir's face told Verdun he'd have to work harder at disarmament. It was the smile that gave him pause.

Apparently, the terrorist had an ace up his sleeve.

"I'm afraid you and those six men hiding in that broken down hangar are a no-go, as you say." Samir walked toward Verdun, clearly enjoying the commando's discomfort. Verdun backed up, trying to keep a healthy distance between them.

"Wait a minute, Samir. Looks like we got off on the wrong foot."

"You might say that, yes." Samir kept walking. Verdun kept backing up.

"What do you want us to do?" Cass's voice came through his earpiece.

Annoyed by the question, Verdun ignored him. What the fuck could he do? If Cass shot him and Samir let go of that switch, they'd be scraping them both off the dirt. Not only that, but the virus would either be lost, or the explosion would release the vector.

However this went down, they were fucked.

How long did a virus survive once dispersed? What had the CDC said during Covid? He couldn't remember.

Shit. It wasn't gonna matter. Not if he was dead. A calm settled over Verdun. He wasn't going to die, not tonight. The commando had a card up his own sleeve. He stopped and looked behind him. He and Samir were a couple dozen yards from the plane.

Verdun turned back to his adversary and said, "You think you can fly that thing?"

Samir's smiled would have frosted Hell. "I know I can."

"Well, then." Verdun bowed and swept his arm toward the Cessna. "Be my guest."

Samir walked past him, wariness replacing his smile as he marched toward the cargo door. Verdun studied his progress, mentally calculating how much time he'd have before the terrorist got that plane off the ground.

If he got it off the ground.

"What the hell's happening, Verdun?" Cass asked. "Tell me you got a plan."

"Oh, I got a plan," Verdun murmured. "Tell Thomas to be ready."

Cass let his breath out in a relieved sigh. "Roger that."

Verdun waited while Samir inspected the cargo area. "Everything there? You likey?" *Might as well make him think I give a shit.*

Samir climbed inside and moved forward to the cockpit. He settled into the pilot's seat and hit some switches. The propeller started to spin and the engine roared to life. Damned if the terrorist didn't know exactly what to do. Strike one for Team Verdun. Verdun was tempted to ask where he learned to fly, but decided against it. *Probably went to flight school in the US of A, just like the piece of shit 9/11 attackers.*

Samir nodded in satisfaction and turned. Just then, the sound of gunfire erupted near the hangar.

"Incoming," Cass yelled.

Torn between helping his men and making sure Samir didn't lift off, Verdun leapt into action and sprinted toward the hangar. "Report," he roared into his mic.

"Taking fire from all sides," came the reply.

Shit. Shit. Shit. Did Samir enlist his al-Shabaab buddies in an ambush? Verdun closed the distance to the hangar, keeping some kind of cover between him and whoever was attacking his guys.

"Thomas, report."

"I'm pinned down."

"Dammit!" Everything was going to shit. If Thomas couldn't get free to do what was necessary, they wouldn't be able to stop Samir.

Midstride, he changed course and sprinted to the plane, sliding his Glock out of his holster.

First, he had to kill the fucking jihadi.

52

"Looks like we're late to the party," Derek said, nodding at the two men near the cargo plane.

Leine scanned the airfield through binoculars. "It's Samir and...is that Verdun?"

"Yeh. Looks like him."

"Now we get backup? But how'd they know where to find Samir? The sitrep I sent Miller didn't say where we thought he was headed."

"Aerial photographs?" Dani asked. "Maybe a surveillance drone?"

Leine shook her head. "Miller couldn't have gotten his guys in place that fast."

Samir climbed into the cargo plane. A few minutes later, the engine sputtered to life and the turboprop started to turn.

"Shit," Leine muttered. "He's going to fly that thing out of here."

Seconds later, multiple muzzle flashes and near-continuous gunfire erupted near the hangar. Verdun hesitated, then broke into a flat-out run toward the hangar.

Leine bolted out of the SUV and wrenched open the cargo

door revealing the Russian merc's weapons stash that Derek and Amira had transferred from the armored SUV. The other three joined her.

"The Russians must have used the explosion to pinpoint Samir." Leine snatched up a PP-19 Vityaz submachine gun. The mercs were well equipped—in addition to the PP-19, there was a VSS carbine, two Dragunov sniper rifles, several AK-74Ms, fragmentation grenades, semiautomatic pistols, and a variety of explosives. And that was just her initial assessment.

Derek pocketed a couple of fragmentation grenades and loaded up on ammunition. "Add a drone with thermal imaging, and they beat us here."

"Why didn't Miller send the drone?" Dani asked as she grabbed a Dragunov, a Makarov pistol, and two frag grenades. "We could have used a little help from above." She gave Derek and Eunice an apologetic look. "No offense, guys. You two were amazing."

The two trackers had worked their magic, chasing Samir to the abandoned airfield. But it had taken precious time. Eunice loaded up with mags for her AK-74, in addition to the pistol she already carried.

"At least the plane's still on the ground," Eunice said.

"Not for long." Everyone finished loading and Leine shut the door. "Eunice, Amira, and Dani, fan out, see who or what we're dealing with. If they're not Verdun's guys, shoot them. Derek and I are going after Samir."

The three women moved out in opposite directions, headed for the hangar. Derek gave Leine a look as they started for the cargo plane.

"What?" Annoyance edged her voice.

"You're going to try to take him alive, aren't you?"

"Got a better idea? How else are we going to find out who's been screwing with us at the CIA?"

"I say we blow the plane. Send Samir and the virus to Hell in a ball of fire, never to be seen again."

"And never find out who the traitor is? What if we release the vector? What then?" She nodded toward a shredded wind sock on a pole at the end of the field. "The wind's picking up. That virus has been engineered to spread, Derek."

"Aviation fuel burns pretty damned hot. I say it's a safe bet that virus would be out of commission. End of story."

"Maybe you're right. But what if you're wrong?" Derek opened his mouth to argue, but Leine had enough. "Let's take care of what's in front of us, all right?"

"Roger that."

They went in low, using what they could for cover.

"We're at the hangar," Eunice reported. "I see ten—no, eleven—combatants with automatic weapons."

"Can you tell which guys are Verdun's?" The last thing they needed was to kill a friendly.

"Affirmative," Eunice replied. "The merc's armor is distinctive. Five enemy, six belong to Verdun."

"If you've got the shot, start picking off anyone who isn't one of Verdun's team." Leine and Derek were fifty yards from the Cessna when Verdun pivoted midstride and started back for the plane and Samir.

"Amira's down," Dani called over her mic, the rapid gunfire drowning her words.

Derek growled, "I'm going in," and split off, headed for the hangar.

Leine ran for Samir and the cargo plane, keeping Verdun in her periphery in case he didn't recognize her. She had to stop Samir from taking off, hoped that's what Verdun had planned.

The plane started to taxi, its cargo door still open.

If I can just get on that plane...

Verdun cut right, headed for the cargo door. Leine pumped her arms and poured it on, closing the distance between them.

They both reached the cargo door at the same time. Verdun dove inside, and Leine followed. Without a word, they moved forward, headed for Samir and the backpack.

"Dead man's switch," Verdun mouthed, pantomiming a switch.

Leine nodded. Samir had rigged the pack.

Shit.

Samir didn't yet know they'd boarded, was concentrating on getting the plane in the air. The rough terrain helped cover their movements. Verdun took one side, and Leine the other, approaching the terrorist from behind.

The commando signaled he would subdue Samir while she contained the switch. She nodded that she understood.

As they drew closer to Samir, she realized he no longer had the switch in his hand. She scanned the cockpit. Where was it?

By the look on Verdun's face, he realized the same thing.

Had he rigged the pack to explode if it moved? That didn't make sense. What if the plane hit turbulence?

Kaboom.

Either way, they had to subdue Samir before the plane lifted off.

By the look on his face, Verdun's intentions were plain—he was going to kill him.

Samir twisted in his seat to look behind him. His eyes narrowed. He dove across the console, reaching for the backpack. Verdun brought his weapon up, his finger curled around the trigger.

"No!" Leine yelled. From her position, she could see that Samir had the switch in his hand. A red light glowed in his palm.

A semiauto appeared in Samir's free hand and he fired.

Leine and Verdun dove for cover. He fired again, and his slide locked.

He was out of ammo.

Verdun lunged forward, and Leine aimed for Samir. Verdun's fingers closed around the switch as Leine fired. Samir moved at the last minute, and the bullet carved a hole in the pilot's headrest.

Verdun and Samir struggled briefly, as Samir tried to choke him out. Leine aimed at the terrorist but couldn't get a clean shot. Verdun threw him off with a kick to his torso. Samir fell back toward the cockpit, while Verdun grabbed the switch and wrenched the pack free.

Leine raised her pistol and yelled, "Who's your contact in the CIA?"

She tracked his movements as Samir struggled to his feet. He opened his mouth to say something when his head exploded. Bits of brain and bone spattered the windshield. He fell to his knees, then pitched forward onto the floor.

Leine spun around as Verdun escaped the plane through the cargo door with the backpack. She headed for the controls to power down the engine, when Eunice shouted.

"Get out, Leine—"

Leine lunged from the cockpit and sprinted for the cargo door. A moment later, an explosion shook the plane.

53

———

Dani was the first to reach Leine, but Derek was close behind. Leine tried to sit up, but she almost blacked out and abandoned the attempt.

Her ears rang, and every bone and muscle in her body was talking to her in strong terms. She opened her eyes to see Dani working feverishly—doing what, she didn't know—her recruit's concern for her obvious. Part of Leine looked on from a distance, amused by the fuss she was making.

The other part of her hurt like hell.

Leine attempted to rise once more and this time was able to sit up with Dani's help. She waved away her ministrations, annoyed she even had to try. "I'm fine, Dani. Really."

Seconds later, a horrible screeching sound broke through even Leine's damaged eardrums, and she turned to see. The cargo plane—a gaping hole in its cockpit—had continued on its trajectory. The screech of metal against metal announced when the plane met the chain link fence, snapping part of the propeller off as the rest of the plane sheared through. The broken propeller twisted what was left of the chain link into a gnarled, misshapen mess before coming to a grinding stop. Gun drawn, Derek sprinted to the open cargo door and disappeared inside the wreck.

Leine felt for her radio, but it was gone. "Samir's dead."

Dani relayed the message to Derek as she dabbed at a cut on Leine's shoulder with a piece of her own shirt.

Leine patted her hand and said, "Leave it. I'll be fine. Nothing a little R&R won't help." The former assassin tried to smile, but it was too much work. She coughed, bringing on a hefty dose of pain in her back. She stifled a groan. *Not another broken rib.*

Derek reappeared a few minutes later, concern etching his face. "You all right, Basso?"

"Never better," she replied, using one of his favorite phrases. "How's Amira?"

"She's all right," Dani said, "although it looks like the bullet she caught is lodged in her shoulder."

"And Eunice?"

"She's good. She took out two of the mercs. She's staying with Amira."

Relief swept through Leine. She hadn't lost any of her team. "The Russians?"

"All dead," Dani replied. "Except for the lead guy. There's no sign of him."

"Are you sure?" Felix escaped? How?

Dani nodded. "I'm sure. I searched for him specifically."

A fitting end for Felix's crew, although she wondered about Felix's deserting his men when they needed him most.

Well, the guy was a mercenary. She shouldn't have been surprised.

At that moment, the scene on the plane when Verdun shot Samir followed by the explosion came back to Leine with alarming intensity. "Where's Verdun?"

"Right here, ma'am." Verdun stepped forward carrying

Samir's backpack, which he sat next to her on the ground. "How many vials did you say Samir had?"

"Seventeen, at last count."

"Well, we got nine." He rummaged inside the pack and pulled out a thermos. Then he unscrewed the top and showed her the interior.

"Nine? Where are the other eight?" Had Samir hidden the rest? Or did he sell them?

Derek glanced back at the wrecked plane. "I checked what I could. There was nothing on board."

Verdun screwed the thermos cover back on. "Guess we'll have to be on the lookout."

Leine gestured to Dani and Derek. "Help me up, will you?" When she was on her feet, she said, "Dani, send Miller a sitrep. Tell him I'll call him later." She turned to Derek and said in a low voice, "Give me a minute with Verdun, okay?"

Derek nodded and followed Dani back to the hangar to check on Amira and Eunice.

Verdun returned the thermos and slung the pack across his shoulder as Leine and he started back for the hangar.

"Why'd you kill Samir?"

Verdun frowned. "You're welcome?"

Leine stopped, working to control her anger. "He could have given us valuable intel."

"He also could have killed you." His anger rose to match hers.

"He was out of ammo. What was he going to do? Hurl himself at me? And who the hell fired the RPG?"

Verdun looked down. "Afraid that was my guy. He was supposed to fire if shit looked bad." He shrugged. "You gotta admit, from his perspective, shit looked bad."

"Yeah." Leine narrowed her eyes as she tried to think through everything that had transpired up to that point in the operation. Her brain needed rest—it had just been through major trauma—and she couldn't make sense of her thoughts. But something niggled the back of her mind, something that had to do with Verdun.

She'd work it out with Miller later.

54

Matt Price closed his laptop and got up from his desk, intending to leave for the day. The door to his office opened, and Paul Miller walked in carrying a file.

"I was just leaving." Matt unzipped his messenger bag and slid the computer inside. "Something you need?"

"Sit down, Matt."

An alarm bell went off in Matt's brain, but he kept his expression impassive and did as instructed.

"There a problem?" he asked.

Paul pulled out the chair across from him and sat. "You could say that."

"What about?"

"How do you know Verdun King?"

Matt frowned. "We've used his services before. He and his company came highly recommended."

"That's not what I asked. How do you know him?"

"I don't know what you mean—"

"Cut the bullshit, Matt. You and Verdun have a history together. I just want to hear it from you."

Matt sighed. Busted. He wondered how much Miller knew. "How did you find out?"

"Straight from the horse's mouth."

Miller's answer surprised him. Verdun would have gone to the grave with anything that compromised their relationship. Then it hit him—if he'd given up Matt, it could only mean one thing. "Verdun's dead, isn't he?"

Paul Miller nodded. "This morning in Mombasa."

Matt shook his head, the impact of Miller's statement sinking in. "How?"

"That isn't important."

Which meant he was targeted by the CIA. "What's going on, Paul?" Matt's anxiety spiked. What else did Verdun tell his executioner?

"What is important," Miller continued, ignoring Matt's last question, "is what he said before he died."

Shit was about to get real. Matt's hands started to shake and he clasped them together. Maybe he could pull it out—make Miller see his reasoning. His sound, patriotic reasoning.

"What did he say?"

Miller sighed. "That you and he were working together, running Samir."

Matt smiled in disbelief. "What? That's crazy shit, Paul." He watched his boss for something, anything that would tell him he could find a way through this. "You didn't actually believe him?" Perspiration dotted his upper lip and forehead, belying his words.

Miller crossed his arms and stared at Matt. "As a matter of fact, I did. The person who saw him last found five vials of the virus on him. He was on his way out the door, Matt. On a fucking cargo ship bound for Yemen."

"You have to believe me, I had nothing to do with him stealing the virus. Nothing."

"But you don't seem surprised."

"Hell, yes, I'm surprised." Matt summoned up a boatload of mock indignation, realizing he was sinking fast. "I trusted him. *We* trusted him."

"I'm afraid he offered quite a bit of evidence that you were in on his decision to take out Samir at the airfield, steal the virus, and sell it to..." He checked the file. "ZeniGen Pharmaceuticals?"

What the hell? Verdun threw him under the bus. "That's a lie."

"He had something else he wanted to tell you, too. Something I'd rather not repeat."

By now, Matt was fuming. How could that bastard dump the whole frigging mess on him? Then it hit him. The person who found Verdun in Mombasa must have told him Matt ordered Verdun's assassination. "You made Verdun think I betrayed him, didn't you?"

"He folded right then and there. Offered to spill on all sorts of operations you two did together off the books."

So Verdun had caved under pressure and offered Matt up as the sacrificial lamb. Hoping to make a deal for himself, he got smoked for the effort. Matt closed his eyes. No two ways about it.

He was fucked six ways to Sunday.

Miller put the folder down. "Why, Matt? Was it the money? Are you that much of a cliché? My God, with your experience you could've gone into the private sector and made a killing in personal security or some shit, I don't know. Anything but this."

Miller's assessment stung.

"You want to know why?" Matt said, his anger building. "I'll tell you why. All day long, every day, we get intel from every part of the world. Actionable intel. Things we could do to make the world a better place. And you know what we do with it? We fucking sit on it, waiting for the right time, the right administration, the right fucking stars aligning, *something*. Yeah, we act, but so many of the assholes get away with it."

"Like who, for instance?"

"Like Bashar-al-fucking-Assad for one."

Miller raised his chin in acknowledgement. "Yeah, he's a real asshole, for sure."

"Right? So me and Verdun, we thought, why not? Let's figure out a way to take the motherfucker down—something that couldn't be traced back to the US." Matt glanced at Miller, realized he had the man's attention. *Might as well swing for the fences.*

"And? Your idea was to use Samir?" Miller prompted.

Matt nodded. "At first we made a deal with him to steal the virus from the Russians en route. But then we found out he and Yusuf Al Shami were good friends—fucking Yusuf Al Shami—so we had him talk Yusuf into selling him a vial—gave him the money, told him where to take it once he had it, the works."

"And the tac team that showed up and killed the Russians and Yusuf's bodyguards?"

"That was Verdun's idea. A way to ensure Samir got away with more than just a vial."

"He certainly did that. But what was the endgame? Leine's team neutralized Verdun's men."

Matt took a deep breath and let it go. Miller looked fascinated. Maybe he'd be able to pull this one out. "Yeah, that was unexpected. I didn't know he was going to do that."

"Because his guys didn't know about Leine and her team." What Miller left unsaid was that if Verdun had known, then Leine and her recruits would likely have suffered more casualties.

The worst part, though, was that Miller knew Matt had lost control of the op and hadn't told him.

Matt tried again. "The main play was that we'd help Samir

go back to Syria, pay him to use the virus against Assad's regime."

"And one vial wouldn't be enough."

"What do you think?"

"What happened at the airfield?"

Matt shook his head. "That I can't tell you. After Samir rabbited out of Beni Haddad's camp with no forwarding address, I figured that was it. Once it was clear Samir had gone rogue, I switched the op to catch and kill, which Verdun's guys are particularly good at. Apparently, Verdun had a different idea."

"Apparently." Miller stood.

At the look on his boss's face, Matt's spirits rose. Miller was going to use this as a teaching moment, let Matt go with a stern warning, maybe a reassignment. He could feel it.

"So is that it?" he asked.

Miller nodded. "That's it for me. What you do from here on out is up to you." At that moment, the door opened and the embassy's legal attaché entered the room. "Bradley will escort you to the plane waiting to take you back to DC."

Matt glanced from Miller to the LEGATT and back to Miller. His spirits plunged.

He was fucked.

55
___

US Embassy, Tunisia

The young man led Sasha into a small room with a long, sturdy table and two chairs. The walls were painted an unimaginative cream and gray-green, reminding her of a military installation. A security camera had been mounted in the corner near the ceiling, like a spider's web.

"Have a seat. The chief will be in to speak with you shortly."

Sasha had caused quite a stir at the American embassy with her story of being groomed as a CIA asset, and having information on the vaccine for a Russian super virus. The chief of station was on his way to meet with her this very moment.

As soon as she'd walked into the Americans' temporary Libyan embassy in Tunis, she knew she'd made the right choice. All the way to Tunisia, while riding in the back of a transport truck, she'd argued with herself, wondering if she was doing the right thing. She still harbored feelings for Tony. Time would take care of that. He was part of her past. Now that she had made the decision to give the Americans the vaccine, she'd felt a deep sense of calm.

The door to the room opened, and a man walked in. He closed the door and turned to face her.

Sasha's jaw dropped in surprise.

"Tony?"

He walked over to the security camera and turned it off. Then he came to the table and pulled out the chair across from her.

"Hello, Sasha."

Confused, Sasha searched his face. He looked haggard, as though the world was crushing him. Otherwise, he appeared the same as he had at the conference—some gray at the temples, a little soft around the middle, but still fit, with large, strong hands and intense blue eyes. A flicker of affection reared its head, but she tamped it down.

Anger quickly took its place and she crossed her arms. "I am supposed to meet with the chief of station, Paul Miller. Why are *you* here?"

Tony set the manila folder he'd been holding on the table. The label read *S. K.* She assumed they were the initials for her name, Sasha Kuznetsova.

"I'm Paul Miller."

Speechless a second time, Sasha snapped her mouth closed. Paul Miller was Tony? She'd been groomed by the head of Tripoli Station? She rose and started to pace, unable to process her swirling thoughts.

"I understand that this is a shock—"

Sasha spun in place and glared at him. "You killed my friends."

Paul nodded, his expression grave. "That wasn't supposed to happen."

"Oh? And what was supposed to happen? Were your thugs supposed to kill me?" Growing more agitated, she resumed pacing. "Boris and Ilya didn't deserve to die." She stopped, turned. "Tell me what your men were doing there."

Paul closed his eyes and sighed. "They were hired to upload a virus into the lab's computers."

"This virus, was it supposed to steal the work that had been done there?"

Paul nodded.

She crossed her arms again. "And this is why they shot Ilya. Because he was going to transmit that information to another site."

"As I said, there weren't supposed to be any casualties."

"What about Boris?" She needed to hear how he would justify his death.

"Another unanticipated loss. Look." Paul leaned forward, clasping his hands on the table in front of him. "I'm sorry about your friends. I take full responsibility. The CIA used a private contractor to do the work. That's on me. But ultimately what we did was right. I firmly believe that."

Sasha walked to her chair and sat down. "But how can you say that? Two innocent people are dead because of what you did."

"Three," Paul said, his voice quiet.

Sasha nodded. "Three." She'd live forever with the guilt of causing the gunman's horrific death. "I thought he was there to kill me."

"You weren't supposed to be at the lab." His tone softened. "And neither was your friend, Ilya. Those men weren't supposed to hurt anyone."

Tears sprang to her eyes, and she wiped them away. She searched her pockets for a tissue but came up empty. Paul pulled one from his own and handed it to her.

"So now what?"

"Now we debrief you, and start the paperwork for your defection."

"And the vaccine?"

Paul sighed. "That's up to you. We've taken care of the terrorist who escaped with the vials, but only recovered a portion of the virus. We assume release of the missing vials is imminent. Your vaccine will mean the difference between life and death for millions."

"We haven't proven its efficacy yet."

"You said it worked in your experiments."

"On rats, not people. There have been no clinical trials." *Except for one.* Sasha shuddered at the memory of Subject One's horrific death.

"It's what we've got. What *you've* got. Your call."

There was really no choice. She dug inside her pocket for the flash drive and slid it free, setting it on the table. "It's all there."

"Thank you, Sasha."

She held his gaze, trying to intuit what he was thinking. "And what of us?" Left unspoken was the question she most wanted to ask: *did you ever care for me?*

Paul returned her gaze. "That's also up to you. For what it's worth, I meant everything I said."

"Everything?"

He nodded. His eyes conveyed the stormy emotions raging inside him. At least, that's what Sasha chose to believe. What did they say? Eyes were the windows to the soul.

These were windows to *his* soul.

Part of her wanted to leap out of her chair and throw her arms around him. The other part told her to be still, let him work for his absolution. He'd been responsible for the death of innocents. *Don't give him the satisfaction of knowing you'd forgive him anything at this moment.*

Sasha allowed herself a small feeling of relief. She'd be able to help the world with the vaccine if the virus was ever released, and the man she'd been in love with for the past year and a half had confessed to loving her back.

Things were looking up.

56

———

Leine Basso handed her pack to the pilot, who stowed it inside the hold of the Russian transport plane. She checked the time—thirty minutes to liftoff. She'd be in London in a few hours. From there, she'd hop a flight back to LA, but first, she was going to take a little R&R. She turned and smiled as Dani and Amira joined her. Amira had her arm in a sling.

"Hard to believe it's time to go home." Dani shook her head. She gazed into the distance at the shimmering mirage visible on the tarmac. "So much has happened. Have you heard anything about Joan's condition?"

Leine nodded. "She's stable, but she's got a long way to go to recover. Traumatic brain injury is no joke. Therapy will be her world for some time." Leine had requested that Miller provide the best medical care available for Joan as she convalesced, as well as a stipend and a vehicle for Maude to chauffeur her to and from the therapist. No sense making Maude pay for petrol and wear and tear on her own car. Plus, she'd have to take time off work. A stipend was only fair for her help during the op.

"I just wanted to say thank you for giving me another chance." Amira captured Leine's gaze and held it with her own. "And for the tools to help me work through the trauma."

Leine shook Amira's hand, careful to avoid disturbing the wound in her shoulder. "You're welcome. Good luck with finding the right person to work with." Amira had promised to search for an expert who dealt with soldiers experiencing PTSD. Dani offered her support, too.

"You two take care, all right?" The three women embraced. Leine was the first to disengage, fearing the moisture in her eyes would morph into something embarrassing.

"If you see Derek or Eunice in the future, please tell them I enjoyed working with them both." Dani smiled. "They taught me so much. Those skills are going to come in handy when we track ISIS."

"No doubt," Amira agreed.

"I will." After her CIA-sanctioned foray to Mombasa to have a "chat" with Verdun, Leine had returned to Nairobi to say goodbye to the two trackers. They were on their way to South Africa, following the purported money behind the pangolin smuggling ring. Eunice asked Leine if she'd like to tag along, but she'd declined.

She really needed a break.

As for the virus, the Kenyan government, assisted by the WHO, had successfully contained the outbreak in Kibera by initiating a robust contact tracing program. They'd stopped the virus's spread in its tracks. Initial reports were that fewer than thirty had died.

But three of the vials were still missing.

Leine waved to Dani and Amira as they returned to the hangar, then boarded the plane. She grabbed a row of seats and stretched out, thankful for a few hours to catch up on her sleep.

She wanted to be well rested. Santa was scheduled to meet her in London, and she didn't anticipate leaving the hotel room for a couple of days, at least.

EPILOGUE

The pangolin scratched at the hollow log for its dinner, its ultra-long tongue burrowing inside, setting the ants that called the rotting bark home swarming. Halfway through its evening repast, the pangolin's tongue tasted something strange. Curious, it rocked the log, attempting to break whatever it found free of its confines.

A metal box slid out of the log and onto the ground, the top of it coming free, spilling its contents onto the dirt. The pangolin licked at the interior and the mysterious contents, but found both tasteless and hard. Unable to consume its find, the walking pinecone lost interest and returned to the log to resume its meal, leaving the three glass vials exposed to the elements.

***NOW AVAILABLE: THE NEXT BOOK IN THE UNPUTDOWNABLE Leine Basso thriller series, *Fatal Objective*.

Leine Basso's missing.

She's not answering her calls. Or texts. Lou and Santa fear she's been compromised. According to her contact on the op she's fine, just busy.

When she finally responds it doesn't sound like her. The two men who know her best aren't buying it. Something isn't right.

Leine Basso's missing.

And Lou and Santa are going to find out why.

Get Fatal Objective now.

Be the first to know when the next Leine Basso is available: Join DV's Readers' List

ACKNOWLEDGMENTS

Author's note

The Kurdish fighters mentioned in this book, although fictional, are based on actual military forces who took Kobani, Raqqa, and several other towns during the Syrian civil war, wresting control from ISIS through sheer willpower and fierce fighting. Their efforts, alongside US air support and other allied forces, helped turned the tide when all appeared lost. To find out more about the brave women of this Kurdish militia, check out the book *The Daughters of Kobani* by Gayle Tzenach Lemmon.

The 2014 Yazidi genocide carried out by ISIS in Iraq and Syria informed my depiction of Amira's traumatic experiences at the hands of terrorists. Several thousand Yazidis were believed to have been killed that summer, and more than 6,000 women and children were captured. To date, close to 3,000 Yazidis remain missing.

The Leopard anti-poaching rangers are based on several groups of all-female organizations that fight poachers and protect Africa's disappearing wildlife. Eunice is an amalgamation of several women in their ranks. For more information, search for the Black Mambas Anti-Poaching Unit (South Africa), the Akashinga (*the Brave Ones*) Rangers (Zimbabwe), the Lionesses (Kenya), former US vet Kinessa Johnson and VETPAW (Veterans Empowered to Protect African Wildlife), and more.

The character of Felix is based on members of the Wagner Group, a well-documented force of mercenaries bankrolled by a Russian oligarch and rumored to be supported by the Kremlin. They have a large presence throughout Africa and around the globe. Similarly, Verdun King's character is based on several accounts of for-profit "security specialists" operating throughout the world.

In addition to the above references, a heartfelt shout-out to the following people who made A PLAGUE OF TRAITORS possible:

Thanks to first reader, brainstorming best friend, and supportive partner extraordinaire, Mark Lindstrom, without whom life would seriously suck; to my amazing editors Ruth Ross and Laurie Boris, whose superhuman attention to detail make my books so much better, and help me look much more accomplished than I am; to TSODA 134 and friends, for his/their extensive knowledge of all things weapons/war/explosives/military training/etc., and who provide these books with a deeper authenticity than I could ever muster; to friend and adventurer Mike Carnevale for being my boots on the ground in Kenya, and coming up with some great ideas for my characters' actions; to friend and fellow suspense author Carmen Amato, for her invaluable knowledge of all things CIA; to former Ambassador, and current friend and prolific author, Charles Ray, for reading an advance copy and lending me much-appreciated support and advice in my writerly endeavor; to my Advance Reader

Team (ART), because they ROCK; and last but not least, to my intrepid writers' group, Jenni, Ali, and Michelle—working with you through the years has been a pleasure.

Writing is never a solitary endeavor.

ALSO BY D.V. BERKOM

LEINE BASSO CRIME THRILLER SERIES:

A Killing Truth

Serial Date

Bad Traffick

The Body Market

Cargo

The Last Deception

Dark Return

Absolution

Dakota Burn

Shadow of the Jaguar

A Plague of Traitors

Fatal Objective

KATE JONES ADVENTURE THRILLER SERIES:

Kate Jones Thriller Series Vol. 1

Cruising for Death

Yucatán Dead

A One Way Ticket to Dead

Vigilante Dead

CLAIRE WHITCOMB WESTERNS:

Retribution

Gunslinger

Legend

ABOUT THE AUTHOR

DV Berkom is the USA Today bestselling author of action-packed, riveting action-adventure and crime thrillers. Known for creating resilient, kick-ass female characters and page-turning plots, her love of the genre stems from a lifelong addiction to reading spy novels, thrillers, and action/adventure stories.

A restless soul and adventurer at heart, she spent years moving around the US and traveling to exotic locations before she wrote her first novel and was hooked. More than a dozen books later, she now makes her home in the Pacific Northwest with her husband, Mark, and several imaginary characters who like to tell her what to do. Her most recent books include Claire Whitcomb Westerns *Legend, Gunslinger,* and *Retribution,* Leine Basso thrillers *A Plague of Traitors, Shadow of the Jaguar, Dakota Burn, Absolution,* and *Dark Return.* DV's currently hard at work on her next book.

For more information, visit her website: www.d-vberkom.com. To be the first to hear about new releases and subscriber-only offers, go to: bit.ly/DVB_RL

www.ingramcontent.com/pod-product-compliance
Lightning Source LLC
Chambersburg PA
CBHW051213190726
48288CB00006B/1946